To:
Linda

Thanks for asking for a copy of my book!

Your mom's friend
Marie

PIECES
of the Past

Marie DeSantis

In Loving Memory of my sisters :
Carole Muncy Benson and Rita Aucter Muncy.

CHAPTER ONE (MAY 1987)

The chilly wind had replaced the pleasant breeze of just a short time before and the shadows were getting a little longer. They had walked along the river's edge for hours now, enjoying the feel of the rushing water as it danced against the rocks and mixed together with the sand beneath their feet. They had talked about their plans for the future together, and how, at least for awhile, they would be together. But all that was in the warmth of a beautiful May day, and now all that warmth and brightness was beginning to fade. Jenna was becoming more and more concerned about the worry she may have caused her family, leaving the way she did without so much as a word to anyone. But, she was with Tom, her very best friend, her protector, the one she hoped to spend the rest of her life with. Nevertheless, the unwelcome concerns were growing in her mind, and she tried to block them out as she stuck her toes into the rushing water. As she gazed into the water she couldn't help but think that maybe she had been slightly impulsive to go along with this idea of Tom's. Maybe she should have given the whole situation a little more thought, but it always came back to the same reality, that if she had refused to go with him she might lose him forever.

Early that morning, before the rest of the family had gotten up, she had hastily packed four bagels, a package of cream cheese, a few apples and bananas, a box of cookies, and as many cokes from the refrigerator as she could carry in a large plastic bag. She left by the back door and practically flew past her mother's small greenhouse that had been an anniversary gift from her father to her mother a few years ago. As she caught the familiar fragrance of the first roses of the season just starting to bloom, she almost hesitated to enjoy the wonderful aroma, but she thought better of it. She had to hurry, if she didn't she might change her mind. She was to meet Tom at the river's edge at their pre-determined time of seven A.M. Their meeting was to take place a short distance behind her house and just a little ways downstream. It was just a short run but she arrived there breathless with anticipation. In her heart she knew this wasn't the right thing to be doing, but her impulsive nature was taking control of her better judgment, which it often did. Besides, Tom had said he was leaving regardless of whether she went with him or not and she knew he meant it, and she couldn't let that happen.

The river this morning seemed to take on a particularly iridescent glow as the silver water dashed against the rocks, and the trees on the far side danced in the early morning breeze creating swaying shadows on the sunlit water. The majestic trees that lined the banks were in full bloom, and scattered here and there between them were the late May purple and yellow wildflowers. Three deep purple lilac bushes a few feet apart added to the scenic beauty this morning, and as she brushed by them, she had the strongest impulse to break off some of the tender branches and take a bouquet to her mother. She had done that so many times before, but not today. She had always felt a strong pull toward the river, and in her sixteen years she had spent many a pleasurable time on its shores. As a little child she had waded in the clear, clean water with her family and had picnicked countless times in the nearby nooks that bordered the shores. As she grew older, she and her friends would swim in the protected area that her father had roped off for them. She and Tom had walked along the sandy shore many, many times as they grew up together in this small town. It was a place where they could come and talk, share their secrets, and think about their future together. As she looked up and down the shoreline, she realized just how much she loved this spot. How could she leave this place? Should she turn around and go back home? No, there was Tom walking toward her a ways downstream. When he saw her he broke into a run and was at her side in a very short time. After a quick welcoming hug Tom took the bag of food, he could see it was too heavy for her to carry very far. He had hurriedly stuffed a few items of clothing in his backpack before he left his house this morning and he had remembered a flashlight, money he had been saving, some matches, but little else.

Tom, as usual, had his baseball cap on backwards, and his black wavy hair was sticking out the sides. This was the look that Jenna had always loved about him, the casualness, the warm smile, and the way he always would light up when he saw her. She knew she cared deeply about him, and she was sure several of the other girls in school shared her interest in him. After all, he was the best-looking boy in school, but she knew he only had eyes for her. They both knew there would never be anyone else for either one of them, they were that closely intertwined. The bright smile hid his true feelings this morning as he removed his cap, brushed back his hair with his hands, and replaced his cap again - backwards.

Jenna felt a rush of excitement as she looked up at his attractive young face. She loved being with him, and now they would be together for keeps. Everyone would understand eventually, they would just have to. There were so many years yet to go, two more of high school for both of them and four years of college, at least for her. They couldn't possibly wait that long, they needed to be together now! But, there were her parents, they would be worrying.

Seeing what looked like indecisiveness in her eyes, he said, "Don't worry, Jenna, I'll take care of you. I have enough money on me, and I think we can make it to that old inn before dark. Remember, it's right on the river a few miles out of town -- you know, the one old man Lawson owns. I'm pretty sure it's still in operation!"

Jenna nodded in agreement, all the time hoping he hadn't noticed her nervousness and the hesitation in her eyes.

"Did you have a problem getting out of the house?" Tom asked quietly. "Did anyone see you leave?"

"No, but I did feel so guilty..."

"Look at me!" Tom stopped abruptly and put his hands on her shoulders. "If you want to go back, I'll understand. This is my problem, not yours. I should have just left alone and got in touch with you later. I shouldn't be putting you through this!"

"Don't feel that way, I'm going with you because I want to! I couldn't bear it without you!" she said as she quickly hugged him, then turned to face him again. "I'd just die if I couldn't see you every day."

"Everything's going to work out, you'll see, just trust me!" he smiled as he gave her a quick kiss on her forehead.

"I do trust you - I really do!" she whispered, as she forced a cheerful smile and clutched his hand, and together they started their journey to they knew not where.

───────

"Wonder if they've missed us yet," Jenna said rather thoughtfully. They had been walking for several hours now. "Wonder what they're thinking," she said almost to herself. She looked away as she spoke because she didn't want to meet Tom's eyes.

She was such a pretty girl, her long blond hair tied in the back in a ponytail with a pink and blue scarf that framed a very attractive face. She had enough natural coloring that makeup was never required, and in her case, never desired. The blue in the scarf exactly matched the blue in her eyes, and her slender, well-rounded body fit perfectly in the Calvin Klein jeans and pink sweatshirt she was wearing. She had tied a navy blue wool cardigan around her waist, although she was sure she wouldn't be needing it. The weather had been quite warm for some time now.

"I'm not going back no matter what!" exclaimed Tom, as he sat down on a large rock, only to discover too late that it had been very recently immersed in the waters of the rushing river leaving it quite damp.

"Darn it all!" he jumped up quickly, realizing how much he hated the feel of damp jeans. "Oh, well, they'll dry out - only wish all my problems were that simple!" he remarked with a crooked smile, which meant he too was a little uneasy about the whole situation. In his haste to get away from the condition at home he hadn't really been thinking too responsibly. It was just beginning to enter his mind that possibly his problems couldn't be solved by his sudden decision to run away, and just maybe he would be presented with larger issues as a result of this rash action. Also there was Jenna to consider, she was with him now, trusted him, just what was he dragging her into? And what would her family think of him after taking her on this little escapade? Probably they would be very angry with him and probably he shouldn't have even told Jenna his plans but should have just disappeared and wrote to her later.

"If you're leaving, I'm going with you!" Jenna had cried earlier when Tom had told her he could not stand living alone with his drunken father anymore. She knew it was wrong, but she couldn't bear to think of the possibility of losing Tom. Maybe he'd never come back to River Valley. Maybe he'd meet someone else and forget all about her.

They had known each other since second grade, when Tom's family had moved to River Valley from New York City. Michelle and Bill Wilson were tired of the hectic pace of the big city and decided that this small upstate town, nestled just below the southern Adirondacks, was just the right size, the ideal place for Tom to grow up in. Bill Wilson was a postal employee with a mail delivery route, and transferring upstate from the city had been a rather easy transition. He had actually enjoyed the slower pace and friendlier atmosphere of small town living as he went from door to door delivering mail each day. Michelle was a stay-at-home wife and mother who thoroughly delighted in her daily household chores, keeping her two men happy, and tending to her ever-bountiful flower garden.

Tom remembered growing up in a happy, though rather reserved home. Being the only child, he, of course, got all of the attention. His mother was a very attractive woman who had married rather young to a man fifteen years her senior, but in spite of the age difference, they had seemed to be quite happy together.

At the time the family moved to River Valley, Tom was about to enter first grade. He had immediately noticed the little blond girl the first morning he had walked into the classroom. During the first play period, he accidentally-on-purpose managed to get as close to her as possible. His big chance came when she dropped a colored pencil on the floor and he bent over to pick it up for her. As he handed it back to her he noticed that she had the prettiest blue eyes he had ever seen. They were practically inseparable from that moment on, sharing everything throughout the years, turning to each other in every little crisis. Neither one could imagine growing up without the other. They had both spent many happy hours at each other's homes and, as a result, the two families had become rather friendly, but with reservations on the part of Jenna's mother, Helen. She liked Tom but would have preferred that he and her daughter not be quite so attached to each other. She had hoped that Jenna would associate more with the offspring of what her mother considered the upper class of the town. But this was entirely her perspective, for Jenna knew no class-distinction and cared little about wealth and status.

Everything went smoothly until the day Michelle was diagnosed with breast cancer, and almost immediately life changed for the Wilson family. She was in and out of hospitals for a little over two years, and along with putting up with the unpleasantness of chemotherapy, nothing was ever the same for the family again. Bill started drinking, moderately at first, but more and more as time went on. Instead of being at her side the night she died, he was in a local bar drowning his sorrows. It wasn't that he didn't care, he just wasn't able to cope with the situation. Tom was only twelve at the time, but it was he who was at his mother's side when she passed away. A neighbor, Frank Smith, had been kind enough to take Tom to the hospital that afternoon and stay with him, because it was apparent that his mother would not live much longer. After everything was over, the neighbor took him home and stayed at Tom's house to await the appearance of his father to give him the sad news. He staggered in about one A.M. in a drunken and incoherent state. When told that his wife had died that evening, he became belligerent and ordered Frank from the house. With guilt-ridden rage he threw himself on his bed and moaned in anguish, as Tom watched silently. Then his anger turned to deep sorrow and he tearfully held Tom close to him for what seemed like hours.

"Why wasn't I with her? Why did I let her down? She needed me and I let her down!" he cried over and over. "At least you were there. Thank God for that, at least she wasn't alone. I'll never forgive myself!" He was inconsolable and Tom thought he would never stop sobbing. Having no siblings made Tom feel especially alone now. If he had only had a brother or sister to turn to in his grief, it would have been so much easier.

For the next few weeks father and son shared their grief together, and Bill sustained from drinking completely. Tom, though still very shaken from the loss of his mother, found consolation in the fact that his father was staying home at night and spending time with him, obviously trying to make up for the last two years. But it didn't last. Within a couple of months Bill was back at the bars, and before long was drinking heavier than before. Tom felt trapped, very unhappy and very alone, with no one to talk to, no one but Jenna, and the two of them became closer than ever.

Jenna's family tried very hard to console Tom and his father and they were invited over to dinner often the first few weeks, or Helen would bake extra bread and cookies and take them over to the Wilson home. Even when it became evident that Bill was drinking heavier than ever, she still continued to try to help, until one day, when he was obviously very drunk, he ordered her out of the house telling her they weren't accepting charity any longer. She didn't go back again, but she felt sorry for Tom, and she couldn't help but notice his sad face each time he came to see Jenna.

Helen was a model wife and mother. She adored her two daughters and her husband and made sure that their every need was met. She was very proud of her husband's status in the community and thoroughly relished the fact that most of the people they mingled with on a regular basis were what she considered to be of the highest caliber; doctors, lawyers and business owners. The family had a maid to tend to housework which freed up Helen for her much-loved social climbing role. Her bridge club met twice a week, but she also found plenty of time to do volunteer work and, in spite of her high-minded attitude, she truly enjoyed helping the less fortunate.

Occasionally the subject of Jenna's companionship with Tom would come up. Helen liked the boy, she just didn't want the situation between the two of them to become serious.

"I want to do what's best for my girls," she would quietly tell her husband when he questioned her noticeable reservations about Tom. "It isn't that Tom's not a nice enough boy, but they've just been too close for too long. She spends so much time with him that she hasn't given herself a chance to meet some of the nice comfortable boys in the community." That was her polite way of saying she would have preferred Jenna associate with the sons of their wealthier friends.

Jenna's father, on the other hand, was very fond of Tom and always made him feel welcome when he came to see his daughter. He was almost like the son he never had and a close-knit bond had grown between them. He knew of his situation at home, everyone did, and his heart went out to the young boy, knowing what he must be going through. At one point he attempted to talk to Tom's father about trying to get help for his problem. He even offered to go with him to AA, but was flatly refused. It seemed to Jenna's father that Bill justified his drinking problem by the feeling that he had let his wife down, and now she was gone so it didn't matter anymore. Jack knew that Bill was apparently so engulfed with guilt that it over-shadowed any fatherly concerns that he should have had for Tom.

"He's a good kid, Helen, Jenna could do a lot worse, a whole lot worse! He always gets her home when we tell him to, and it's obvious he thinks the world of her. And besides, she has a mind of her own, she has to decide who she wants to be with," Jack would remark in Tom's defense every so often when Helen would mention that she disapproved of the two of them spending so much time together.

"But she's only sixteen!" Helen would persist, "but I suppose you're right - at least she's not changing boyfriends every week like some of her friends. And I know, he's a good kid, I'm just thinking about her future, how much easier her life would be if she just took an interest in dating some college-bound boys, I'm almost sure Tom will never go to college." Helen insisted she was only thinking of Jenna's welfare.

"You don't know that, and even if he doesn't, he's got a good head on his shoulders, and he'll do right by Jenna. He's a good kid," he repeated.

Helen would just shrug her shoulders, knowing that her husband would always come to Tom's defense, even though she herself really had nothing against the boy. She just hoped they wouldn't do anything crazy like running away and getting married.

Jack Lauren was a very successful physician, well-liked by everyone and revered by his patients. He never lacked for patients, and was always well-booked months in advance. He was kind, sympathetic and sincerely loved his work and the people that depended upon him. He had met and married Helen in his first year of medical school and Jenna had come along less than a year later. He had known since he was very young that he was adopted, but was never completely told of the details. A few times he had attempted to bring up the subject of his true identity, but he never seemed to be able to gather any clear information, it was almost as if the subject was taboo. He had been told that both his biological parents were dead, and that would end the conversation. He, of course, had a natural curiosity about his biological background, but he was never so overly concerned that he cared to question his parents too deeply. All through his growing-up years he had loved his adoptive parents, regardless of whether or not he shared their blood and genes. At least until the day when he might decide to probe further into the identity of his birth parents, that was enough for him.

His adoptive father, although completely open for whatever his son decided to do with his life, had more or less assumed he would follow in his footsteps and go into the business world someday, but the young man had other ideas. He had always had a compelling need to help people, and he knew from the time that he was very young that he wanted to be a doctor, and his parents couldn't have been more supportive. After high school he went first to a state university and then on to Columbia University Medical Center in New York City, graduating with high honors.

Jack's adoptive mother was extremely proud of her son's success and wished many times that his adoptive father could have shared her pride. Widowed since Jack was sixteen years old, she had just recently started to live with him and his family when it was discovered she had heart trouble and Jack had insisted that she move in with them.

"It's really not necessary," she would say to her doting son, "I can still manage by myself, just check on me occasionally and I'll be fine." She had sold her big house years ago and had moved into a small apartment that she knew would be much easier for her to take care of. It was for a few years, but then the intermittent chest pains started and she herself became a little fearful being alone. As much as she hated to give up her independence, she finally realized it was becoming too difficult to live by herself so she reluctantly gave into his pleading.

Although she was a devoted mother and grandmother, she would, at times, become very quiet and go off by herself as if in deep thought. She had her own little suite of rooms in another part of the house, and she was spending more and more time there. She had her own bathroom, which led directly from her bedroom, a tiny kitchenette, and a small living room which opened onto a back porch. She spent many an hour on that back porch doing her crocheting, mending for the family, or just plain reading a good book. It was a pleasant situation and for the most part she was quite happy. Her granddaughters added to her contentment as they were always popping in to check on her. Although she would certainly never have admitted it, she always favored Jenna, possibly because she was the first born, but mostly because Jenna always seemed more concerned about her. She never forgot to stop in to chat for a moment and kiss her grandmother goodnight every night, and it was a ritual that Mary cherished. Both girls were deeply devoted to their grandmother, spending hours with her as they were growing up. And she doted on them, taking them shopping with her, occasionally to a movie, baking chocolate chip cookies together, or maybe just sitting on the porch while she told them fascinating tales from when she was a young girl.

Jenna was thinking of her now as she held Tom's hand and walked wistfully in the sand. Would it make her grandmother cry when she found out her granddaughter was missing? Would it possibly cause her to have a heart attack? She was getting sadder by the moment. She shuddered as she thought of that possibility and she knew she had to get her mind off those kind of thoughts or she wouldn't be able to go on.

"Hungry yet?" She forced a smile at Tom. "I am. Let's sit awhile and have a snack, O.K?"

"I guess I am too, more thirsty than hungry, though."

"There's cokes in the bag, that's why it's so heavy."

Reaching into the bottom of the bag he took out two cokes, opened one and handed it to Jenna. The soda was spurting out of the top all over their hands, due to all the jostling in the bag during their long walk. They quietly wiped their hands on their jeans and proceeded to take a sip.

Tom set the bag down on a large rock and she solemnly took two bagels from it, then proceeded to spread the cream cheese on them.

"You like the cream cheese spread real thick, don't you? This is our favorite, cinnamon and raisin, Mom just got them yesterday, so they're nice and fresh. Sorry, I forgot all about napkins." She just missed dropping the bagel in the sand as she handed it over to Tom. He reached out quickly and rescued it.

"We're roughing it, remember, we don't need napkins. Hey! These are good! I could live on bagels."

When Jenna didn't respond, he glanced her way and could see that she was deep in thought again. She sadly wondered what her mother thought this morning when she discovered that not only the bagels were gone but her daughter was also. She visualized her mother calling all her friends in case she was supposed to meet them earlier before going to school, or maybe she would just assume she had something to do that she hadn't been told about. Her mother knew that, at sixteen, she was practically grown-up and very responsible. At least she had always been responsible- until now.

Last night when Tom had told her he was running away from home and asked her to go with him, she was filled with excitement and anticipation. But now that the day was coming to an end, she was getting homesick and she decided she missed her family.

"Let's drink from the same can of coke, that way they'll last longer," Jenna offered, feeling tears starting to sting her eyes. She took a sip and offered it to Tom.

"Sure, but please don't worry, Jen, we'll be OK," Tom optimistically retorted, seeing her wet eyes, "Once we get out of here and find jobs we'll get by just fine!"

"They must know by now that we didn't go to school today," Jenna almost whined. "What do you think they'll do when we aren't there at dinner tonight?"

"My old man will only be drunk anyway, he probably won't even notice!" Tom replied rather sarcastically. "But your folks, that's different, they'll probably worry, but I'm sure your father will know you're with me and I know he trusts me."

Jenna knew that was true, her father did trust Tom. And she knew they would be quite sure they were together since they would both be missing. She looked up at Tom and smiled. Maybe it wasn't so bad after all, she thought, as they trudged along the shore just relishing being together, albiet bittersweet.

"There'll be a full moon tonight, so we can still see pretty well where we're walking," Tom said much later. Jenna folded her arms across her chest and shivered. The coolness of the evening made her thankful she had grabbed her sweater at the last minute before leaving home.

"You know, I could have sworn Lawson's Inn was around here. Do you suppose it's been closed or torn down?"

"I don't know, I had never heard of it. When did you last see it?"

"A few years ago, and it was right next to the river, I'm sure of it. Gee I hope it's still here."

At that point they were very close to the highway, which in a few places ran in close proximity to the river. Glancing to the left at a spot between the river and highway, Tom spotted a clearing, In the deepening twilight it was hard to make it out at first, but, as they got closer they saw remnants of a rather large building next to the highway that apparently had been ravaged by a fire, and not too recently either. A good portion of the chimney was still standing, and black, charred spirals seemed to reach proudly to the sky. It was not what Tom had hoped to see.

"That must have been the inn," he solemnly remarked, "I

don't remember ever hearing that it had burned down." He glanced apologetically at Jenna, who looked as though she was about to cry.

Not knowing what else to say at the time, he blurted out, "We could check and see if there's a spot there somewhere where we could get shelter for the night. It's worth a try." The dejected look on Jenna's face was almost more than he could take.

They silently walked over to the burned building and were suddenly startled by a small animal running across their path.

"It's a rat!," Jenna screamed. "Oh, No! We can't stay there, there's probably rats all over the place, and snakes and all those horrible things!" Now she was crying! Tom put his arm around her and felt her whole body tremble as he tried to comfort her.

"Don't worry, Jen, everything will be OK. We'll keep walking for a while, we'll find something." He didn't believe a word he was saying, but he knew he couldn't demonstrate his fear to Jenna. She quietly wiped away her tears, and bravely grasped his hand again.

It was slowly getting darker by the minute, and the new uncertainty of where they were going to spend the night, and what they were going to do tomorrow, was becoming increasingly disturbing. Just where were they going to sleep, now that their hopes of comfortable beds in a nice warm inn were dashed?

And what were they going to eat when their meager food supply was gone? The entire situation was becoming frightening to say the least.

Tom was getting a little more concerned as time went by, but was trying as hard as possible to hide it from Jenna. He forced himself to look very confident as he said, "Maybe I should have never got you into this mess Jen, but I promise if you stick with me things will work out. We can't be very far from Allenville and I'll start looking for work right away. I'll get something. I used to help my uncle in his store and gas station. I used to unpack stuff, price it and put it on the shelves, and I also pumped gas. So, with that experience, I know I can find something!"

Jenna looked over at Tom's jet black hair protruding out of the sides of his baseball cap and had all she could do to keep from crying again as she said, "I know, but it's just a little strange to be doing this. I never ran away before, you know, and I'm a little scared!! Aren't you?"

She glanced up at his handsome young face, thinking of how much she cared for him, and how now they would be together forever, but the prospect of this togetherness had taken on bittersweet undertones. She had confidence in him and knew somehow that he'd look out for her. But then he was just a high-school kid just like her in spite of his brave front, and she knew that her confidence in him wouldn't keep the darkness of the night from approaching very soon with its ensuing cold, along with the fear of not knowing what awaited them.

They had left the river's edge and were walking closer to the road now. The rocky steep banks had made it impossible to walk alongside of the river so they had moved inland a little. There wasn't much traffic on the country road, hardly anyone lived here, but each of the two times that a car passed, Tom thought momentarily about flagging them down, but he always changed his mind. It was almost as if they were in this thing too deep now. They were walking within the cover of the deep forest, several yards from the highway, and Tom knew they couldn't be spotted unless they made a serious effort to be seen.

More time passed and the full moon was providing some light. With the help of the flashlight Tom had taken from his backpack, it wasn't too difficult to see where they were going as they walked hand-in-hand over the brush, pausing whenever necessary to climb over a fallen tree.

"We aren't getting lost, are we?" Jenna looked up at Tom knowing full well what his answer would be.

"Of course not!" Tom answered with full certainty, not being too sure himself, but not wanting her to worry. "We're following the road, no way can we get lost as long as we're between the road and the river." The confidence in his voice comforted Jenna, and she even managed a slight smile. *"That makes sense,"* she thought to herself.

The chill of the night was something neither one of them had fully prepared for. Jenna had buttoned her sweater around her and Tom was thankful he had worn his heaviest sweatshirt but they both could still feel the cold. They had been away from their homes at least thirteen hours now.

They were unable to spot either the road or the river at this point, but they knew they were not that far away. They were approaching a large clump of pine trees which seemed to form a deep green oasis in the middle of the tall maples and elms. There was no way to avoid walking through them, and they were far enough apart that the moonlight could still seep through. The brown pine needles made a plush, aromatic carpet at their feet, with the pines extending their green, scratchy arms in every direction.

"Look!" Tom grabbed Jenna's arm and pointed. "I think we're in luck!"

They didn't see the small light-colored cottage at first, it was hidden by the trees, but the small shack behind the house was in full view and directly ahead of them, and looked like a likely place to spend the night if they were able to get into it. Looking around carefully in every direction, they quietly approached the shack. Cautiously, Tom tried the door. It opened with a slight push and squeak. It was rather dark inside, but with a quick sweep with the flashlight they could both see the place was neat and uncluttered. There was plenty of room for the two of them to spread out on the hardwood floor. What they didn't see was a bearded, gray-haired man several yards from the shack who was watering his newly-planted vegetable garden by the light of the moon.

At the sound of the opening and closing of the door he turned suddenly and looked in the direction of the shack. Thinking it was possibly the wind, although he realized he wasn't aware of any, and knowing the door wouldn't have opened that easily anyway, he quietly walked over to the shack. Opening the door with one quick move he was surprised to see two terrified young people standing in front of him. Jenna started to whimper and Tom put a trembling arm around her. He made a weak attempt at trying to act real brave and protective, and they both knew it was too late to try to run. They had been caught red-handed!

"Well, what have we here? What are you kids looking for anyway? You're trespassing you know! This is private property!" he said, trying to make his voice sound harsh. But upon seeing the frightened looks on the two, standing like frozen statues before him, he quickly mellowed. Scrutinizing them more closely he could see they were just a couple of youngsters, scared to death.

From out of nowhere a German shepherd dashed up to his master and when he saw the two strangers started to bark excitedly.

"That's enough, Scout," was his master's firm command and the dog responded by laying down on the grass next to the shack.

"Did someone send you here?" Jake realized how ridiculous his question was the minute he uttered it. Who would send two kids to find him? They had to be as bewildered to see him as he was to see them. Too frightened to be surprised at his question, Tom attempted to be calm as he spoke, but was unable to control the quiver in his voice, "No one sent us, mister. We were just looking for a place to spend the night. We'll go away; we're sorry we bothered you."

Jenna, still whimpering, blurted out, "Yes, that's all, we didn't know anyone was here. We kinda thought it was just an empty shed --we'll find another place. Please let us go, OK?" The old man was still standing in the doorway, blocking their escape, and they knew they didn't dare try to get around him. For all they knew he could be dangerous, or at the very least, a little weird.

He smiled as he realized how frightened they both were. "Aw, come on now, do I look like I'd hurt anyone? I better shave off this beard!" he chuckled. "I'm just not used to finding strangers in my shack!"

He stepped forward and reached out his hand to Tom who reluctantly took it. He concluded by their panic-stricken faces that they were telling the truth and had stumbled onto the shack accidentally. He lived alone and nowadays kept mostly to himself, and at least pretended to like it that way. It seems it had taken two children to discover his remote sanctuary!

"I don't know what you're doing here but now that you're here, come on in and have something warm to drink. And take that frightened look off your faces, you're starting to scare me!" he joked. He turned and stepped out the doorway onto the ground and motioned for them to follow him.

He certainly seemed harmless enough, and since they needed shelter for the night it appeared to be their best offer. He certainly didn't look or act like a monster, he had a very kindly way about him, but they both knew looks and actions could be deceiving. They would keep a close eye on him!

"Come along now. I have a phone if you want to use it!" He knew these two frightened kids were running from something, and he was treading softly so as not to scare them away. He would try to help them through whatever turmoil they were facing that had brought them to the middle of nowhere in the darkness of the night. He knew he had to instill confidence in them that he was their friend and they had nothing to fear. He was sure he had never seen either of them before, but living the way he did, avoiding social situations, that was not surprising. He knew very few people, he was very lonely, but he had his reasons for living the way he did. He was still a rather attractive older man, in trim physical shape despite his age, with a sizeable amount of healthy gray hair and a softness to his eyes that revealed only kindness. He never really liked living alone, but he had become accustomed to it over the years, and it had become his way of life. He often thought of all the wasted years, there were no children, no family anywhere. Seeing these two young people made him realize even more what he had missed.

Even though they were both still a little frightened at this point, they obediently walked behind him to the front porch of the little cottage.

"Welcome to my humble home, kids. It's not the Taj Mahal but it's comfortable. Scout and I like it here, even if we are way out in the sticks. Now, come in and make yourselves at home!"

The full moon was now sending forth light that was almost close to daylight and they could easily pick out the details of the small cottage. The boards of the porch and steps looked as if they had been recently painted gray. A steel-framed lounge chair and a small table were setting at the other end of the little porch. The door to the cottage was painted green as were the window frames. All around the porch were rose bushes, not yet in bloom, but seemingly patiently awaiting to usher in the warm weather. There were two bunches of what looked like lavender on either side of the steps and small bushes were planted here and there on raised ground with stones for the border. Two lavender lilac bushes stood in the front of the house on either side of the walk. They were in full bloom and, even in the moonlight, Jenna thought they were the most beautiful lilac bushes she had ever seen. The man who lived here apparently had a green thumb.

Ushering them to the front door, he motioned them in before him. Jenna entered first, and though still a little apprehensive, couldn't help but feel the warmth and friendliness of the room. The brown leather sofa looked very appealing after their long walk and when she was invited to sit down she did so without hesitation. She observed immediately that the house with its impeccable cleanliness reminded her of home and how even her mother would approve of the owner's housekeeping. The place was small, but ever so cozy. In one corner was a television on a high bookcase that took up an entire wall, and with more books than Jenna had ever seen in one spot. A comfortable padded rocker sat next to it on the brown and green colonial carpet. At one end of the living room there was an open doorway into the kitchen, and on the opposite wall the log in the stone fireplace was still a bright red but with no flames, apparently having been burning for some time. The old man was obviously very proud of his home and willingly gave them a quick tour, of which Tom showed little interest, but much cautiousness. All in all, though rather small, the little cottage was indeed very inviting.

Suddenly the old man turned to Jenna, "You know, I'm hungry, how about a snack?"

Jenna felt a closeness to this old man that she couldn't explain, there was something different about him that made her feel that way. He had such a warmth about him, and when he smiled at her she could feel a genuine kindness and concern.

Meanwhile Tom, who had been standing in the living room with a watchful eye, slightly annoyed at Jenna's quick acceptance of the old man said, "We'll be on our way in the morning, mister, just looking for a place to spend the night. Didn't mean to bother you none." He was more cautious than Jenna, who by now was completely calm and quite taken with this old man.

As the three of them walked back into the living room they could feel the cool evening breeze floating into the room through the screen door with its tantalizing aroma from the lilac bushes, and Jenna breathed deeply to catch all she could of the pleasant fragrance.

"Aw, Come on," he said as he turned to Tom and put his hand briefly on his shoulder, taking note of his cautiousness. "You have nothing to fear from me, so relax! I was young once. Come on out into the kitchen, let me fix you some cocoa!", the owner said, turning his head and smiling to himself as he walked toward the refrigerator. "Sit down, both of you. Do you like doughnuts? Just made some this morning, and they are darn good!"

Slowly and obediently they sat down at the table and watched as he poured the milk into a saucepan and set it on the heating element. He put a plate with four delicious-looking doughnuts in front of them and quietly watched as the two young people seemed to be scrutinizing him more thoroughly. Jenna's fright had almost completely disappeared, but Tom was still a little uneasy about this stranger whose territory they had invaded.

After he had poured the hot cocoa into their two mugs their host said, "So- what should I do about you kids? You obviously are not where you should be right now!" Scanning the two sitting before him he paused a minute before he continued, "Like I said, there's a phone in there. I have the strangest feeling that you're running away from home, am I right?" Jenna and Tom looked at each other but didn't answer.

"Just as I thought! Well, you certainly aren't going anywhere tonight. Drink you cocoa and help yourself to the doughnuts. By the way, have you two got names? I'm Jake." He pulled up a stool and sat next to them. Scout stretched out on the floor and quickly went to sleep.

Rather reluctantly Tom said, "She's Jenna, I'm Tom."

"Well, Jenna and Tom, isn't this better than being out there in the cold tonight?" he said with a teasing grin. They couldn't help but agree and they both silently shook their heads yes.

"Not bad are they? Made them this morning!" he proudly stated again regarding the doughnuts.

"They are good!" Jenna said between bites, managing a wide smile. "You mean - you cook?"

"Well, I fired my cook, and my maid quit on me so now I do everything myself," he laughed.

Jenna laughed too. Jake could see he had won her confidence, but Tom was still a little suspicious, he would keep an eye on him.

They took their time eating and drinking the cocoa, with Jenna alternately asking questions of Jake and answering a few of his questions. She was feeling very comfortable in his presence now, much to Tom's disapproval. He considered her much too accepting, too quick to take people at face value. It took him a while to trust, his home environment had taught him that, and this old man would have to win his trust before he would feel secure around him.

"Have you lived here a long time?" Jenna was asking.

"Yes, for quite a few years. I used to live out west, but this is my home now."

"How come I've never seen you before? Do you ever come into River Valley?"

"Oh, so that's where you live!" He said quickly, then realizing his mistake he answered, "Occasionally, when I need to stock up on things or pay a couple of bills.."

Jenna felt a very slight kick under the table coming from Tom's direction, and she immediately terminated her questioning.

Fearful that if he said the wrong thing he might scare them out into the cold night, he got up from his stool and started to walk out of the kitchen.

"I'm going to get some blankets and pillows and we'll make some sort of sleeping arrangements between the sofa and the extra bedroom," he said nonchalantly as he walked into his bedroom and came back with two khaki blankets, sheets and pillows.

"We'll let Jenna have a bedroom so she can have more privacy, and Tom, you can sleep on the sofa. I'm assuming you're pretty tired after your walk. Don't forget, there's a phone on the table over there, you're welcome to call your folks. It just might be a good idea, you know! And don't get any wild ideas about running off into the night," he said as he looked directly at Tom. "You're safe here, I promise! Now if you don't mind, I'm going to bed. I like to read for awhile before I sleep, so don't mind the light, and we'll talk in the morning." With one last reassuring look at the couple he disappeared into his bedroom once again.

They were both extremely tired after their long walk and Jenna looked at Tom and said quietly, "Let's get some sleep. You don't have to worry, he won't hurt us, I know he won't!" For just a moment she glanced at the phone, but turned away quickly.

"You're probably right - I think what we really have here is a lonely old man who's almost glad to have some company. But, we'll still leave in the morning!" Tom whispered, stifling a yawn. "And just to be on the safe side, I'll sleep with one eye open, and when you go in your room lock the door, OK?"

Jenna was secretly pleased over Tom's cautiousness, but really thought it unnecessary. She went into the bedroom, lay down on the bed and within minutes was sleeping soundly. Tomorrow was another day, they would worry about what to do then.

CHAPTER TWO (1987)

"Oh please find her -- please! You're wasting precious time here, you should be out there searching!" Helen Lauren was pacing back and forth in her elegantly furnished living room, nervously wiping tears from her eyes as she tried to concentrate on the endless questions being asked by the local authorities. .

"She never gave me any indication that she was unhappy, I can't imagine where she could have gone - she's probably - probably with that Wilson boy if he didn't go to school either. If he's dragged her into something I'll never forgive him!" she shook her head as she tearfully butted her cigarette. The local police had been called when Jenna had not returned home from school, and upon further investigation it was determined that both she and Tom had never reported to school that day. They wanted to know what Jenna was wearing this morning, if she had said anything that could have indicated impending unusual behavior; if she had acted differently the past few days, if they had argued, and other pertinent questioning that only served to distress her mother that much more.

"I - I didn't see her this morning, she was gone before I came downstairs, I can't say what time she left the house. When - when she wasn't here when I came down, I guess I just assumed she had gone to her girlfriend's house or had to get to school earlier than usual. I should have checked, oh, why didn't I check? I just assumed."

"So you have no idea what she was wearing?" the police were asking Helen.

"No, - No, not this morning. But she always dressed nice for school, usually a skirt and sweater or nice top. And she must have been awfully quiet too, I can't remember hearing anything." Helen pondered sadly. She realized that Jenna must have left the house without breakfast, and now she wondered if her daughter had a problem, something weighing on her mind. She wished she had talked to her more, possibly to help to surface anything that might have been bothering her. She considered herself a model mother but couldn't help but think that maybe she could have prevented all this heartache if she had been a little more attentive.

"This is certainly not normal behavior for her. Where is she? Why is she doing this? What if something bad has happened to her? What if -"

"Try to stay calm, Mrs. Lauren. It sounds like she might have had a plan in place," the officer stated. "Try not to worry - we'll check every lead and we'll be talking with Tom Wilson's father too. It looks to me like they're most likely together. Now, promise me that you'll stay here and let us do the work, we're trained for that, you know, and you need to be here when she comes home."

Helen agreed that her daughter and Tom were most likely together, but as she intermittently paced the floor and sat in the blue, wide-armed overstuffed chair drinking more coffee and inhaling profusely on another cigarette, she couldn't help but think that the possibility existed she might never see her daughter again. Since the police had told her that Tom was also missing, she at least found comfort in the fact that hopefully they were together. She admitted to herself that she wasn't overly fond of Tom, but she knew he cared for Jenna and was certainly watching out for her if he was with her. She just had to believe Jenna would be found or come back on her own. The police finally left when the questioning ended, leaving her with every assurance that they would find her daughter. She set her coffee cup down and stared out the side window, hoping, just maybe, she would see her running across the backyard, as she had seen her so many times before.

Jenna's father had left to make his hospital rounds, and although he was very concerned, he knew his daughter's disappearance was well covered and he had every confidence in the local police. He knew the best thing he could do was to remain calm for the sake of the women in the house, and to go about his business and keep his mind as busy as possible. He promised he'd be back home as soon as he finished his rounds and Helen had told him she would phone him immediately if there were any new leads or updates. All of their lives had been turned upside-down by Jenna's sudden disappearance and each of them was trying to cope with the situation in their own way. One common thread was the intensive distraught feeling they each had of not knowing what had happened, had she come into foul play, or had Tom and her just decided to run away together. Naturally, she prayed it was the latter.

She jumped as the phone rang. The police had just left, it couldn't be them. Maybe it was Jenna calling home - maybe she wanted her to come pick her up somewhere. With renewed anticipation she ran to the phone and silently prayed it would be her daughter on the other end.

"Any news yet?" It was Jenna's father calling between rounds.

"No - nothing - the police just left," Helen practically whined from disappointment. "They're checking with Tom's father now. Oh Jack, what will we do? I've called all her friends, no one's seen her - I don't know what else to do - I feel so helpless - I wish you could come home - could you - please?"

"I've got two more patients to see, and I'm hurrying, so I'll be home in less than half an hour, I promise!"

"Maybe we can go out looking for her, I mean them. Even the police are pretty sure she's with Tom, maybe we can spot them somewhere. But then - they told me to stay here - maybe I should - oh -, please hurry - I'll feel so much better if you're here!" She was close to sobs again.

"Try to stay calm, Helen. If she's with Tom, she's safe, I'm sure of it! Is Mom OK? Is she with you?"

"No, she must have gone to her room. I don't know what she's doing - just hurry!" She hung up the phone and walked back to her watch window, more nervous than ever.

She was right. Jenna's grandmother had more or less confined herself to her quarters since she had learned about Jenna's disappearance. She was very devoted to her granddaughter, and was extremely distressed over the situation. She knelt at her bedside and silently prayed for Jenna's quick and safe return. It would seem that the two women should be together at a time like this but there had always been a tense feeling between the two of them. Helen was never happy with the fact that her mother-in-law lived with them. Because of this, the older woman felt like an intruder most of the time and, as a result, when her son was out of the house, she spent most of her time in her own space watching television or knitting or anything to occupy herself.

She looked up just in time to see Shiela walking through the door. Shiela always knocked, but this time she didn't. She had been very quiet since first being notified of her sister's disappearance, but now her grandmother could see her sad eyes and tear-stained face, and as she walked closer, she reached out quickly to hug and comfort her. She always came to her grandmother when she was especially unhappy or distressed, and right now her mother was much too preoccupied to even realize how her youngest daughter might be feeling.

"I yelled at her because she was in the bathroom so long last night, do you think that's why she ran away?" Shiela sobbed on her grandmother's shoulder.

"No, I don't think any such thing!" the older woman smiled. "It has nothing to do with you, honey. I'm sure she's with Tom and she'll be found soon. We just have to be brave and help each other, OK?"

"I just never thought I'd miss her so much!" she cried as fresh tears rolled down her cheeks and she hugged her grandmother tighter.

"Everything will be alright, I just know it - I just know it!" She tenderly brushed her granddaughter's hair with her hand as they sat quietly on the sofa.

Tom's father, on the other hand, was almost totally incoherent when the police began to question him. Not finding him at home, they questioned a neighbor who told them he was most likely at the bar on the corner. They parked outside of the bar and the younger of the two policemen walked in and found Bill Wilson propped on a bar stool. He was told that his son had never gone to school that day but he was in such a stupor that nothing penetrated and he didn't fully understand the questioning.

"Do you understand, your son didn't report to school today. Do you have any information whatsoever as to where he may have gone?" They repeated the question several times before the incoherent man finally understood. "Did you see him at all this morning? Did you have any communication with him recently that might give us a clue to his whereabouts?"

"I saw him this morning, I think it was in the kitchen, and then I heard the door and I thought he was going to school," Bill finally stated with slurred words. "You mean he didn't go to school? Where is he? Why didn't he go to school? Shouldn't you be out there looking for him?"

"We're doing our best, but we need as much information as we can get. Do you recall what he was wearing when he left the house this morning?"

Bill admitted he had no idea what Tom was wearing or any indication as to where he might have gone.

"Jenna Lauren is missing, too, and we're more or less assuming they're together," the officer said. Bill confirmed the fact that they were very close and most likely were together if she was unaccounted for, too.

"We'll keep you informed," said the officer as he headed out the door.

As Bill began to rationalize the seriousness of the situation he started to sink into a deep emotional sadness. The past few years were flashing through his mind, he was fully cognizant of the fact that he hadn't been much of a father. Even before his wife and Tom's mother had died, he had become an alcoholic, and hadn't even tried to resist the temptation to drink every night. Luckily he had been able to sober up enough most mornings before going to work, but he had been warned, and he knew there was a strong possibility he might lose his job.

After the police left he sat deep in thought for some time. He started thinking of Tom, and how depressed he looked all the time, and he knew he was largely responsible for that depression. The more he contemplated the situation the sadder he became. *'Maybe he won't come back, maybe I'll never see him again,'* he found himself thinking. *'Somehow I've got to straighten up my life, I've got to change, I'm losing my son, I've sunk so low, I've got to stop drinking -'* He could feel hot tears welling up in his bloodshot eyes and he lowered his head and cupped it with his hands and cried. Tom was all he had left. If he lost him there would be nothing left for him. He was going to get help for his problem. He would go to AA as his son had begged him to do so many times. He would turn his life around and be a real father again - he knew it would be difficult, but he had finally made up his mind, he didn't want to live this way any longer! He had made his decision and in his heart he was determined to stick by that decision.

He threw some money on the bar, got off the stool and headed for the door. Once he was home he made himself some black coffee, consuming two cups as soon as it was brewed. The impact of what the police had told him had hit him like a brick. As soon as he found himself completely in control, he grabbed his keys and walked briskly to his car. He would join in the search, after all this was his son!

CHAPTER THREE (1952)

It was a warm spring morning in early May of 1952. The robins had arrived especially early this spring, and the trees were starting to show bold hints of green. No one could have asked for a more tranquil and beautiful beginning for a new day. The sun was shining and spreading it's golden hue all over God's earth. The day appeared to be heaven-sent.

"Mary, what do you say we go to that new restaurant tonight, the one that just opened last week?" Joe said hurriedly as he picked up his briefcase and started toward the front door. He was wearing his new navy blue suit this morning with a striped red and blue tie, and as usual he looked impeccable. Mary glanced at him approvingly, and thought how lucky she was to have such a handsome and considerate husband.

"Sounds good to me! I'll be already to go when you get home - about six, right?"

"Possibly a little later, I've got a client coming in at four-thirty, so I may be a little late, but I'll come home as soon as I can."

He smiled as he gave Mary a quick kiss on the cheek and walked out the front door to his car in the driveway. Mary waved to him as he drove off, then slowly walked back into the kitchen and poured herself another cup of coffee and took it out onto the back porch to enjoy the peacefulness of the morning.

Her two beautiful white and lavender lilac bushes were nearly in full bloom, and she smiled to herself as she caught the fragrance of their flowers. She put her coffee cup down on the small table and sat down in the padded wicker chair next to it. She loved her back yard and marveled at the handiwork of nature all about her. She never tired of watching the squirrels and birds as they scurried about and flew from tree to tree and she was always elated to see the little sprouts of her many perennials as they popped through the ground each spring.

How she wished she were watching children running instead of squirrels. She had been told by at least three doctors that she would never be able to bear a child. Her heart ached every time she thought about it, because more than anything in the world she wanted to have a baby of her own. Joe shared her desire, she knew he would make a perfect father, but she seemed to be unable to become pregnant in the twelve years of their marriage and the longed-for blessed event never happened.

Her next door neighbor, Ellen, often brought over her nearly two-year old energetic little boy. He had a bright, contagious smile and ran gleefully to Mary the moment he saw her, and they were obviously very attached to each other. He had adorable blonde curls that bounced as he played and Ellen had been unable to cut them off, even after hearing people commenting on what a cute little girl he was. Mary loved watching him run and squeal with joy while he played as she and Ellen chatted. The two of them had become very close over the years, running back and forth to each other's house for morning coffee or just on the spur of the moment. Now and then, on a warm, lazy afternoon, they would put the baby in his stroller and take long walks in the nearby park, sometimes stopping along the way at the local market to pick up fresh vegetables for dinner. Mary was about ten years older than Ellen, but the age difference didn't deter them from becoming great friends. As she sat there this morning on her back porch she couldn't help but think how her and Ellen were closer than some sisters, and how very fortunate she felt to have her as a friend. She thought about giving her a call to share a cup of coffee with her, but she decided against it as the baby may still be sleeping and the phone ringing would probably wake him up.

She put her head back in the chair and found herself happily anticipating the dinner date with her husband that evening. They hadn't been out to dinner together in some time, almost two months. They usually went out much oftener than that, but Joe had been so bogged down at the bank that he had come home real tired most nights. She always understood and always waited for him to make the suggestion, and she was elated that he had this morning. She would wear that new black and white dress with the solid black short-sleeved jacket - that would be perfect! The new black patent-leather pumps would go well, too; that is, if they didn't pinch her feet, she hadn't worn them yet. Spending the evening over a carefree dinner with her handsome husband was just the ideal way to end a perfect day. She closed her eyes and smiled to herself. Life was wonderful!

After she lazily finished her coffee she walked back into the kitchen and started to wash the breakfast dishes. She switched on the radio and started singing along with the song currently being played when she heard a loud noise. She ran into the living room and glanced out the front windows and seeing nothing unusual she dismissed it as a street sound or possibly one of those sonic booms she had heard people talking about. She finished the few dishes, and pulled the plug in the sink to let the water out. Was that smoke she smelled? She turned and glanced quickly at the stove, thinking she had possibly left the burner on. No, it had been turned off. Suddenly she heard sirens! - loud sirens! - coming closer and closer! Running to the living room side window she pushed back the drapes that had completely covered the window and saw large mounds of gray smoke billowing out of the house next door - Ellen's house! Just at that moment she saw brilliant red flames leaping out of one of her windows. She gasped as she ran frantically out her front door and nearly flew the few yards to the front of Ellen's house. Ellen was frantically running out of her front door holding the baby. He was screaming at the top of his lungs, apparently very frightened by the loud noise and the ensuing agonizing distress displayed by his mother. Terror-stricken Ellen quickly handed the baby to Mary and before she could be stopped, ran back into the house, obviously not thinking clearly and believing that she had time to save some of what she perceived to be her precious belongings.

"NO! Ellen, NO!." Mary screamed, "Don't go back in

there! Ellen, please come out!" Mary started to run after her but then thought better of it since she was holding the baby. She could feel the intense heat and knew she had to keep him safely away from the heat and smoke.

The flames were leaping out the front windows now and engulfing the porch as Mary continued to scream for her friend to come out. She held the baby very tightly and tried to cover his face so he wouldn't breath in the smoke. She was starting to choke on it herself.

Ellen must have called the fire department herself to have it arrive so swiftly, and they immediately started turning their hoses on the house, but Ellen was still in there amidst the violent and swift-moving flames. Mary was aware that something had been tossed from an upstairs window, but that was unimportant right now and her only concern was that Ellen get out alive.

"There's a woman in the house!" Mary screamed running to the firemen, "For God's sake, get her out!! Don't let her die in there -get her out!!"

"Maam, we're doing everything we can! Please get yourself and that baby back as far as you can and out of the way of the hoses! We know she's in there and we'll do our best to get her out!" the fireman yelled above the crashing and crackling noises all around him. Meanwhile the baby continued to scream in fright and Mary intermittently attempted to comfort him amidst her own panic. Neighbors were running out of their houses now and standing in groups to watch the excitement. Another fireman was roping off the area to keep onlookers from coming too close.

Frantically, Mary realized Ellen's husband had to be called. She quickly handed the baby to her neighbor, Jean, and ran back into her house to use the phone. Almost unable to dial, she finally got through to the hospital where Ellen's husband Tim was a doctor. She felt very relieved that the hospital was so close.

"Please, Please, this is an extreme emergency! Please tell Dr. Rogers to come home immediately - immediately, do you hear?"

"I'm sorry, I believe he's - let's see-with a patient. But I'll page him if you think it's necessary," the slow-talking receptionist said on the other end of the line.

"Yes - it's necessary! Page him immediately! His house is on fire - Hurry!!" Mary hung up the phone and ran back out the door, praying that the rather dim-witted girl would get the message to Tim quickly.

She desperately wished there was something she could do to help Ellen, but she knew it was hopeless. One fireman had ran into the burning house but was forced back by the flames. Another one was attempting entrance through a side window with one of the hoses trained above him to keep him wetted down, but flames shot out at him and he was thrown to the ground.

So much of the house was engulfed in fire now and the heat coming from it was intense. All the while another hose was trained on Mary's house to keep the fire from spreading. And Ellen had still not come out of the burning building!

Two other firemen had ran around to the back of the house, and through the kitchen window spotted a lifeless mass lying on what was left of the kitchen floor. Not thinking of the danger to himself, one of them forced open the back door, and with flames leaping at him, pulled the partially charred body out of the house and onto the back porch which disintegrated beneath them. Badly burned and screaming with pain, he collapsed near the burned victim. The body he had so desperately tried to save was still burning when three more firemen reached the back. One of the firemen took off his coat and threw it over the burned body, extinguishing the flames, then the three of them gently picked up the lifeless bundle and moved it out onto the grass and leaving just the head partially exposed, wrapped it in a large, canvas-type cloth. Meanwhile several ambulances had arrived and the injured fireman was being given oxygen and treated for his burns. Attendants carried him to one of the ambulances and he was immediately whisked away to the hospital.

Another attendant bent over Ellen and checked her pulse. There was no heartbeat and she apparently had succumbed from the combination of smoke inhalation and extremely severe burns over her entire body. Nevertheless, they attempted artificial respiration on her to no avail. Very gently the firemen carried her to the front of the house, and lifted the lifeless body into the back of a waiting ambulance.

"Tim! Tim!," Mary screamed amid the sirens and confusion. She had spotted him next to the ambulance as Ellen's body was being loaded. He was just standing there, clearly dazed, as he watched them lift up his wife and close the back doors. She saw him reaching his hand out and attempting to touch her, then pulling back quickly with a look of horror on his face. Viewing what was exposed of her badly burned head could have left no doubt in his mind that his beloved wife was dead. A fireman was solemnly speaking to him, obviously confirming that grave fact.

Mary was no more than thirty feet from him, but with all the noise and confusion he apparently could not hear her calling his name. He had not once looked in her direction. His eyes had been fixed on his dead wife and nothing else - not even his flaming house!

"Tim! Tim! I have the baby, he's with me!" she screamed again, but with the siren starting to bellow on the ambulance she could hardly hear herself. She wanted so desperately to get to him, comfort him, and let him know his son was safe. Huge hoses, piles of debris, and water-soaked ground were in front of her with every step. Some hoses were still pouring gallons of water on the house battling the remaining flames, and a small river was running out into the street. She glanced down to watch where she was stepping and when she looked up again, she could see Tim quickly turning away, and just as suddenly, he disappeared amidst the fire trucks and ambulances!

Perhaps he was going to follow the ambulance. She was sure that was what he was going to do. He'd be back later and she and Joe would be there for him then, and assure him that his son was safe with them. How must he feel, she thought, choking back the sobs! The ambulance with Ellen in it had pulled away and Mary turned and walked slowly back to her house. Jean saw her coming and brought the now-motherless child to her. Trembling and sobbing bitterly, they embraced for a long moment with the whimpering child between them.

"Tim was here. I saw him, but he left. The poor man - it must have been dreadful seeing his wife like that! But he'll be back, I'm sure he'll be right back as soon as he can," Mary gasped through her tears.

Neither of them wanted to be alone, so they went into Mary's house and collapsed on the living room sofa. Nothing could be done now but to take tender loving care of the baby until his father returned to him. The hose that had been trained on Mary's house had left water dripping from the wet walls and large puddles on the floor but that was very unimportant in comparison. That could all be fixed.

"Mommy, Mommy, I want Mommy!!" cried the confused little boy as he ran toward the front door. Mary realized she had to gather some control over her own emotions, as this child needed all her attention right now. The two women took him into the kitchen, gave him cheerios and milk, and watched as he gulped them down, seemingly unaware of the heartbreaking drama that had unfolded shortly before. After he had finished eating, he fell asleep in Mary's arms, much to her relief, and she laid him on the sofa.

"I don't know how Tim will ever explain to him about his mother," Jean said, "but I suppose God will help him find the right words."

The two women walked silently out onto the front porch and looked over at the devastation that was once their neighbor's house. The firemen were still there, pouring water on the charred remains of what had once been a very well-cared-for cape cod. There was nothing left to prove that a sparkling white house with dark green shutters had once stood there. It had nearly burned to the ground in spite of the efficiency of the local fire department. Mary couldn't help but wonder what had caused the fire in the first place. The loud noise she had heard - was that an explosion? She knew there was a kerosene stove in the kitchen which Ellen used frequently, and she had heard that they could explode! Could that have been the culprit that had killed her best friend and wrecked the lives of her little family? She thought about speaking to one of the firemen, but she knew it was too early. There would have to be an investigation, and besides, did it matter now? What had happened couldn't be undone!

As she sadly surveyed the mess, she noticed a few feet away, nearly covered with mud, a small wooden box lying on what used to be a beautiful front yard.

"That must be what Ellen threw out the window," Mary exclaimed as she stepped through the mud to retrieve it. "It must have been important to her. I'll take it in for Tim." Wiping it with her apron, she took it into her house and carefully placed it on a kitchen shelf.

"I do hope Joe gets home before Tim comes back," Mary nearly whispered as she gazed straight ahead. "I think it would be so much easier if we were all here together, and especially since Joe and Tim are so close. Poor Tim, he adored Ellen, they were such a perfect couple, and now - this little boy - without a mother...." Mary put her hands to her face and choked back the tears.

"I'll make us a pot of tea," Jean said comfortingly, knowing how close Mary and Ellen had been. She put her arms around her friend and whispered, "and then we'll just sit here and wait."

"Yes, we'll just sit and wait," Mary echoed sadly.

CHAPTER FOUR (1952)

The sun was setting over Puget Sound as the aircraft circled over beautiful downtown Seattle and headed toward the airport. The tall, handsome doctor in his late twenties was momentarily entranced by the electrifying colors of orange and rose lingering on the water and the western sky. He realized he had never seen such a beautiful sunset and, for just a brief moment, the beauty of it had overshadowed his fears.

He had boarded a plane in Albany several hours earlier. Try as he may he couldn't remember how he got to the airport. Did he drive himself or did someone take him? In fact, everything was pretty much of a blur until the plane was ready for takeoff. He just sat there in his window seat in dumbfounded bewilderment. As the plane went into the clouds it dawned on him that he didn't even know his own name. The stewardess had poured him a drink and he sipped it, nervously gazing out the window, staring at the landscape below but not really seeing it. He had a pounding headache, his palms were sweaty, and his mind was a total blank. He looked straight ahead and to either side at all the passengers seemingly very comfortably settled in their seats for the trip. They were either chatting with the person beside them or busily reading the newspaper or a magazine. No one seemed to have a confused or distressed look on their face, they all seemed to know why they were on the plane. So, why didn't he? He looked at the side window and saw a hint of his reflection. That must be me, he thought,. Hey, I'm a fairly young guy, I can't be developing dementia, or can I? Maybe if he just put his head back and tried to rest everything would come back to him. He pushed his seat into the reclining position and closed his eyes. Try as he may there was no recollection of anything.

"Got business out west?" broke the silence as the man beside him attempted conversation.

"Well, - no, not really." Slightly irritated that he was

disturbed from his deep concentration, he attempted politeness.

"Oh, I saw your white lab coat, and I guess I assumed you were in the medical profession, or something along those lines. Nothing wrong with just taking a vacation, though! Wish I were!" the man said as he seemed to be putting something in his wallet.

Not wishing to further the conversation, the young doctor turned and looked out the window again, but his companion's remark had struck a chord. Just what was he doing with this white lab jacket on? Why was he wearing it? And shouldn't he have a wallet too? He reached for his back pocket and finding no wallet there, he put his hands into his pockets on either side of his lab coat and pulled out a crumpled up boarding pass and a small picture of a woman and child, but no wallet. Amazed at his discovery he stared at the picture, hoping for a spark of recognition. Who could they be?

"Must be your wife and kid, huh," remarked the man beside him.

"Uh, yes," was his confused answer as he hurriedly put the picture back into his top pocket, not feeling the need or desire to attempt an explanation. Perhaps the man was right in his assumption - he only wished he knew!

Then glancing at his boarding pass he thought long and hard for a moment. He was momentarily paralyzed by the stranger's name on the top of the ticket. If that was him why didn't it ring a bell? He quickly read his destination as Seattle -- perhaps he lived there and was going home. Or worse yet, could he be running from something, possibly the law? Exactly what had happened to him that had so thoroughly stolen his memory and left him in such a traumatized state? Should he go back to Albany and attempt to piece together this puzzle? But how could he with no wallet or no money? He abruptly decided it might be in his best interest not to have any identification on him until his memory returned. Without identification he felt somehow safer, no one would be able to prove who he was when he didn't even know himself. If that was his name on the top of the ticket he was sure he would eventually remember who he was. This was probably just a temporary state of amnesia and he would have total recall in a day or two. He was sure Timothy Rogers would not be a stranger to him for very long and that name would continue to be indelibly engraved on his mind as his only connection to his identity. He quickly wadded up the stub, reached across his traveling companion and tossed it in the waste bag the stewardess was carrying down the aisle.

'For the time being, I'll just be Jake,' he silently decided to himself, picking the first name that came into his mind. *'Just as soon as my memory returns and I know who I am, I'll gladly assume my true identity. But just to be on the safe side-.'*

He knew he hadn't lost his intellect, just his memory, and hopefully, he thought, by the time he arrived in Seattle everything would be clear to him. It was very frightening not to be able to recall one thing from before arriving in Albany. And this white lab jacket, certainly not normal everyday attire, what could that mean? He tried to think of all the occupations that would require a white jacket of this sort. A druggist, a chemist, a doctor or medic, and probably others he couldn't think of. And no wallet, either? What was he doing without his wallet? And the picture of the pretty woman and little boy, were they his family? If they were, could they be wondering where he was at this moment? He knew he had a scheduled flight because of the stub he just threw away, but was he leaving from home or going home? If there was no return ticket, that must mean he lives in Seattle, doesn't it? So many questions circled in his mind and he could feel his head spinning! He had never felt such desperation in his entire life, and he wished he could just fall asleep and when he awoke be able to recall everything. That was a possibility. He would try to sleep! But try as he may, sleep evaded him and he just sat there hopelessly gazing out the window, seeing nothing!

The trip was long and uneventful. Thankfully, the whir of the engines had lulled his co-passenger to sleep. As soon as he heard him softly snoring, he took the picture out of his pocket again and stared at it for a very long time. These two beautiful people must be very important in his life, or why would he have their picture in his pocket, when he didn't have so much as a comb on him? She is so pretty, he thought, and that adorable little child looked about two or three. Why can't I remember?? If only this were a bad dream and I would suddenly wake up and everything would be normal! But it's not a dream, it's real, I'm on this plane and I don't know why or who I am!!

There was a temporary landing in Chicago, a few passengers got off, then they were in the air again. The only real break was when the stewardesses served what the airlines called dinner. It was a macaroni and egg salad with ham and cheese chunks mixed in. The young doctor ate very little but found that the hot coffee hit the spot and seemed to relax his nerves slightly. At least the man to his right was still asleep. He knew he was not in the mood for idle conversation and was thankful that he hadn't been prodded for more small talk. They had been flying for hours when the pilot announced that Mount Rainier was to the left, but no one seemed to be too interested. Soon the seat belt light came on and the stewardesses announced they were preparing for landing. As the plane was descending, panic seized him, and he found himself saying a silent prayer.

'Please Lord, let there be something here in Seattle that will jog my memory and make me remember the man whose name was on my ticket. Why am I here and what am I supposed to do now? - where am I supposed to go? Is this my home? I am totally lost!! Please help me!!'

He got up from his seat, patiently waited in line in the aisle, thanked the stewardess on his way out, and, in total bewilderment, deplaned.

CHAPTER FIVE (1952)

At least he didn't have to wait at the baggage counter since he didn't have any luggage with him. He suddenly realized that nothing in this airport looked at all familiar to him. Had he ever been here before? He knew he must have looked rather odd, not carrying any kind of luggage, as everyone around him was struggling to balance two or three bags as they attempted to make their way through the crowded airport. An elderly lady, trying to juggle a rather large suitcase, dropped her carry-on practically at Jake's feet, where it opened and the contents spilled out on the floor. She was nearly in tears as she bent down to retrieve her belongings, some of which were rolling across the floor under the feet of the passersby. Several people hurried by, trying not to step on anything, but no one stopped to help her - no one except Jake.

"Let me give you a hand," he said with a smile as he bent down next to her. People were scurrying by so fast that in their haste they were kicking a few of the articles, and Jake found himself dashing to retrieve lipsticks, hair rollers and various other articles of a cylindrical nature that had escaped from their paper bag, and various other articles of a cylindrical nature. He handed them them back to the very relieved lady, who by that time was finding it rather amusing herself. She thanked him and quietly told him she was glad there was still some chivalry left in the world. Continuing his walk along the long corridor he attempted to blend in with the crowds and followed them down the stairs and out the nearest exit. Stepping out onto the sidewalk he discovered large parking lots in all directions except one, so that seemed the logical way to go. In spite of the distress he was feeling he couldn't help but notice the beautiful white-capped mountains looming in the distance. Turning in one direction he caught a glimpse of Mount Rainier and was in momentary awe at its majestic beauty. He stood quietly surveying his surroundings for a few moments to try to get his bearings, as people continuously hurried by him completely unaware of his forlorn circumstances. There was a Howard Johnson restaurant and inn down the street to his left, and another two-story motel across the street. At his right were several smaller not too progressive-looking businesses that seemed to stretch forever. He walked along slowly looking for clues that would possibly explain what he was doing here. There certainly was no point in hurrying, as far as he knew he had nowhere to go. He could see tall buildings looming in the distance so he knew that the airport was located somewhat out of the hubbub of the large city, for which he was thankful. In this less intimidating area it might be easier to find his way around.

Now and then someone would give him a brief smile as he walked along the sidewalk and he politely smiled in return. Possibly he had been here before, and he suspected that maybe he even lived here somewhere in the city, but, if so, why wasn't there some little spark of familiarity? If this was his home at least the mountains in the distance should be a recognizable landmark to him. Then a thought occurred to him; with a little luck he might possibly run into someone who would recognize him. But how embarrassing would that be if someone recognized him when he wasn't even sure himself who he was? Perhaps he had just visited in Albany, New York and now he was coming home. Should someone have met him at the airport, and would he have known them if they had? He decided he had never in his life felt quite so vulnerable. He felt like a man without an identity. The stub of the airline ticket that he had thrown away had listed a name that most likely belonged to him, but that person was as much of a stranger to him as the people he was meeting on the street. Desperately he looked around for something familiar, something that might shock him out of his amnesia. But it was to no avail, nothing rang a bell, it was just an ordinary street filled with unrecognizable buildings and strangers.

He walked by a fruit and vegetable market and a kind old wrinkled man offered him a apple, but he declined the offer, not knowing whether it was a gift or if he was expected to pay for it. Slightly embarrassed over the fact that he was penniless, he shook his head and gave a weak smile and walked away as quickly as he could.

Then he had an idea! Spotting a phone booth on the corner he decided to flip through the white pages for the name that had been listed on his ticket. He discovered to his perplexity that there were at least two and a half pages of Rogers, and several T. Rogers. The addresses meant nothing to him, and even if he could call those numbers without having to deposit money, exactly what would he say if someone answered on the other end.

'Hello, I believe my name is Tim Rogers, but I'm not absolutely sure and I don't know where I live,-- are you missing anyone?" or *"Hello, this is Tim, is it OK if I come home now?"* He laughed to himself thinking how ludicrous those words would sound. An overly suspicious person might even call the police and he decided he didn't need that at this point.

Besides, there was just as much of a chance that he lived on the other side of the country. It suddenly dawned on him that since he had flown out of Albany, New York that he could call Albany information and ask for the phone number of the person named on his ticket. That would be a start! Oh, sure! He would do that if he had a dime to dial the operator! And what would he do even if he got a phone number. It could be his number or belong to someone with the same name, that name was certainly not that uncommon. And even if he called and got an answer, again what would he say? For all he knew a tracer would be put on the call and he would be in big trouble if his suspicions were confirmed and he really was wanted for something. He decided the best thing to do was to walk away from the phone booth, and think of another plan of action.

He started to cross a street and inadvertently stepped on some chewing gum which had been tossed by the curb - adding insult to injury. He attempted to scrape it off the bottom of his shoe on the side of the curb and continued on his perplexed walk. He didn't know where he was going and what he was going to do when he got there! He was going to have to find a job immediately if he expected to eat. He would take anything for the time being, he told himself. Anything at all would suffice right now.

He had walked a couple of blocks further and, just a short distance up the street, on a building set a little off by itself, he spotted a faded red and white sign with the words Nell's Coffee House in large black letters. Possibly he could bargain for a cup of coffee while he bought more time to think about what he should do next. Filled with uncertainty he walked slowly, hesitating a moment before he cautiously opened the squeaky screen door.

What was he doing? He was actually going to ask for a free cup of coffee. Here in a totally unfamiliar place he was about to beg! On top of that he was homeless. How had he sunk so low?? He knew what he really wanted wasn't the coffee, but an unencumbered, free mind with a clear knowledge of his past. He had to have had a past-everyone has a past! Why couldn't he conjure up even the slightest remembrance of anything from that past?

As he was closing the door as quietly as possible, trying to avoid the squeak and hoping he wouldn't be noticed, he couldn't help but notice the rather run-down condition of the establishment. There was one lone man at a table way in the back. He had his head down reading a newspaper and didn't bother to look up when Jake walked in. The only other person in the restaurant was a rather large, pleasant-looking lady behind the counter, busily cleaning off the cooking area. As he approached the counter with a rather hesitant smile he said, "Maam, I'm sorry, I seem to have lost my wallet, but your coffee sure smells good. Could I offer some kind of assistance, maybe sweeping up or washing dishes, in exchange for a cup?"

The large, round-faced woman behind the counter turned slowly, paused for a moment, then wiped her hands on her blue-striped apron. It looked like she was in the process of cleaning up for the day. Her face was heavily made up, but there was a softness and kindness behind the make-up that Jake spotted immediately. She was quite wrinkled, her gray hair was done up in a bun in the back and he surmised she was probably in her late sixties or early seventies. She walked with a slight limp, and with the extra weight she carried around he concluded she must be quite tired by the end of the day. Suddenly that kind face broke out into a wide, toothy smile.

"Oh, I guess I can spare a cup, probably would be dumping it soon anyway. Sit down, you look tired. How about a cinnamon doughnut to go with it?"

"I would be ever so grateful, you see I --"

"Now, don't just stand there, have a seat. And no need to explain to me, things happen!" she smiled again as she poured him a steaming cup of coffee and placed the doughnut on a plate in front of him. "There's more where that came from, so don't be bashful, now. I'm going to keep cleaning up, but if you want more coffee, just whistle." With that the trusting lady turned back to her closing-up tasks, but she couldn't help but wonder about this handsome stranger. True, he looked a little disheveled, but the honesty in his blue eyes captivated her and she somehow knew she couldn't turn him down. The white medical-style jacket threw her off a little at first, but she realized that didn't have to mean anything in particular. He was wearing a pale blue shirt beneath it, and the five o'clock shadow on his deeply tanned face told her he hadn't shaved too recently. His black hair was thick and a little wavy, and she watched as he ran his hand nervously through it. She didn't want him to catch her watching him so she turned around and started cleaning around the coffee pot. She could see he was very disturbed about something, and she guessed correctly that he desperately needed a friend.

He sat silently as he sipped the delicious coffee and munched slowly on the doughnut. He felt a little guilty about the whole thing, and he hoped that he in no way had frightened this kind lady by approaching her in the manner in which he did. She certainly didn't appear to be annoyed or frightened, in fact she seemed to look rather pleased. As he took the last bite of his doughnut, he couldn't help but gaze around the room again and see that the place was in a rather neglected condition, but was still clean and orderly. And he sensed a warmth and coziness in this little coffee shop that he couldn't explain. Faded blue curtains hung at the windows and the flooring was worn in a path from the door to the counter and tables. Business must have been rather good here for some time to wear the flooring away like that. The padding on the stools was ripped in places, and the pink and gray counter top had lost all of its Formica shine and was severely scratched and worn. The tables and chairs clearly needed to be refinished, they were past the state of worn, and the dingy plastic pink roses in the little vases on each table desperately needed replacing with something fresh and colorful. Nevertheless, the little restaurant had a certain aura of comfort and appeal, probably due to the friendliness of the owner.

"My name is Nell," she offered, as she turned back to the counter and reached out her hand to him, "everyone likes to call me Nellie, but I prefer just plain Nell. This here is my place, I've had it for twenty years now. Done quite well too, I might add. Being close to the airport has helped a little, I'm sure, but I get mostly neighborhood trade. But now and then a pleasant stranger like you pops in. How's your coffee, and what's your name?"

"I'm - uh - Jake," he retorted slowly, using the name he had previously decided upon. "And maam, your coffee is great! But I really mean it, let me help you clean up this evening. I'm sure you could use some help and - I don't know how to say this but I really have no place to go."

"No place to go?" she repeated as she reached for the coffee pot to give him a refill. As she poured the coffee her heart went out to him. *"Homeless?, he certainly doesn't look the type"*, she thought to herself.

"I bet you just flew in, is that it?"

When there was no reply, she took a couple of steps closer

and continued, " I have a friend who runs a boarding house just down the street, if that will help."

He put his head in his hands for what seemed to her a long time before he spoke. Without raising his head he said, "Thank you Maam, but you see, like I said, I've lost my wallet, so I wouldn't be able to pay for a room. Can you tell me if there's a rescue center in the area, or - a shelter of some sort - somewhere where I could spend the night?"

His voice sounded so desperate she knew she had to help him. She had never turned anyone away and she was not about to start tonight. She was well known all around the area for her big heart, and trying to help people even in a small way was her specialty.

"You sound like you could use a friend, maybe I can help," she said softly.

He sat quietly for a moment longer then raised his gaze to meet hers. He saw a sympathetic, genuinely concerned, grandmotherly-type lady with a warm, contagious smile looking down at him. She had no reason to trust him - a total stranger - but she somehow knew she could. He could tell she was sincere in her offer to help him.

The man in the back had left and they were alone now. For a moment he thought hard about confiding in her about his amnesia, but he soon put that idea to rest. For all he knew she might be frightened and go to the police and, if there was the slightest possibility that he did have a problem with the law, he better not say anything to anyone, not even this compassionate stranger!

"Just down on my luck, I guess, sure could use a job if you know of any."

Wiping off a portion of the counter, and hesitating for a moment before she spoke, she said, "How handy are you with fixing things and painting - stuff like that?"

"Actually, I consider myself pretty handy - for small jobs anyway," he answered rather quickly.

"Well, if you're not particular, I could use some help repairing this place, shaping it up a little. My husband died twelve years ago, he did all the repairs. I've had a few neighborhood kids helping me from time to time but I never could really depend on them. And a carpenter just charges too much, so I just let it go. I realize the place is in quite a sorry state." She glanced around at her tired establishment with a mixture of love and defeat in her eyes.

"Nothing that can't be fixed with a little effort and elbow grease, and I'll be grateful for anything right now!"

Her eyes penetrated his as she looked squarely at him and said, " Now I can trust you, can't I? You don't look like the sort that would give me any trouble, but this is the fifties after all and one can't be too careful these days."

He could understand her concern, him being a total stranger, and he reached his hand out to reassure her. "I certainly understand, maam, I realize you've never seen me before today, but I can assure you you're safe and I won't give you any trouble. I'm trustworthy and I'll do a good job for you. And, believe me, I truly appreciate your offer. It's very kind of you."

Reaching for his outstretched hand, she smiled and said, "If it pans out I could give you twenty dollars a week and all the food you can eat." There was something about this young man, something very honest and sincere, and she felt an instant rapport.

Jake couldn't believe his ears. He never expected to find any kind of a job this quickly. This would hold him over until he discovered his purpose for being here, which he was certain would be revealed to him before much longer. He listened as she continued on.

"Now, you need a place to sleep. There's a cot in the back room. I live in the connecting house so don't feel that you'll be in my way if you use that room." She motioned toward a closed door on the back wall. "As soon as you're through with your coffee I'll show you. It's small, but sufficient. My husband, toward the end, when he was getting pretty sick, would go in there when he was feeling tired and rest for awhile before he would come back out to work. It came in handy for him, poor man, he should have rested more than he did. He always worried about leaving me with all the work out here, but he only went in there during the slow times. He was a good man - I miss him terribly!" Her eyes were getting misty as she spoke.

He hadn't finished his coffee yet but he got off the stool and followed her through the doorway. Just as she had said it was small. There was the cot, a place to hang clothes if he had any, and two small screened windows on the back wall, so the place had plenty of light and ventilation. A door at the end of the room led to a very small private bathroom with a seat, wash area and a tiny corner shower. It was cramped but it would do just fine for now, at least he wouldn't be out on the street. The relief must have shown on his face as he looked at his angel in disguise and thought how the God who works in strange and mysterious ways had really heard his silent prayer. Maybe not exactly as he had originally wanted it answered, but at least he was going to eat, have a roof over his head, and some money coming in every week; until he discovered where he really belonged. He decided he was going to do everything in his power to help this miraculous lady! She had given him his first real ray of hope and he wasn't going to let her down.

"Thank you so much, maam, I am ever so grateful, I can't tell you how much you've helped me, and I promise I'll get this place in ship-shape condition in no time," he smiled in relief as he gazed at his benefactor. "You have no idea what you have done for me!"

"Think nothing of it, happy that I could help!" she smiled warmly as she walked back out into the restaurant. There was something very promising about this young man that seemed to be in such desperate straits. She knew instinctively she had nothing to fear from him, and that possibly he could become the answer to her prayers. She had seriously considered selling the restaurant, it was becoming too much of a burden for her, but now she would just wait and see. Maybe once he had the place repaired and looking more presentable again she could manage to hang on to it. And just possibly she could convince him to stay on and give her a hand in running the place. It seemed as though he had been sent to her at precisely the right time and the entire undertaking could be very beneficial to the both of them. Time would tell. It seemed that God had blessed them both simultaneously!

Jake still couldn't believe his good fortune. The desperation he had felt earlier had disappeared, at least for now. He was so relieved that he wanted to give Nell a big hug, but decided against it, maybe that would be going too far. He was about to take a final sip of his coffee, which had gotten cold, but Nell was right there with the coffee pot for a warm-up. "I'm going to fix you the best roast beef sandwich you ever had! And there's apple pie, fresh, made it this morning!" She was beaming, and it was hard to tell who was the most relieved, her or Jake.

"That sure sounds great, Nell. I am a little hungry!" he admitted sheepishly. He found it almost impossible to believe his good fortune, it was almost as if they had been waiting for each other to come along. And there was so much warmness in the gaze that passed between them that he knew at that moment he had found a friend and a home away from home!

CHAPTER SIX (1952)

Bill Woodrow was just about to leave his office for the day when his intercom buzzed. He had wanted to get home a little earlier today and he hoped this call wasn't something that would hold him up too long. He enjoyed his job, it gave him a tremendous feeling of accomplishment, but he was tired tonight and just wanted to get home, grab the evening paper and sit back and relax.

"This case is right up your alley, Bill," his supervisor was saying, "It's a little offbeat, but you'll solve it in no time, I'm sure. Stop by my office and I'll fill you in on the particulars."

What could he say but "I'm on my way," as he put his coat back on the hook and walked down the long hallway to the chief's office. Since he was considered one of the top investigators at the Seattle Missing Persons Bureau he seemed to always be nominated when the case at hand was more complex than usual.

"What is it this time, Wally?" Bill said as he sat down in the chair in front of the chief's desk.

After butting his cigar and shifting papers around on his desk, Wally began, "We got a call from a little upstate New York town, River Valley to be exact. The authorities there informed us that a young doctor in the local hospital, by the name of Timothy Rogers, presumably came here to Seattle for a medical symposium, never showed up for it, and never returned home, or at least no one knows of his whereabouts. And there's a twist to the story - it seems. On the morning in question, May 6th to be exact, he was called at the hospital and was told to rush home because of an emergency. That emergency turned out to be that his house was on fire, and later the authorities learned his wife was killed in the fire. There was also a little two-year boy - he survived the fire."

He had Bill's full attention now as he continued, "Upon questioning his next-door neighbor it was determined that he was at the scene of the fire, at least momentarily. She said she saw him for

53

just a moment and then he was gone. She said she was quite sure of the time when she saw him and if she was right then exactly an hour and a half later he was boarding TWA Flight 97 out of Albany, New York, with a stopover in Chicago, and a final destination of Seattle. The boarding list has been confirmed, he was on that plane! Question is, what's he running from? It may be possible he thinks he is wanted in connection with the fire, but that's not the case, they've found the definite cause and it was purely an accident, a kerosene stove explosion. Strange thing, though, he wasn't even around to attend his wife's funeral!"

"That certainly is strange! Sure makes him look guilty about something! But it's definitely just a missing person's case, nothing criminal attached to it, right?"

"No, nothing criminal at all! I've been strongly assured of that, although I have to admit I'm skeptical. If he had nothing to hide why did he take off like that? But right now the most important thing is to find him, if he's still alive, so that little boy has at least one parent!"

"And you want me to look for him here in Seattle or in Chicago? You know he could have gotten off the plane there quite easily," Bill said.

"The stewardesses were questioned and they said they were 100% sure he didn't deplane in Chicago, a few had gotten off, but one stewardess in particular said she remembers serving him dinner later. Besides she said he was very handsome and she couldn't keep her eyes off him." Bill and Wally gave each other a sly smile.

"That should happen more often - sure would make our job a lot easier!" Bill quipped.

"You got that right!" Wally laughed, "Anyway - It seems he has just disappeared off the face of the earth. They've already checked with the hotel in downtown Seattle, where the symposium was held and he never showed."

"What about relatives? I assume they've checked that all

out, too."

"According to his neighbor, she wasn't aware of any relatives, at least he had never mentioned any, only his wife, now deceased, and, of course his little boy. According to his records at the hospital he listed his wife as next of kin. That's why they're stymied at that end, I guess they've checked out every possible clue they could come up with. So they naturally assume he must be here in the Seattle area somewhere, and they want us to proceed with the investigation at this end, just physically look for him everywhere. By the way, they sent us a picture." Wally handed the picture to Bill and he studied it for a minute, then he tucked it in with the rest of the investigative papers.

"OK, I'll start by checking the airlines again and all the hotels and motels in the area more thoroughly, he has to sleep somewhere. I'll show the picture around to car dealers, eating places. gas stations, boarding houses - doesn't sound too difficult. I'll start first thing tomorrow," Bill assured his boss, as he picked up the folder of papers and started for the door.

"Good! I'm sure someone will have seen him. Keep me informed!"

"Will do," Bill promised as he walked back down the long aisle.

'Poor little boy, he thought to himself, *'I've got to find his daddy as soon as I can, I hope nothing bad has happened to him.'* Suddenly he couldn't wait to start.

CHAPTER SEVEN   (JULY 1952)

"Jake, I'm so glad you stopped in for coffee that evening," Nell smiled sincerely as she handed him his weekly twenty dollar bill. "I didn't know anyone could do so much in seven weeks time. You've fixed the roof, repaired the front steps, put new flooring all through the place, repaired chairs and tables and painted everything in sight. It goes on and on, is this the sort of stuff you did for a living?"

"I don't think so - I mean - yes, in my spare time, I believe," he stammered.

This was the first direct question about his past life Nell had put to him all the time he had been there. She seemed to respect his privacy and hadn't even asked where he was from or his last name, but he knew she must have wondered. He would catch a questionable gaze from her occasionally, but there was at the same time a warm feeling of mutual respect growing between the two of them. Jake was quite contented now, he was well fed, had his own little room in the back and twenty dollars a week certainly was ample pay along with free room and board. In fact he had been saving the majority of it.

'Jake Miller - that's my full name now - Jake Miller. Someone's bound to ask and as long as I don't have to show proof it'll be fine,' he thought to himself as he lay on the cot that night. It was really the first time he had given some thought to the fact that he didn't have a last name. No one had asked, not even Nell, so he had had no occasion to require one. He had thought momentarily about using Rogers, the name on the ticket, but quickly decided he'd better not, for obvious reasons. He slept very soundly that night and awoke the next morning with almost a sense of relief. He would just have to create a whole new identity and in case his memory never returned he would just have to start over as a new person. But he couldn't help but wonder, was someone waiting for him somewhere, wondering

every moment what had happened to him, and had they notified the authorities? And why wasn't someone looking for him? A month had passed without even the slightest hint of recall. He had prayed each night for some small recollection, some little token of remembrance - but nothing had come to him! Didn't anyone care?

He had gone to a nearby phone booth one day and called Albany information and asked for the phone number of Timothy Rogers. He was informed there were four Timothy's and twenty-eight just plain T. Rogers. He decided to start with the numbers that had the full name. He dialed the numbers of one of the Timothy Rogers but there was no answer. He tried the next number. At the sound of a woman's voice he quickly hung up. If he was married could that have been his wife? He was annoyed at himself for panicking so quickly - maybe if she had heard his voice she would have recognized him. He tried to call again but this time she didn't pick up. He tried a third number and this time when a female voice answered he found the nerve to ask her if Tim was at home. She sounded very old and quite sarcastically told him she had been a widow for fifteen years. He half-heartedly tried the fourth number and nervously repeated the same question.

"He's at work, he'll be home about five-thirty," the young voice on the other end answered. "Do you want me to have him call you?"

"No, thank you, I'll try again later," he lied. If that Timothy Rogers was at work it certainly couldn't be him. He had run out of change and out of luck as far as attaining any information, at least for the time being. He crossed off the two numbers that he knew not to try again and stepped out of the phone booth and started to walk slowly back to the restaurant. He told himself he would try to call each day at least two or three of the phone numbers listed under that name, and with each call he would ask for Tim. Eventually, maybe someone on the other end would say, "We don't know where he is, he's missing!" At least that would be something he could follow up on. He knew his searching could take a long time. He would have to try every one of those numbers in the Albany area, and also start checking all the T. Rogers in the Seattle phone book, of which there were many!

CHAPTER EIGHT (1952)

Bill Woodward had really gotten involved in the case. He sincerely wanted to find that missing man so that little boy would have his father back. The thing was, there was the strong possibility that the man in question may have met with foul play, although, as of that moment, there had been no criminal report matching his description. He realized this could become a long-term or completely futile search.

He was sure he had canvassed the entire Seattle area in regard to anything that a Timothy Rogers might have had access to. Three months had passed since he had started the investigation in the middle of May; it was now the middle of August, and he had not uncovered a single lead. He had shown the picture in every gas station, used car dealer, eating place, laundromat, boarding house, hotel and supermarket that he had come across. No one could recall ever having seen him. The airport and the hotel where the symposium was held had been checked and double-checked, nearly everyone had been questioned and shown the picture but to no avail. He had become aware of the fact that the Seattle police had also been informed about the missing man, possibly even before he had been put on the case, and were also doing their own search. Apparently, they hadn't come up with anything either. He wasn't used to working a case like this, he had always uncovered something by this time, and he was beginning to become quite frustrated over the entire situation.

Feeling especially perplexed one afternoon as he was driving along a side street several blocks away from the airport, he spotted a coffee shop and decided he could use a cup of the hot liquid. Maybe it would settle his ragged nerves. As he was getting out of the car he realized this was one eating place where he had not questioned anyone or shown the young doctor's picture. Might as well kill two birds with one stone, he thought! He started to rummage through his briefcase for the picture. Where was it?. He had shown it at least a hundred times all around Seattle, and he always had it with him when he was working. Then he remembered - Wally had asked for it that morning to show to some realtors he was meeting with, and he had not come back to the office before Bill left. *'Wouldn't you know it?'* he thought to himself, *'But, then what would an up-and-coming doctor be doing in this part of town anyway. But just to be on the safe side I'll stop back another day with the picture.'*

Opening the door to Nell's Coffee Shop he stepped inside and took the first seat at the end of the counter. A heavy-set lady came up to him and with a big smile handed him a menu.

"Just coffee, maam," he said.

Nell poured his coffee and set it in front of him. "I've got fresh doughnuts, sure you wouldn't like one?"

"Not today, maam, thanks anyway," he said looking out the window, wondering why he had taken the time to stop here in the first place. Not that the coffee wasn't good, but he should be getting back to the office, he'd been away from there for several hours now, and he knew he had quite a bit of paperwork to take care of before he went home. He took a few more sips, left the money on the counter and started for the door. The heavy-set lady saw him get up to leave and in a very pleasant voice said, "Have a great day, stop in again!" He turned, gave her a quick wave, and as he was closing the door, he heard her voice again,

"Oh, Jake, there you are, I wondered where you disappeared to."

"I was in the back room checking to see what we needed to order. I'm sorry, I didn't mean to leave you out here alone, but I noticed that it wasn't busy, so I grabbed the opportunity."

"No problem, just one lone customer and he didn't stay long. Didn't seem to be too friendly either. Guess he didn't like my coffee much. Seemed to be in a big hurry."

"Where do you suggest we go from here?" Bill asked Wally one late afternoon. "This man is certainly a master at elusiveness, or he's dead, or he's using a disguise and alias, and if that's the case he could be anywhere in the world by now!"

"Those are possibilities, I agree, -- or he may just go back home on his own. Let's just put it on the back burner for now and give it a rest. Besides, I've got another case for you, - there's this woman looking for her husband, down in Federal Way. She says he's been gone a month, and she claims he just went out for a pack of cigarettes."

"Guess he didn't tell her where he was going for those cigarettes! I'll take it - it's bound to be a little more exciting than this last one!" Bill laughed.

CHAPTER NINE (1953)

The restaurant was not only looking one hundred percent better, but business was improving. Customers commented on the new improvements and Nell always gave credit where credit was due. She always let Jake know how much she appreciated all his hard work. The tables and chairs had all been repainted in country blue and white, checked blue and white curtains hung at the windows, and shiny new gray and white tiles brightened up the floor. Even the contents of the white vases on the tables had been replaced with authentic-looking flowers intermingled with sprigs of greenery. Two part-time waitresses had been hired when it had become too much for Jake and Nell to handle. One came in at eleven till two and the other worked from four to seven. To Nell's delight, satisfied customers were coming and going most of the day,

In one of their frequent conversations Nell had mentioned a son who lived down in Tacoma. Edward was a good boy, she had said, but very lazy and had never offered to give her a hand with the restaurant. In fact he rarely came to visit.

"Not completely his fault though," she had said, "that wife of his, she pulls him around like a puppy. I don't think he can even think for himself anymore. Never did care much for Claire - don't like to feel that way, but that gal is sure cold and calculating."

"That's too bad, Nell, you deserve better, he just doesn't realize how lucky he is to have a mother like you. But he may come around yet, you never know."

"Not while he's married to her, he won't," a grim-faced Nell answered. "Why you seem more like a son to me than he does!"

Jake continued stacking frozen hamburgers and steaks in the freezer as he listened to her talk and heard the sadness in her voice. He couldn't imagine why a son would ignore his mother, especially one like Nell.

"That's nice of you to say, Nell, but it's a two-way street you know! You've been awfully good to me. I don't know what I would have done that day without your kindness and concern. You took me in when I was desperate! That cup of hot coffee and cinnamon doughnut were sure heaven-sent!" He stepped over toward her and gave her a quick peck on the cheek.

"Thanks, I needed that!" she said with a little laugh. "But I would say it was a double blessing. Guess I never told you but I was seriously thinking about selling this place. It was becoming too much for me to handle, and then - thank God, you walked in and saved the day! It was almost like a miracle!" He could tell she meant every word of it. He really was becoming like a son to her, not by blood maybe, but as an honest, considerate, hard-working replacement for the mostly-absent Edward. They had established a mutual respect and trust for each other that was uncommon for two heretofore total strangers to find in such a short time.

Jake had been doing much of the actual running of the restaurant now, since the majority of the repairs were done. He found that he really liked everything about restaurant work. Was this maybe what he had done before? He was doing all the bookwork, all the ordering, cooked, helped to wait on tables and assisted with the cleanup. His days were very busy, but he found he never tired of it.

He was starting to make friends among the customers who dropped in on a regular basis. Frank Maley, a postman, stopped by every morning on his way to work and he and Jake had become acquainted while Jake served him his morning coffee and toast. Frank was really into athletics, all kinds, from baseball to bowling to golf, and he convinced Jake that he should join his bowling league, which Jake promised to do in September. They closed most evenings by seven, on weekends they stayed open a little later, so he knew bowling one night a week wouldn't pose a problem.

There was another customer that seemed to be dropping in

on a regular basis. She was like a breath of spring compared to the mostly middle-aged and elderly people that patronized the restaurant. Sandy was petite, hazel-eyed and blonde, a very attractive twenty-year-old lady who had lost her young husband a year ago in an auto accident. She hadn't had any desire to even as much as look at another man since his death, and she more or less assumed she never would. The fact that she was only nineteen when she lost him didn't sway her, she was so sure that her life was over as far as dating and marriage were concerned. It never occurred to her that she might meet someone that she could really love again. She had had some extra time one morning so she stopped in the little restaurant on her way to her job in a nearby bank, and when she spotted Jake wiping off the other end of the counter she couldn't believe her eyes! He was definitely the best-looking man she had seen around here in as long as she could remember. She felt herself staring at him and when he turned and spotted her, she immediately blushed and turned her gaze away. Feelings of guilt consumed her - she should not even be noticing him! But it had been a whole year, maybe it was alright now if she considered finding happiness again. After all, nothing could bring her young husband back. She had been through it all, the sorrow, the unending tears, the hopelessness. Of course, some days were better than others, some days she realized she even felt happy.

For some unknown reason this morning had started out as one of those days. She was glad she had taken a little extra time with her makeup this morning and she knew her long, blond hair fell just right on her shoulders. The forest green suit with the pale green blouse she had chosen to wear today helped to highlight her hazel eyes, and she was feeling extra good about herself.

"What can I get you, maam?" he said as he was walking toward her with a warm smile that would make any female, any age, sit up and take notice.

"Ah - just coffee, I guess -" she stammered, hoping her red face wasn't too obvious. This sudden surge of adrenalin was something she hadn't experienced in a long time.

Jake gave her a wink which only added to her nervousness, then turned around, reached for a cup and poured the coffee and sat it in front of her. Just where did this beautiful young woman suddenly come from?

Sandy had managed to regain her composure, at least momentarily, and reached her hand out across the counter to him.

"Hi, I'm Sandy Burrows, I haven't stopped in here in quite a while, but I had extra time this morning," she smiled, wondering why she felt the necessity to explain, "Gee, the place looks great! I'm glad Nell decided to get it spruced up. The last time I was in here it was getting pretty run down." She knew the reason why she hadn't stopped in in such a long time was because she had stopped going anywhere or doing anything except going to work each day, then going home each night and watching television with her mother. She knew that for the past year she had almost ceased to live. Just the sight of this handsome young man made her realize that maybe now it was time to rejoin the human race.

"Nice to meet you Sandy, I'm Jake Miller, and I've been giving Nell a hand." It was nice to see a fresh young face for a change and he wasn't oblivious to the fact that she was very pretty, and he found himself wondering if she was unattached. A quick gaze at her ring finger told him she wasn't wearing a wedding band.

"I work near here - in a bank - so I have to walk by here each morning, but I haven't stopped in in months, I'm usually running late, you know how that is - but it's amazing that I haven't seen you around." She knew she was stammering and she couldn't hide the fact that she could become very interested in this handsome stranger, in spite of her year-long sorrow.

"Well, uh - I've been staying pretty busy right here, been here close to a year now, and I'll probably work for Nell until a really great opportunity comes along or Nell tells me to leave, whichever comes first!" he laughed.

Just then a customer sat down at the other end of the counter, and since Nell was busy, Jake reluctantly went to wait on him.

"Be right back," he smiled as he walked away. He secretly hoped she wouldn't leave until he could get back to her. Sandy watched him walk away, and felt a little stirring within her that she hadn't felt since before her husband had died. There was something about this man, something very exciting, something worth pursuing - *'and to think he's been right here for nearly a year, why didn't I stop in sooner,'* she scolded herself. *'Well, let's just see what happens!'*, she happily thought to herself as she finished her coffee, gave him one more lingering glance, and slowly got up to leave. She could have sat there a few minutes longer but she didn't want to appear too obvious and maybe scare him away.

'I do believe I'll need this refreshing cup of coffee every morning from now on,' she smiled to herself.

Jake turned and looked in her direction just as she got up from the stool. His eyes followed her out the door and he found himself hoping that this would become an every-morning ritual. But Sandy had already decided that it would.

CHAPTER TEN (AUGUST 1953)

Jake was quite comfortable with his life now! He hadn't even looked at the picture that was still in the pocket of the lab jacket that hung, nearly forgotten, at one end of the small area he used as a closet. The last time he had looked at it he was still unable to conjure up any recollection of the faces of that beautiful young woman and adorable little boy. He had concluded that the best thing he could do was to move on with his life. If his memory returned some day he would deal with it then.

With his wages from the restaurant he had been able to pick up a second-hand automobile, a 1948 Oldsmobile in great condition, only five years old, with the automatic shift which in 1948 was a fairly new innovation in driving. The day he picked it up was about his most exhilarating high since he had arrived in Seattle. He was beginning to feel like he really belonged to the world.

Just as he had hoped, Sandy Burrows had become a morning regular at the restaurant. She made sure her schedule gave her time to stop at the restaurant. The day was incomplete if she didn't get to see Jake before she went to work. She always had a cup of coffee, but that was secondary, sometimes she didn't really want it - it was just a good excuse! When she saw Jake walking toward her each morning with her coffee in his hand she could hardly contain her excitement! She knew that, at least for her, this was developing into something more than friendship. He was always very friendly and attentive to her but other than that really gave no outward indication of any special interest in her, or so she thought.

Jake was being cautious. He was still deeply concerned over the fact that his past was a mystery to him, and, as attracted as he was to Sandy, wasn't sure just how involved he should become. Still when she walked through the door each morning, he knew the sudden exhilaration he felt upon seeing her could only mean one thing. That lovely girl with the blonde hair and hazel eyes had really made an impact on him, and he realized he was the happiest he had been since he had arrived in Seattle. Could he be falling in love? But - what if there was someone waiting for him, maybe even married to him, and someday the truth about his past would all surface - what then? Should he throw all caution to the wind and pursue his interest in Sandy, or just keep the relationship as strictly friendship?

A whole month went by before he decided that just spending a quiet evening together wouldn't need to be construed as anything more than just a friendly date. After all they were good friends by now, talking every day, what harm would there be in spending a few hours alone together?

When she stopped in the next morning, he took her coffee to her as usual, smiled, then found he was a little nervous when he confronted her, but forced himself to continue anyway.

"Would you like to go to a move tonight?" he blurted out as he sat the cup down in front of her.

Sandy could feel her heart racing as she looked up into his handsome, tanned face and tried to answer as casually as she could, " Well, yes, I'd like that - that would be fun! The early movie starts at seven - is that okay?" Finally, he had asked her out!! She was beginning to think he never would! She spent the rest of the day in happy anticipation of their date together, hardly able to keep her mind on her work.

Jake finished up in the restaurant a little early that night. He had told Nell he had something he had to do and asked her if she would mind closing alone. She gave him a sly smile, she hadn't been blind for the past month. She could see there was something developing between the two of them, and it pleased her to see it happening.

"Of course I can close alone, did it for years. You go and have fun!" she said as she winked at him, and he knew she knew. "She's a lovely girl - you two look great together! See you tomorrow morning!"

"Glad you approve!" he laughed. "She is pretty wonderful,

isn't she?" Jake said with a smile as he gave Nell a quick peck on the forehead and then walked through the door to his living quarters. *'This isn't really a date -- just a way to get to know each other better,'* - he kept telling himself, but deep inside he knew it was going to be the start of much more!

She had given him her address and he drove to her house promptly at twenty of seven. She had been in such a happy state all that day at work that she had to force herself to concentrate on what she was supposed to be doing. Invasive thoughts of Jake and their impending date kept her at the height of excitement. As soon as she got home she started primping. Her mother encouraged her to at least eat a sandwich, but Sandy couldn't take the time. And she wasn't hungry, she was much too excited! She tried on at least three different outfits before she decided on black slacks and a light blue light-weight sweater. She tied back her blonde hair with a blue ribbon and put on just the right amount of makeup - not too much - she didn't want to look overdone. When she saw Jake drive up and park in front of the house her excitement was almost more than she could stand. When she opened the door Jake thought she looked like an angel, and was happy that he had finally decided to see her outside of the restaurant. She gave him a contagious smile that she had not been able to erase from her face from the moment he had asked her out. She quickly invited him in and introduced him to her mother and after a few pleasantries she glanced at her watch and reminded him that the movie would be starting soon. Any feelings of guilt or betrayal that she might have had previously regarding her deceased husband had dissipated and all she could see now was Jake. It was a wonderful world after all!

They saw each other regularly after that, every morning at the coffee shop and at least five nights a week. Sandy decided she needed one night, usually Sunday night, to catch up on her sleep and

Jake tried to understand. Usually they went to a movie, or sometimes they would drive into downtown Seattle and listen to the symphony when it played outdoors in the park. They enjoyed sitting in their lawn chairs on those warm nights, holding hands and listening to the strains of Bach and Beethoven, with an occasional Sinatra melody thrown in for good measure. Or they would just walk in the park, feeding the squirrels and the ducks and enjoying nature together. Whatever they did, it was the being together that mattered, and they both knew this was becoming much more than a good friendship.

"Did you live here in Seattle your whole life?" Sandy asked Jake one night as they sat quietly on a park bench. She had been wanting to ask him for some time now, and had been a little surprised that he had never mentioned anything about his family.

Jake, momentarily stunned, didn't quite know how to answer. She had never approached the subject of his past before. How could he tell her that maybe he had always lived here but he didn't really know for sure. He knew any answer he gave her would lead to more questions, and he had almost forgotten that those questions were bound to come up sooner or later. Realizing that if he said he had always lived in Seattle she would probably want to know what part of the city he was from. So he decided to take the easier way out.

"No, I - I'm originally from back east. Just decided to try my luck out here."

"Just like that? Gee, that was brave to come out here with no job in mind or anything. At least I assume you weren't planning on working for Nell, right?"

"No, but I was lucky she hired me right away, and I didn't have to spend time looking for something," Jake continued, as he tried to act as nonchalant as possible.

"What about your parents, brothers or sisters if you have any, don't you miss them?" Sandy was genuinely concerned about him being here in Seattle all by himself.

"My parents died a few years back, and I have no siblings,

so there's really no one to miss," he said, hoping that would end the conversation. For all he knew his parents could have been alive and well and he could have had a dozen brothers and sisters somewhere.

"No cousins or aunts and uncles, no one like that?"

"A few scattered ones, I guess, but no one that I was ever close to. Hey! - enough about me, how about a hamburger?"

"Sounds good to me!" Sandy was seemingly unaware of Jake's nervousness upon being questioned about his past. She was happy to believe anything he told her, but she couldn't help but feel a little sad that he obviously had no one - no one but her and Nell now. But she decided right then and there that she was going to stick like glue, she was falling in love with him, and she fervently hoped it was mutual. She would make sure he would never be alone again!

CHAPTER ELEVEN   (1954)

Summer in River Valley could be either very pleasant or extremely muggy, and the July of 1954 had chosen the latter. The humidity was at an all time high and those who were lucky enough to own air conditioners were running them at full blast. Very few homes had them though, mainly just the very wealthy.

But the extreme heat and humidity weren't the only demons plaguing the community. Poliomyelitis, (or infantile paralysis, as it was commonly called), had reached epidemic proportions in many parts of the country and was running rampage among the citizens of River Valley. There had already been three deaths within a few weeks in this small village. Everyone, particularly parents of small children, were on guard and in a state of panic over the alarming rate at which this frightening disease was spreading in the area. There had been articles in the paper from time to time that someone named Jonas Salk had developed a vaccine against the disease but it was still in the experimental stage and had not been fully released to the general public as yet. There was an ongoing study, however, where over a million children were injected with either the polio vaccine or a placebo, but four-year old Jack Rogers was not among them and therefore didn't have even the fifty percent chance of protection against the disease.

He had been quietly playing in the back yard one afternoon. Mary noticed that he seemed extra quiet that day, that he didn't seem to have the energy that he usually had. He had been quite wistful at the breakfast table, and although usually very hungry in the morning, he had eaten very little this morning. He had a very tired look around his eyes but, other than that, he didn't appear to be sick and when he wanted to take his little red truck out to play in the sand pile, Mary saw no reason to deny him. As she watched him from the kitchen window, she was suddenly astonished to see him tearfully struggling to make his way toward the back door, and she quickly ran around the corner of the kitchen cabinets to meet him as he came into the house and fell at her feet. Brushing his hair back and looking down into sad, wet eyes she gathered the little boy up in her arms and sat down in the nearest chair.

"Mommy, it hurts - all over -- Mommy - Mommy!", he cried as he snuggled closer in Mary's arms. As she brushed her hand across his forehead she discovered he was burning with fever. He pointed to his throat in an effort to let her know that hurt him, too. Very alarmed, she decided not to wait for any more symptoms to surface. Her thoughts immediately focused on infantile paralysis. Could her little boy be coming down with the dreaded disease that was terrorizing River Valley?

Grabbing the phone with one hand and still holding the sobbing little boy with the other arm she quickly dialed Dr. Quinn's office. When his nurse-receptionist answered she nearly screamed into the phone.

"This is Mary Lauren. My little boy has a high fever and sore throat - and, - it seems to be hard for him to breathe. I'm so afraid ---"

"Bring him in immediately. Do you have transportation?"

"No - I don't, I'll call my husband to come home."

"No, that would be wasting time. I'm going to send an ambulance to your house immediately. I'll have Dr. Quinn meet you at the hospital. And try not to worry. It may not be what I know you are assuming. Have him lie down until the ambulance gets there. And it won't hurt to pray!"

The phone clicked on the other end and Mary felt very alone and helpless. Realizing she may be needlessly imagining the worst scenario, she forced a smile as she lay the little boy on the couch. She left him long enough to pour cold water on a washcloth, wring it out and put it across his feverish forehead. The cloth became warm rather quickly due to the little boy's high fever. She knew she had to try to remain calm so as not to upset him any more than necessary.

"You know that big white car that makes that funny noise?

Guess what? You're going to ride in it in just a few minutes. Won't that be fun?"

"Are you going too, Mommy?," Jack questioned in a teary voice.

"Of course I am. Daddy and I will be right there with you! Listen! I think I hear it now!"

In a matter of minutes the ambulance arrived, loaded the little boy and prepared him to be whisked to the hospital. She quickly called Joe while the attendants were getting Jackie ready for transport. Mary hugged him and assured him she'd be riding in the ambulance with him.

Fortunately Joe arrived home just as the ambulance was pulling out of the driveway. Tears streamed down her face as Mary rolled down the window and quickly told him of Jack's symptoms, but was careful not to mention her dreaded fear of what it might be. Joe tried quietly to reassure her, then closely followed the ambulance carrying their son. He couldn't get his mind off the dreadful plague that had taken over the valley. What would they do if something happened to this precious child? Although the adoption wasn't final yet, as there was still the possibility of his father returning, they loved Jackie as if he were their own. He had been put in their care, of which they were more than willing to take on at the time, but should his biological father come back for him someday, they knew they would have to give him up, because, of course, he should be with his own biological family. It would leave a tremendous void in their lives if that happened, but they knew they would never lose him completely. They would always keep in close touch somehow.

Joe pulled in behind the ambulance, quickly parked his car and rushed to where they were unloading Jackie. The attendants pushed the gurney through the open doors and into the hospital. A team was at his side within seconds to examine and evaluate his condition. The curtains were pulled around him and Mary and Joe were asked to stand outside. The wait was long and agonizing, but finally the doctor appeared.

"I'm sorry folks, I sure wish I didn't have to tell you this," Dr. Quinn hesitated, as he led them away from Jack's bed. The look on his face confirmed Mary's worst fears. All she could think about was the three who had already died from this disease right in this community, two of them little children. She knew others were hovering on the brink of death, and she was horrified to think that the same thing could happen to her little boy.

"Oh, No!" she cried. "What can we do, will he be alright? Anything at all, it doesn't matter, doctor, just make him well!!"

"The best thing we can do for Jackie now, is to try to remain calm, although I realize how hard that is. The disease is affecting the muscles of his respiratory system and making breathing a little difficult. The only alternative I see at this time is the iron lung, believe me, it's a lifesaver. Hopefully we'll catch it before it gets worse. He will be enclosed except for his head, and it will help him with his breathing. Don't worry, I'm going to make the recommendation that you stay with him -". The doctor stopped short when he saw Mary start to sway.

Joe put a hand on each of her shoulders, and Mary turned her head slowly and looked up at the doctor.

"You said hopefully you'll catch it, what does that mean?", Mary said quietly as the tears rolled down her face. She glanced toward the curtain a short ways away that was pulled between her and her little boy.

"It means we'll do everything we can for him. But let's not waste time. I'm going to start making the arrangements. You can stay with Jackie until we move him."

At that, Mary quickly dried her tears, pulled back the curtain, and, forcing a smile, hugged the little boy.

"Everything's going to be alright, Jackie, the doctor's going to make you feel better. You'll see!"

All kinds of thoughts crowded their minds. This was without

a doubt their son lying in that bed, they had raised him, nurtured him and loved him completely for the past two years now, but there was always the thought of Tim. Tim, his real father - if he was still alive somewhere he would want to know. But where was he, what had happened to him?

Mary knew that immediately after the fateful fire two years ago, his disappearance had been probed to the fullest extent by the River Valley police, the New York State Police and the Seattle Police Department. They had interviewed numerous nurses and doctors and health care workers at the hospital and discovered only that he was scheduled to be at a medical symposium in downtown Seattle the next day after the fire. They had traced his flight to Seattle, that much she knew for sure, but upon checking the hotel where the medical symposium was to be held they found him to be a no-show. The airlines, train and bus stations had all been thoroughly researched in case he had decided to leave Seattle. He could have purchased a car, but none of the local dealers had any record of a Tim Rogers in their recent sales. It was a mystery - it was as if he had dropped off the face of the earth. It seems everything had been fully scrutinized except for the small local Seattle restaurants and coffee shops.

She had learned that, after a while, since it was not a criminal but a missing persons case, the local law enforcement departments decided to hold off for further clues, or the possibility of the eventual return of the man in question. But, two years later, it was still a mystery - Tim has never returned.

It seemed like hours had passed as they sat quietly waiting, each trying to reassure the other. Joe had gotten them each a cup of coffee, at least it was something to do with their hands, and the warm liquid was comforting to a small degree.

"The doctor would like to see you both," quietly stated a pretty redheaded nurse, as she walked to where Joe and Mary were sitting. Terrified by what might be awaiting them, but doing her best at gathering composure, Mary rose slowly from the brown leather chair, took Joe's arm and followed the nurse to where Dr. Quinn was waiting.

"You can sit by him now. He's a frightened little boy, of course, so if possible try not to let him see your concern," said Dr. Quinn as he led them down the hall and into the room where the long steel contraption known as the iron lung was housed.

"I want you both to know he'll be getting around-the-clock care. I think we're in pretty good shape here and as you know early detection is always the best medicine, and we caught him in the very early stages." He gave a reassuring smile as he consolingly put his hands on each of their shoulders for a moment, then slowly walked from the room.

Each day Mary kept a continual vigil by the side of the iron lung, relieved only by Joe for a few hours after he came home from work. His small limbs were being massaged several times each day by physical therapists and the doctor assured them there was a gradual improvement every day, in fact he stated that he wished every case that had been brought in had been as encouraging as Jack's. Even his happy and captivating smile was resurfacing, and the color was returning to his cheeks. Knowing how devastated the entire community had been since this terrible plague had started, Mary and Joe were extremely grateful that their son's case had been one of the lighter ones reported.

"Mommy, can I go home now?" he said one morning as Mary walked into the room. He looked unusually bright and alert and he could move his legs without pain and Mary had been told he was making a remarkable recovery. Last night had been the first night she had gone home to sleep, she had been keeping a faithful vigilance every night in a lounge chair by Jack's bed, but he was improving so dramatically that Dr. Quinn had almost forced her to go home and get a good night's sleep.

"Maybe not today, honey, but it will be soon. Dr. Quinn says you are getting much better, and Mom and Dad can take you home before too much longer, but we have to wait until the good doctor tells us its OK!"

"Can I play in the dirt with my trucks, huh - can I, Mom, - as soon as I get home? I'm kinda sick of this place. It smells funny too - I want to go home!"

His childish impatience was music to Mary's ears, she was so grateful he had recovered from what had attacked so many others, some even fatally. She hugged him and assured him it would be soon.

The only damage that seemed to have been done to his little body was a slight limp, but he was still the same bright, happy little boy that he had always been. His relieved parents thanked God and counted their blessings, extremely happy that their precious child had been restored to them, and with such minor complications.

September and much cooler weather returned to River Valley, welcomed especially this year, because the number of new cases of infantile paralysis was rapidly declining, and everyone was starting to breathe a little easier. It had been such an immensely hot summer with the death toll from the disease rising one more to four, but there were also a few still in wheel chairs or on crutches that would possibly be left with permanent damage to their limbs. It was very possibly the worst crisis that had ever affected the small community as a whole, and everyone was glad that at least for this year the problem was diminishing. Supposedly, Salk's vaccine was going to be put into general use within a year or two and hopefully stop this dreaded disease in its tracks.

Jackie was very excited about entering nursery school, and life in the Lauren household was returning to normal. When Mary took him to school on his first day and walked with him to his room to meet the teacher, she couldn't help but think of how quickly he was growing up. How fast the years would fly by from now on!

CHAPTER TWELVE   (1956)

The year was 1956, time was moving along, and Jake had definitely made a place for himself now, he had bought some new clothes, among them a couple new sport jackets, several coordinating slacks, and at least a dozen neat-looking shirts. He and Sandy had been inseparable for nearly three years now. Sometimes she would come and help him out at the restaurant, just so she could be near him. It didn't matter as long as they had the companionship of each other. The subject of marriage had not come up, Sandy was hoping, but Jake seemed to be stalling and at times she wondered why. She wasn't going to rush him, he had to be the one to bring up the subject, and she was beginning to think he might never ask her. She was feeling impatient but she was determined not to show it. He seemed to be in deep thought sometimes and just as she would start to ask him what he was thinking he seemed to change and suddenly become his old congenial self. But she sensed some inner turmoil, that try as she may, she could not seem to relieve.

Every Sunday morning they went together to the ten AM services at the local Baptist church which Sandy belonged to. They stood side by side, holding hands, as they sang the lovely old hymns and listened intently to the inspiring messages in the pastor's sermon. They both realized that their mutual strong belief in God had brought them even closer together. It had become a beautiful relationship and they knew they were in love, but Jake was still harboring indecisive feelings about his past, the past of which Sandy was still not aware of. He had told her his parents were dead and he had no other close relatives that he knew of. But she was not aware of the fact that he really couldn't remember anything about his life before he landed in Seattle. A few times he almost weakened and attempted to bring the subject up, but he would always change his mind, not being too sure of what Sandy would think of him if he told her of his amnesia. She might even think he was living a double life, or had been in deep trouble somewhere and had came here to escape - it just wasn't worth the risk.

Meanwhile, Nell's health had taken a downslide, she was having chest pains now and then, her breathing would become labored at times and she was keeping to her bedroom more often. This kept Jake extra busy at the restaurant; he often worked past the 7PM closing time, sometimes not finishing up the cleaning tasks until around 8 at night, but he didn't mind, he loved the business and the people who stopped by. Besides, Sandy was usually stopping by in the early evening to help him, and they enjoyed working together. Nell would pop into the restaurant a couple of times a day, wait on a few customers, and wipe off a couple of tables, but Jake noticed she was slowing down and tiring very easily.

"Now I can carry that!" she would insist, if Jake took a tray of dirty dishes out of her hands.

"I'll take care of the next order - you know, I'm not helpless!" was another one of her frequent phrases. Jake would usually let her but he couldn't help but notice how quickly she got out of breath and had to sit down.

"The girls and I can handle everything here, Nell, and I want you to take it easy. No need to tire yourself."

Sometimes she would even snap at him, which was not like her at all, but Jake knew she was really just annoyed with herself for not being able to do what she was used to doing.

"I'll feel better tomorrow," she would mumble as she would slowly walk back through the door into her house and Jake knew she had had enough, at least for the time being. He had succeeded in convincing her to see her doctor and she assured him she had been put on heart medication. He made a point of checking on her every evening and he tried over and over again to get her to call her son and let him know how she was feeling.

"I'd rather not bother him - they've got their own lives," she'd quietly explain. "Besides, I'm just getting a little tired, that's all!"

"Well, I'm going to see to it that you take it easy. You need to rest, and I'm going to keep checking on you to make sure you take your medicine, too, understand?" Jake said trying to look stern as he put his hand on her arm.

She smiled as she nodded in agreement, and thought how close Jake and her had become. He knew she thought of him as a son, and she had certainly become a mother figure to him. Jake was always concerned about her and wondered if he shouldn't just try to get in touch with her son himself. But since she was so adamant about it he decided that if she really needed him she'd call him, and possibly it would be an infringement on her privacy if he interfered.

It had been just about four years now since the day he had landed at the Seattle airport in total confusion. How fortunate for him that he had wandered into Nell's restaurant and literally begged for a cup of coffee. This remarkable woman had, in essence, given him back his life. She was paying him one hundred dollars a week now plus a percentage of the profit, and room and board were still included. She had surprised him a year ago by hiring carpenters and having his living area remodeled and expanded by several yards in the back. He now had a small kitchen area, (just in case he wanted to eat in private), a small but sufficient bathroom, and quite a large living/bedroom combination. She had had new carpeting installed and the entire area was immaculately masculine. She had also given him full rein as far as the restaurant was concerned and since she wasn't feeling too well a lot of the time, Jake was managing most of the operation and all of the book work.

Since the business had picked up considerably, Nell had some time ago given her approval to hiring two part-time waitresses, one came in at eight AM and left at two PM and the other one came in at about three for the supper hour. They had long since changed the name from Nell's Coffee House to Nell's Restaurant and they were serving light meals now called blue plate specials. The helpings were quite generous and it didn't take long for word to get around.

But as busy as he was all day, Jake still found time for things that he enjoyed doing such as reading, in particular, anything associated with medicine. He couldn't explain his strong desire to learn the latest medical techniques and treatments. He was particularly intrigued by Jonus Salk's recent development of a vaccine that had the potential of wiping out infantile paralysis forever. He thought of the thousands of people who would live and have productive lives as a result of this contribution. He knew he had an unexplainable urge to become involved in the cutting edge of medical knowledge and research. Most nights after he had come from Sandy's house he would become engrossed in a couple of medical books he had purchased, or check the daily paper for anything related to medical advancement. Then he would lie on his bed in the dark and ponder his intense interest in the subject. Possibly he was meant to be a doctor - or - was there the slightest possibility that he had been one? No, that couldn't be, surely he would vaguely remember something about medical school, hospital surroundings, his patients, or some other association. He determined it was just a deep interest, no different than with someone who was passionate about baseball or acting or some other profession.

Several times he would recall Nell's words to him, 'You're much too intelligent to be working here, much as I'd hate to see you leave, but you're cut out for something much better!' He knew she didn't want him to feel locked in or obligated to her in any way and this was her way of telling him to feel free to leave if something better came along. But for now he was contented, he had learned the restaurant business well, and he felt very comfortable here.

CHAPTER THIRTEEN (JULY 1957)

"You look so handsome tonight, I could hug you!" Sandy squealed as she opened the door and saw Jake waiting on her doorstep to pick her up for their usual Friday night movie date. She had on her favorite white peasant blouse with a navy blue flair skirt. Her long, naturally-curly blonde hair framed her fresh and pretty face, and Jake couldn't help but smile in delight when she appeared. She certainly was an attractive young lady, and just as beautiful inside as out.

"I wish you would!" Jake blurted out with a teasing grin on his face. Quickly he put his arm around her waist and lowered her down the three steps to the sidewalk. Sandy looked up at him with a startled look and they both broke out in hearty laughter.

"Let me know next time you have that sudden burst of energy," she laughed, "I'm not used to surprises!"

"Sorry, honey - guess I got carried away!" Jake whispered in her ear. The warm breath on her ear was too much of a temptation and she lifted her face toward his. He needed no invitation as he looked into her pretty hazel eyes and soon their lips met in a warm, passionate embrace, - then, holding hands, they walked slowly but happily to Jake's slightly rusted Oldsmobile.

"The movie starts at nine," Jake suddenly became serious, "that means we have fifteen minutes to get there." He had hurried with the clean-up at the restaurant, it had been a particularly busy day. But knowing he was going to see Sandy every evening made it all worth while.

"Well, lets not keep Clark Gable waiting!" she laughed as she slid into the seat on the passenger side of the car. Jake parked the car in front of the theater, paid a little over a dollar for both of their tickets, purchased some popcorn, and the two of them walked into the darkened theater. It had become a habit of theirs to always sit in the back row. They both enjoyed this, holding hands in companionable silence as they enjoyed the movie together. The theater was packed and noisy at first, but as the movie started it quieted down and the couple happily munched on their popcorn.

Clark gave his usual superior performance, and two hours later, as they walked out of the theater they decided they were both in the mood for a light snack.

"Hungry enough for dinner? " Jake asked, as he took her hand.

"Not really, let's save that for another time. How about the drive-in down the street? I think I would like something light - like maybe a hamburger?"

"OK! Hamburgers it is!" Jake smiled as he looked over at his lovely companion.

Sandy noticed that Jake seemed a little nervous tonight, she was beginning to wonder if something had happened, or if maybe he wasn't feeling so well. She really had no idea of the surprise in store for her.

They drove to the nearby drive-in and the carhop came out (on roller-skates, no less). Jake had to give the young girl a hand with attaching the tray to the window but it finally snapped in place. He gave her their order of two hamburgers and two root beers and she turned very competently on her skates and wheeled back to the order window.

Sandy surprised herself when she suddenly blurted out, "You know, I'm so glad I met you! What if we had never met? What if I had never stopped in Nell's coffee shop, it scares me to think about it!"

"But you did, and here we are! Some things are meant to be, honey, and our meeting each other was one of those things!" He was about to reach over and kiss her when the carhop appeared at the window with their snacks. He gave her a quick smile, paid her the dollar and fifteen cents, and handed Sandy her root beer and hamburger. For a few minutes they relished their burgers in companionable silence, occasionally giving each other a contented grin.

It was a warm summer evening with a full moon glaring down on them, and Jake had turned suddenly quiet and deep in thought. He had been seeing Sandy for a few years now, and he knew she was the one for him. After all he was approaching his thirty-third birthday, not getting any younger, and this beautiful night in July of 1957 looked as if it had been made just for them. He knew he had been holding out, convincing himself he had to deal with his past first before he could make any commitment to Sandy, but it was beginning to look like his past was lost forever. He knew he had better speak up before Sandy grew tired of waiting and he lost her too.

As they were finishing up their hamburgers, Jake decided it was as good a time as ever as he reached over for her free hand. They both laughed as, startled, she nearly dropped her drink in her lap.

Nervously, he began, "Sandy, something's been on my mind for a long time now, in fact, nearly four long years! You know how much I care for you and how close we've become." He paused for a moment as if to find the right words. He never thought he would be quite this nervous, and he decided the best thing to do was to just get it over with as quickly as possible. Sandy looked up at him, holding her breath in happy anticipation. Reaching across in front of her he opened the glove compartment and, with a sly grin in her direction, he took out a small white box. His hands were shaking slightly as he attempted to open it, finally succeeding on the third try. Holding the tiny, but nevertheless, beautiful diamond ring in his right hand and taking a deep breath he blurted, "so would you consider marrying a poor restaurateur ---?"

"Yes, Yes!" she squealed in delight. "I thought you'd never ask!"

"But you didn't let me finish my speech I've been so meticulously working on."

"I don't care about a speech, honey, I'm just so happy you finally asked. What took you so long? I've been waiting and waiting for such a long time!" she whispered in relief as she snuggled closer.

"I was beginning to think you never would! I promise I'll try real hard to make you never sorry!"

Her third finger, left hand was poised and waiting as he slipped the engagement ring on it and they came together for a ecstatic and lingering kiss.

"Oh, I love you so much, Jake, you'll never know how much I've prayed for this day!," Sandy squealed.

"And I love you! I don't think I've ever been so happy! We're going to have a great life together. And I'm sorry I took so long to come to my senses. I hope you forgive me for that."

"Forgiven!!" Sandy laughed, as they excitedly hugged and kissed again,

"I realize I don't make a pile of money, but with us both working, I think we can make out alright. And my little apartment behind the restaurant is big enough for two - for the time being. Once we feel we can, we'll look for a bigger apartment. Is that OK with you?"

"I don't care, just as long as we're together. Besides your little apartment is fine, I love the way Nell let you fix it up!" Sandy said happily.

"Then, it's settled. That's one detail we've already worked out," Jake smiled.

"What do you think - maybe just a small wedding? I'll buy a new dress of course, probably off-white, and I'd like to carry pink roses, and have all our closest friends there. My mother will be happy to let us use her back yard for a reception - not a very big one, of course. " Sandy was so bubbly and happy she couldn't sit still.

"Anything you want is fine with me," Jake happily interrupted. "And we'll pay for everything. I don't want your mother burdened with any expenses."

"I think a small, beautiful wedding in my mother's flower garden would be perfect! John and I had such a huge church wedding, and I know I don't want to go through all that again. It was nice but it was so much work and so expensive. I certainly never thought I'd be planning another one so soon." She thought briefly of her previous marriage which she had entered into at the tender age of seventeen, and had ended with his death just before she had turned nineteen. At the time she was sure she would never find meaningful love again, but here she was with this marvelous, handsome man who she knew loved her as much as she loved him.

"But that was then and this is now! And I am so terribly pleased and happy to become your wife!" Sandy was becoming so overcome with emotion the corners of her eyes were wet and the tears were starting to roll down her cheeks. Jake was becoming emotional too, and he knew that anything that had happened in his life heretofore, paled in comparison to the happiness he was feeling now.

"Honey, I'll buy you the most beautiful pink roses in the city and I'll call the pastor as soon as we set a date. How about six weeks from now, would that give us enough time?"

"Six weeks from tomorrow - Yes!- that should bring us to the first Saturday in September! Oh, Jake, it'll be wonderful!! I'm going to start looking for a dress right away. And I'll pick up some invitations, and order a cake - and - Oh, I can't wait!!" Sandy was beside herself with joy!

"Oh, and by the way, we have to think about a maid of honor and best man. I'll ask Nancy, my cousin, I think. If you don't have anyone in mind I'm sure my brother would be happy to be best man." Her brother, Jimmy lived in Boise, Idaho with his wife and two children and managed to get over to see Sandy and her mother at least four times a year. "That is unless you have someone you would rather have. Oh! I can't wait to tell my mother, she'll be as excited as I am!"

"Your brother would be great for my best man. I have no one in particular to ask so that's fine with me. Do you want me to call and ask him?"

"No, I'll take care of it. He's due for a visit anyway. Oh! I can't wait to tell my mother, she's been waiting too, just like I have!" she said with a little sly grin.

It made Jake happy to see her so excited and as he took her in his arms he whispered, "I love you Sandy, and I promise you we'll never be apart again!" He sealed his promise with a tender, lingering kiss.

They were both happily ecstatic on the drive home. It seemed to them that nothing could ever go wrong again to spoil the beautiful life they would have together. They hugged happily as he walked her to the door. "I just remembered, I have to open an hour earlier in the morning, so I better go, much as I hate to, but I'll see you in the morning, honey, OK?"

Sandy smiled the smile of a woman in love as she opened her front door and Jake turned to walk to his car. She could hardly contain her happiness as she tiptoed into her bedroom so as not to awaken her mother. She could tell her the happy news in the morning, for now she just wanted to dream about the wonderful life her and Jake would have together!

'Wait till I tell Nell. She'll be almost as happy as we are!' Jake thought to himself as he pulled out of Sandy's driveway.

As he turned in to park his car next to the restaurant he noticed a light on in the front room of Nell's house. It was about one-thirty and Nell usually retired around nine o'clock. Since he was in the habit of checking on her most nights, he was especially concerned to see a light burning. He knew it was highly unlikely that she would still be up at this time. Maybe she had just forgotten to turn out the light, she had been quite forgetful lately. He suddenly regretted that he and Sandy had spent nearly an hour and a half discussing their impending wedding. He should have checked on Nell sooner. Cautiously he opened the door to the restaurant and walked through to the entrance of Nell's house. She had given him a key some time ago when he had insisted that he wanted to make sure she was alright each night before he retired. She had protested, telling him not to worry so much, she would be alright, but she finally gave in and handed him a key.

He no sooner had the door opened when he spotted her on the floor in the doorway between the kitchen and living room. A small rocking chair was tipped over sideways next to her, she apparently was getting up from it or she grabbed it when she realized she was starting to fall. Running over to her he immediately felt for a pulse and discovered there was one, but very faint. Her eyes were closed and her skin was clammy and Jake instinctively knew she had been lying there for some time.

"Nell! Nell!", he called loudly several times but there was no response, she couldn't hear him. His first impulse was to give her artificial respiration, but decided against it when he realized it might do more harm then good. He left her long enough to reach for the phone book on the telephone stand and he rustled quickly through the yellow pages for an ambulance.

"Come quickly to 228 Walton Ave. There's a woman on the floor, I believe she's either had a heart attack or stroke. She has a slight pulse, but she's very gray."

"We'll be right there, see if you can get her to respond." There was a click of the phone and almost immediately one sharp siren not too far in the distance that let Jake know they were on their way. He was grateful for the close availability of the ambulance.

Kneeling beside her Jake rubbed her hands and arms and kept talking to her in an attempt to possibly revive her. When there was no response, he ran to the front door to make sure it was open and the porch light turned on so no valuable time would be lost when the ambulance personnel arrived.

It only took them less than five minutes to arrive, but to Jake it seemed like thirty. They immediately administered oxygen and put her on a gurney for transport. Jake hurriedly gathered up all her medications and put them in a paper bag for the ambulance attendant to take with them. In a flash she was loaded into the back of the ambulance as one of the men informed Jake she would be taken to Harborview Medical Center.

Several neighbors had come out of their houses when they heard all the commotion. They were standing around in groups watching as the ambulance pulled away. It was quite late but there seemed to be no time constraint on curiosity!

"Did Nell have some sort of attack?" Louise from next door was asking.

"I'm not sure but it looks like it's probably her heart," Jake answered. "I'm going to the hospital now and I'll stay there till I get some news."

"Please give her our love if you get to talk to her, we'll be praying for her." Louise said solemnly as she turned to walk back to her house.

Jake locked her front door and walked back through the restaurant. Making sure the sign was flipped to the '*closed*' side and in case he wasn't back in the morning in time to open, he locked the restaurant door and hurried to his car. As he walked he kept thinking that he should have kept closer tabs on Nell, he knew this hot July weather could have bad consequences on anyone with a bad heart. Why hadn't he given her a little more attention? But he knew she would have made light of it and would have told him to stop worrying.

As he hurried to his car, it suddenly dawned on him. *'I didn't get a chance to tell her my news! She would be so happy for us. I just hope I get the chance to tell her.'*

All the way to Harborview, he silently prayed for her life and for a quick and complete recovery. She had been like a mother to him and he didn't want to lose her.

CHAPTER FOURTEEN (1957)

"An elderly lady named Nell Matthews was just rushed here. Could I see her please?", Jake asked as he rushed into the hospital reception area.

"Relative?" was the quick retort.

"No, but a very dear friend, and I know she'll be wanting to see me."

"Sorry, sir, but we're not allowed ---", she started and Jake quickly interrupted her.

"Look, maam, her son is in Tacoma, I'm going to be trying to reach him and I want to reassure her that I'll be calling him as soon as possible. I'll only be a minute, I promise!"

Something in his voice must have convinced the receptionist, and she very softly said, "Well, just a minute, then -through those doors and to the left."

He was beside her in less than a minute. Nell's face was ashen and her breathing was irregular, but at least she had regained consciousness, and just as he walked to her bed, a gurney was being wheeled up beside her.

"She's being taken for evaluation, but you can see her for just a minute," a young doctor was saying to Jake, as the two of them walked briskly alongside the gurney.

Nell was certainly in no condition to converse, and Jake reconsidered telling her he was going to call her son about her situation, and also his own happy news could wait until there was an improvement in her condition.

He put his hand on hers, gave her a reassuring smile, and quietly told her, "I'm right here, and I'll stay nearby in case you need me." Nell managed a small smile and a weak 'please do' but Jake couldn't help but see the frightened look in her eyes.

Turning to the doctor he said, "Keep me informed, I'll be in the waiting room." At that, he let the gurney, doctor and attendants continue on down the hall and he went directly to the phone booth out by the waiting room.

Searching through the Tacoma phonebook he found several Matthews, and a few of them were E. Matthews, so he knew he would have to try them all till he got the right one. Fortunately, the second one he called turned out to be Nell's son.

"Mr. Matthews, we've only met once before. I work for your mother in the restaurant, and I'm calling to let you know she's in Harborview Medical Center, she had some kind of attack, possibly heart. I knew you'd want to get here as soon as you could."

For a moment there was silence at the other end. There was the muffled sound of voices in the background, then a quick, "O.K, We'll leave right away!"

Jake walked back to the waiting room to keep his promised vigil. He would stay at least until her son arrived, then he would go back to the restaurant before the breakfast waitress arrived and get the place opened for business.

About forty-five minutes had gone by and it seemed to Jake that Nell's son should be arriving at any minute. The ride from Tacoma at two in the morning shouldn't take too much longer than that. He would have liked to have gone to check on Nell, but he didn't want to be a nuisance and the doctor had promised to keep him informed.

Almost two hours later Ed and his wife Claire walked through the hospital front door. Jake rose to greet them and as he walked toward them, Ed brusquely said, "Do you know her room number?"

"She's being evaluated," Jake answered as the two whisked past him toward the elevator, not even bothering to ask for preliminary directions.

Feeling a little useless and unnecessary, Jake decided to leave. Her son was here now, it wasn't necessary for him to stay any longer. He only hoped it wasn't too late and she would be able to see and talk to Ed, and possibly their relationship would start to mend as a result of this. Reluctantly, because he had been given no further news on Nell and would have very much liked to have known her present condition, he walked out of the hospital, got in his car and drove back to the restaurant.

It was almost 5AM as he parked his car beside the restaurant and was surprised to discover a large sign on the restaurant door. Covering up the small 'closed' sign which he had left earlier were the letters in large print 'CLOSED TILL FURTHER NOTICE!'

Jake walked to the door and tried his key and to his surprise he couldn't unlock the door. Then it came to him. This is why it took them so long to get to the hospital! They had come here first, changed the lock and put up the sign. From what Nell had told him about them he wasn't too surprised about their priorities. They were obviously more concerned about their own selfish motives then they were about their critically ill mother.

He hadn't thought about himself until that moment. His concern all along had been for Nell and he certainly hoped she would recover and be able to come home. But - what if she didn't recover? He very possibly would be without a home and a job. It seems Ed and Claire were making sure the restaurant would be secured and not fall into the 'wrong' hands in the event their mother did not survive.

Not knowing quite what to do next, he remembered a window that led into his apartment that he could possibly raise. Then he thought better of the idea. It would be breaking and entering and they'd have every right to press charges. He walked back to his car and decided to rest in the back seat for a couple of hours, at least until it started getting light. He knew he could have gone to Sandy's house and camped out on their couch but he didn't want to wake them at five in the morning, besides there would have been a lot of explaining to do. He was unable to sleep so he waited until about seven-thirty and then he drove to Sandy's house. She was more than surprised to see him.

"What are you doing here? What about the restau--"

Jake quickly interrupted, "Nell's in the hospital - critical - her son's with her now but he came by the restaurant first and changed the lock. They put up a sign that says 'closed till further notice' so there's no way I can get in until I see them. So I thought I'd take my favorite lady to breakfast in the meantime."

Any attempt he made at sounding casual fell short as far as Sandy was concerned, and though he managed a smile she knew the sad chain of events was foremost in his mind. He used her home phone to call the two waitresses to inform them they were unemployed, at least for the time being. He explained the situation to them as best he could without going into too much detail.

He shook his head sadly as he walked back to Sandy. "Right now I'm worried about Nell. Everything else will work out," he assured her.

"I know it will, honey. Besides when Nell gets better, and I'm sure she will, you'll still have your job, after all the place still belongs to her."

"That's if she gets better, it sure doesn't look good, but a job can be replaced, she can't!," he said sadly.

After breakfast, which neither of them were scarcely able to eat, he drove her to her bank, kissed her goodbye, and told her he'd see her later in the early evening. He decided to try the hospital again to see if there was any new word on Nell and possibly have an opportunity to talk to Ed.

He decided to make a quick stop at a florist just a block from the hospital and buy a bouquet to take to Nell. He knew she loved roses so he decided on three pink roses in a little white vase tied with a pink and white ribbon. It reminded him of the small rose centerpieces on each table in the restaurant and somehow it seemed appropriate. He paid the cashier and drove the remaining distance to the hospital.

"I'm sorry, Mr. Miller, but Mrs. Matthews passed away a little over two hours ago. Massive heart attack. Her son and daughter-in-law were able to see her for about an hour before she died," quietly said the nurse at the desk.

Jake was taken aback, but regained his composure enough to ask, "Can you tell me where her son is now? Maybe I can be of some help to him."

"I believe he went to make funeral arrangements at the," she paused and looked down at some papers, "Jenkins Funeral Home, down on North."

Not knowing where they'd go after arrangements were made, possibly back to Tacoma, or the restaurant, or somewhere else, Jake decided to try to see them at the funeral home. He left the flowers on a nearby table by the hospital front door, walked to his car and drove to the funeral home. They were about to get back into their car as he drove up and it was obvious they tried to hurry in an attempt to avoid him.

"Could I speak to you for a minute?" Jake almost shouted to make sure they heard him. Ed reluctantly opened his car door and walked grudgingly over to Jake's car.

"First of all, I'm very sorry about your mother, they told me at the hospital. I want you to know I was very fond of her too, and I will miss her very much. She was awfully good to me," Jake said consolingly.

"Well that's not going to do you too much good, now is it? And it was bound to happen sooner or later. Funeral's the day after tomorrow." At that, Ed started back to his car.

"Just a minute - I went back to open the restaurant for breakfast and I couldn't get in, the lock was changed, why was that done?"

"Why? Because it's ours now! I don't want no trespassing! Just so you know - there'll be a FOR SALE on it tomorrow. I want to get rid of it as soon as possible. I realize you live in the back, so I'll let you in long enough to get your belongings out, but that's it! Clear out today - and don't touch anything, I've taken pictures!"

"Looks like you thought of everything, even a camera. Couldn't you at least wait till after the funeral to put up a FOR SALE sign out of respect for your mother?" said Jake, not even attempting to hide his disgust.

"It's ours now, we'll do what we want!" came the curt reply. "I'll go back and open the door for you, but like I said I want you out today!"

Jake knew it was true, it was theirs now, and if they didn't want him to continue to run the place he would just have to find another home and job. He would ask Sandy's mother if he could store what little furniture he had in her basement, then find a room he could rent by the week. That would suffice until he and Sandy were married. He immediately thought of the YMCA, that was fairly close, so he decided to try that first. With no trouble at all he was able to rent a small room with a tiny closet and a bathroom down the hall shared by three other occupants. He knew he wouldn't be there for long so he knew he could handle it for the time being. He had reluctantly asked Ed and Claire if they would wait at the restaurant while he checked the Y. They ungraciously agreed to give him a little time to find a place, and as soon as he was set with the room he hurried back to gather up his belongings, he had really not trusted them to wait. But they were still there. He could hear them arguing and walking around in the connected house. Their grief was non-existent, which Jake viewed as completely repulsive, and he knew their main concern was the monetary value of the restaurant and connecting house.

It took him a couple of hours to sort through his belongings and he had to rent a U-Haul to carry his few pieces of furniture to Sandy's mother's house. Ed had come into the restaurant just as Jake was ready to leave and watched with a distrustful eye as he loaded his remaining belongings in his car.

"I'm in room twelve at the Y, for a few weeks at least, so if there's anything you need to know about the restaurant, or if you have any questions you can contact me in person, I won't have a phone," Jake said in total kindness to the most distasteful man he had ever met, but it was said out of respect for his mother, whom he had so revered.

"You won't be needed!" Ed abruptly replied as he ushered him out the restaurant door. The door was shut very quickly behind him, almost before the screen door had a chance to close.

The FOR SALE sign went up immediately just as Ed had promised, but after two weeks the sign was still in place. He wondered, would Nell be pleased or sad to see her place go up for sale so quickly? He called the realtor incognito just to see what the asking price was in case he was interested and found it to be way out of his reach. He knew there was no way he wanted to haggle with the two of them. He really wanted nothing more to do with the unpleasant couple, so he dismissed the whole idea and decided to move on with his new life.

CHAPTER FIFTEEN   (AUGUST 1957)

One week had passed since Nell's death. He had taken time out from his job hunting to attend her funeral earlier in the week and had been even more disgusted with her son and his wife. Claire sat wiping her eyes continuously, while Ed attempted to appear overcome with sadness. From what Jake knew about them so far it certainly appeared to be fake remorse, but they were quite successful in fooling everyone else. Jake didn't feel that Nell had been given even the slightest proper respect, even in her death, but at least she was not aware of it now. He often thought about her and the restaurant and wondered about their regular patrons who had enjoyed stopping in every day.

He had decided, since he was familiar with the restaurant business, to apply for managerial jobs in that field. Checking the newspaper he spotted quite a few that took his interest, but upon interviewing for each one of them, he decided against them. There was always something that wasn't quite right, either the tone of the interview or the appearance of the restaurant itself. He had run the gamut of the eating establishments, downtown with it's fancier, larger restaurants and the smaller diners and cafes throughout the area. He almost weakened a couple of times, thinking he would give a place a try, but upon listening to his inner instincts, always backed down and changed his mind. He knew he had to find employment, after all he was being married soon, and realized that perhaps he was being too particular. He had been pounding the pavement every moment of every day for a week now, and in spite of the mild recession in the country that he had heard about in the news, he knew there was something out there for him. And there was always something in the back of his mind, a controlling vision, that was convincing him he should possibly pursue another line of work.

Nell had been on his mind a lot lately. It seemed as if she was almost trying to communicate with him. He could feel her presence, especially when he lay down at night and let his mind wander. He recalled how she had told him several times when they were at the restaurant together, "*You're much too intelligent for this line of work, I'd hate to see you go but you really deserve to have a better job than this. Anyone can do this, you're cut out for something far better!*" She had noticed how he had listened intently to diners complaining about their ills, aches and pains and how Jake always had some sort of remedy for their problems. And all this reading of medical journals, where did that come from? Just maybe there was a place for him in the medical world. The more he thought about it the more he was determined to give it a try. Deciding to act on impulse he put an application in the Harborview Medical Center and within a week had been hired as an aide. The pay, at first, was less than he had become accustomed to, but they had promised him periodic raises, and he knew he had to start somewhere. He was surprised at how knowledgeable and comfortable he was around medical procedures and terminology. It was almost as if he could accomplish his duties with very little or no instructions. He even found himself questioning medications and procedures. Realizing this was not within his domain and he had no business disputing the doctor's orders, he decided it best to keep it to himself and not make waves. After all, what did he really know about medicine? And why, if there was the possibility he had worked in the medical field before, was he able to recall medical practices but nothing else connected with his past life? He was beginning to think that maybe there was a connection.

At first he had missed the restaurant but that was now fading into the past. He somehow felt that Nell was responsible for leading him to the hospital and his new occupation. She was still his guardian angel, just as she was the day he walked into her restaurant on the day he arrived, lost and alone, in Seattle.

CHAPTER SIXTEEN (1957)

They had found the will! After much rummaging and practically destroying Nell's neat house they had come across it in a notebook that she kept in top of one of the bedroom closets, way back in. It was almost as if she had tried to hide it.

"Now why did she put it way up there?" Claire had said to Ed in frustrated anger, "why not in a file cabinet or desk like everyone else! Was that miserable woman trying to keep us from finding it?" They were exhausted after their search but not too tired to open it as rapidly as possible to discover the extent of the fortune they were now heirs to.

The house and restaurant were theirs of course, they were sure of that, Ed being her only child, but they were extremely ecstatic to discover she had banked a considerable amount of money, - fifty thousand dollars to be exact, and that was theirs, too.

The lawyer's name listed on the will was Fred Daniels, and Ed wasted no time getting to the phone and making the appointment for the reading of the will. It, of course, had to all be done legally, but with visions of ensuing wealth dancing around in their heads they considered that only a formality. Nell's funeral was the next day, and they knew it would be proper etiquette to wait until after that, as if they really cared! Money was all that mattered, but they could wait a few more days to claim what was legally theirs!

They were able to project the image of bereaved son and daughter-in-law at the funeral, and no one was any the wiser, except, of course, Jake. It nauseated him to see the show they put on for Nell's many friends, and they actually looked embarrassed as they occasionally glanced his way. They knew he could see through them. *'Poor Nell', he thought, 'What a wonderful lady to have had such a wretched son. Had she been my mother I would have cherished her!'*

They had arrived at Attorney Daniels office about half an hour early the day of the appointment, they were so over-anxious to claim their new-found wealth. Nell's funeral had been ten days ago but the attorney was so overbooked that this had been the earliest appointment they had been able to make. When the secretary ushered them into his office, they sat down in the brown leather chairs in greedy anticipation.

The attorney greeted them, and took one last puff on his cigar before he laid it on the ashtray. "I assume you have read your mother's copy of her will," he started.

They both nodded with big toothy smiles and tried their best to appear patient.

"She was a lovely lady, your mother, I respected her highly. We were great friends, hard worker she was, and very kind to everyone!"

He sure was taking his time, purposely fumbling with the papers before him, they thought.

'Skip the baloney - get on with it,' Ed was thinking to himself.

"This will was written ten years ago, but there has been one slight change since then, a codicil has been added, about a year ago," the attorney was saying, and as he looked at the two before him he knew they didn't have the slightest idea of what he was talking about.

"Just what does that mean - a codicil?," Ed was frowning as he asked.

"It's an addendum to the original will. And I'm sorry, but I cannot read the will until all recipients are present."

"What do you mean? We're the only recipients. I'm her only child!" Ed very adamantly stated.

"We're the only ones that have the right to anything she had - it's all our money! She has to leave it all to us!" Claire jumped out of her chair and pointed her finger at the attorney.

"She can leave it to anyone she chooses, it could be you, a charity, a stranger, even a dog pound if she so desired. It is totally her decision, and this will and attached codicil are legal in their entirety, and cannot be changed!" Mr. Daniels replied very firmly.

Claire was still about to explode, but Ed was forcing himself to calm down and listen to what the lawyer had to say.

"There's a Mr. Jacob Miller named in her will. Until he's present I won't be able to divulge any portion of it. Do either of you know how I might get in touch with him?"

"Never heard of him! There must be some mistake, you know, my mother was getting quite senile. Maybe it's just a name from her past - she really didn't know what she was doing most of the time!" Ed lied.

"I do believe she mentioned him to me - like Ed said, someone from her past. I believe he died some time ago, poor old man. I think they were lovers and she just never got over him - but he's dead now!" Claire said very emphatically as she compounded Ed's lie.

"Sorry to disagree with you, but I think you're both wrong. I believe Mr. Miller was the young man helping her run her restaurant. Surely you must have been aware of him," he squinted his eyes as he looked at them, knowing full well they were lying. "Now if you'll just tell me where I can find him, we can get on with the business at hand!"

"I don't know anyone by that name!" Ed insisted.

"Well, it's up to you - as I said before, nothing can be finalized until he's present. I'll do my best to try to locate him myself, but it certainly would be helpful if you could tell me anything. It's in your best interest, you know. Now - if you don't mind, I have other cases to attend to. Good day!" He picked up his cigar and went back to other papers on his desk. After a minute had passed and neither one of them had attempted to leave he very adamantly repeated, "Good Day!!"

They realized they were defeated, there would be no will reading - not today, anyway. Without another word they got up from their chairs and walked out the door as attorney Daniels watched them with a knowing smile. He knew they would have to back down eventually, unless, of course, they really didn't know Mr. Miller's whereabouts, which he highly doubted. He decided he would have to do some investigating on his own - he had ways. Nell had spoken so highly and so affectionately about Jacob Miller at the time she added him to her will, that he was determined he would find him, if the Matthews refused to help. She had even broken down in his office, feeling a certain amount of guilt and sadness over not leaving everything to her son, but he recalled how she had told him, her longtime friend, about all the sorrow her son had caused her and the years and years of neglect he had exhibited toward her. She had wanted very much to help the young man whom she claimed had saved her from going bankrupt and had become her devoted friend. Mr. Daniels had quietly understood.

Claire and Ed had been arguing for the past two days. They were both anxious to get their hands on his mother's money but they certainly weren't about to share any of it with anyone else - least of all a stranger! It was theirs, they had earned it by blood, Jake was an intruder, he had no right to their money!

"Maybe if you had helped the old woman more she wouldn't have left part of her money to someone else - you're the fool! You should have at least pretended to care about her, now see what's happened!" Claire was yelling at him.

"If I remember right, you were the one that didn't want me to see her whenever I brought the subject up! Maybe I would have seen her more if you hadn't been on my back all the time!" Ed screamed back at her.

"You hated her - you know you did! Don't lie to me! You said she always tried to control you, tried to make you go to college, wouldn't let that crowd you hung around with come in the house. How about when you started that fire? She let you stay in jail for three days before she bailed you out. She was always trying to run your life, you said, that's why you hated her! So don't blame me!" If hateful words and looks could have killed, Ed would have been stone dead! In her vicious anger she threw the cup she had in her hands against the wall and watched it shatter into a hundred little pieces.

Ed didn't say another word in his defense. He knew how violent she could become when she was in this state, but he also knew Claire was right. His mother had tried for years to straighten him out, in his heart he knew it was true. But once he was on his own they had just drifted further and further apart. And then he had met Claire - a perfect match. She had been in juvenile court a number of times, ran away from home twice, and had given her family the same heartache Ed had given his mother.

"We'll contest it! Whatever she left him, we'll contest and get it back!" Ed yelled, surprising himself that he was aware of what contesting meant.

"You know, there is the possibility she may have left him just a small amount, a token, like a thousand dollars, or maybe just her favorite rocking chair for all we know," Claire said, suddenly calming down and becoming excited, as if the thought had just occurred to her.

Ed was quiet for a minute, then, as much as he hated to, he agreed with her. "I suppose that could be true! Maybe what she left him is not enough to worry about, and not telling Daniels where he is is holding up our fortune! And how could she possibly leave him anything but a token, - she hardly knew him!"

For once they were in agreement, and Ed couldn't get to the phone fast enough!

When the secretary answered, he was told the attorney was in court and wouldn't be available until the afternoon of the next day.

"Did you find Miller, if you didn't I think I know where he is," Ed said when he talked to Mr. Daniels the next day, feeling a little uncomfortable over having to admit he had known his whereabouts all along.

"Oh, are you referring to the dead lover from the past, you mean he has suddenly materialized ?" The lawyer smirked under his breath.

Ed was silently fuming. He would have liked to punch that man right in the nose! "He's staying at the Y on 27th Ave. Room 12. No phone number. Call me when you can set up an appointment for us."

"Suppose you call me! Don't bother for another couple of days, I'm busy and I can't fit you in until Thursday. Speak to my secretary about a time."

Jake had just arrived home from his job at the hospital and was opening a can of soda when he heard a knock at the door. Sure it was Sandy, as no one else knew he was staying there, (except the Matthews of course), he hurried to answer it. He was surprised to see an unfamiliar older man standing there. Mr. Daniels extended his hand and introduced himself.

"Mr. Miller, I believe?"

Jake hesitantly shook his head and mumbled, "Yes, I am Jake Miller."

Extending his right hand, the attorney said, "I'm Fred Daniels, attorney for Nell Matthews' estate. May I come in? This will only take a minute."

Stunned at first, Jake said, "Of course, come in - I expected it to be someone else."

He invited the attorney to sit in one of the two chairs at the small table, and Jake sat in the other one.

After a minute or two of small talk the attorney began, "It seems you have been named as one of the beneficiaries in Mrs. Matthews will. Will you be able to appear in my office at two o'clock on Thursday afternoon?"

"Why - yes - I believe so," the still-stunned Jake was saying. "But she has a son, why am I a beneficiary?"

Mr. Daniels laughed, "She apparently cared a great deal for you, and she wanted to help you. She was a great lady, as I'm sure you know! Don't tell me you're not interested.-"

"Oh, no, I don't mean to imply that. Of course, I'm interested. I just didn't realize she was going to do anything like that. In fact I'm overwhelmed!"

"I can expect you Thursday afternoon promptly at two, then, right?" Daniels said as he got up to leave.

"Yes, of course, I'll be there," Jake slowly closed the door behind him and just stood there in bewilderment. *"I don't why she thought she had to do that, but I'll treasure any little thing she decided to leave me,"* he thought to himself, imagining it to be, at the very most, an antique piece of furniture or one of the various semi-valuable paintings she had hanging in her living room.

He walked into the attorney's office at two o'clock sharp. Ed and Claire were already there, and the looks they gave him as he came through the door were almost lethal. He sat as far away from them as possible without it looking too conspicuous.

Mr. Daniels opened his safe and took out a large folder. "Mr. and Mrs. Matthews," he started, taking a puff on his cigar before he laid it down in the ashtray. "You have a copy of your mother's will in your possession. The original will states that she leaves her home and attached restaurant and also fifty thousand dollars in her bank account to the two of you. "However, " he paused as he looked at the three people in front of him, noting especially the two that were becoming more excited by the minute, "The codicil which I have in my possession, legalized one year ago, states that she has decided to leave her home and attached restaurant, in its entirety, to Mr. Jacob Miller. It was her -"

Claire screamed as she jumped from her seat. "She can't do that! It's ours! It's all ours! He has no right to anything!" In her outburst of anger she nearly slipped on the floor and had to grab the arm of the chair for support.

Ed was out of his seat just as quickly, and stalked over to Jake with fire in his eyes. "You!! You coerced my mother into giving you her house and restaurant! All the while you worked for her, was that your game?" He looked like he was about to hit Jake when the lawyer broke in.

"SIT DOWN, both of you!!" Daniels shouted. "Or I'll call the police and have you removed! This will and attached codicil is completely legal, it was your mother's wish, and it cannot be disputed, that fact was also very adamantly stated by her! And I can assure you there was no coercion, your mother made it very clear to me that she wanted Mr. Miller to have her home and restaurant. The fifty-thousand dollars goes to her son and daughter-in-law. That's it! It stands as read!"

Claire and Ed were both reluctantly back in their chairs, and Jake was thoroughly and understandably bewildered. He suddenly owned the restaurant he had worked at so diligently in the past four years, and he also owned Nell's house! He almost felt sorry for Ed and Claire, and also a little guilty, as if he had taken what rightfully belonged to them.

"I want you all to listen to something! This is a letter written by Mrs. Matthews to Mr. Miller at the time she added the codicil. It's completely her own words, in her own handwriting, and I can assure you she was completely sound of mind at the time," the attorney said when he could see order had been restored in his office. He opened the envelope in the folder and began.

"Dear Jake,

I know this is going to come as a surprise to you! You can't begin to know what a wonderful friend you have been to me! I was about to call a realtor and try to sell my home and restaurant, it had been on my mind for months and I knew I just couldn't keep it any longer, and I was feeling very badly about it. My husband and I had worked many years on our restaurant, and we had both loved it, and I truly hated to see it go!

Then you walked in my door! You were an angel sent to me from heaven! You worked so hard fixing the place up for me, you worked as cook, waiter and manager and on top of all that you became my very dear friend! You have watched out for me as I find myself getting sicker and weaker and that alone has allowed me to stay in my own home, because I knew you would be so faithful about checking up on me.

I realize this will not set well with my son and daughter-in-law. But it's my home, my restaurant and I will leave it to whomever I please!! And I want to leave it to you, Jake, because you've been so good to me. You have been like a son to me and I will always cherish that! But there is one stipulation! I want you to sell it all, - immediately! There are much better things waiting for you in this life then to run a restaurant, you are much too intelligent for that! Please put it up for sale right away and enjoy the money from it. Follow your dream and have a wonderful life, my son!!

Love always, Nell

Jake could feel tears gathering in the corners of his eyes, he had really been deeply touched by Nell's kind words. The attorney put the letter back in its envelope and handed it to him, then looked squarely at Ed and Claire. They were both glaring at Jake with intense hatred, and Daniels, afraid of a repeat performance either in his office or out of it, very sternly said, "And let this be a warning! There are to be no repercussions as a result of the disposition of Mrs. Matthews' property, as she has clearly made her final wishes known to me, both orally and legally! I can assure you it will be obvious to the law who to point their finger at if there is any trouble!" He gave a stern, long look in the direction of the Matthews, both of whom he observed were still extremely angry.

"Now - if all beneficiaries will come up to my desk."

Jake let the Matthews go first. After they had finished and had turned around to leave, he tried not to notice the hatred that permeated the atmosphere. He had almost wished Nell had left him just a painting or a piece of furniture. Grateful as he was for her generosity, the intensity of the situation he now found himself in was quite disconcerting, to say the least!

CHAPTER SEVENTEEN (1957)

Jake went straight home to the Y after he left the attorney's office. He was still in a state of total disbelief and he felt he had to calm down and mull everything over in his mind before he told Sandy about it. He still couldn't believe it! Nell had thought that much of him! The lawyer had handed him the deeds to both the restaurant and the house before he left his office. He stared at them for awhile, amazed that all that property now belonged to him.

After he had collected his wits, he took a drive over to Sandy's house. It was four-thirty and she had just gotten home from work. She saw his car drive in and ran to the front door in happy anticipation.

"You're not going to believe this!" he said as he kissed her. "I was at the lawyer's this afternoon, Nell's lawyer. I had to meet with him along with the Matthews regarding Nell's will. I didn't tell you about him coming to my room the other evening to tell me I was a beneficiary. Well, to make it short, we now own the restaurant and her house! She left it to me, not her son, - me!"

"You're kidding!! Why did she - are you sure? You mean Nell left you all that?"

"Under the stipulation that I sell it immediately. She wanted me to use the money to follow my dream, as she put it."

Sandy was as surprised as he had been and as they both collapsed on the couch, Jake continued, "It's all perfectly legal, but I can't help but feel a little strange about it. After all I just came into the picture five years ago, but she left this letter for me, obviously just to make sure I wouldn't feel guilty." He handed Sandy the letter and she read it with tears in her eyes.

"Tomorrow I'll go to the realtor that Ed listed the property with and explain to him that I now own it. Maybe I should talk to Mr. Daniels first about how to proceed. But right now, lets have a toast to our new found fortune!"

Ed and Claire didn't go right home. They went to the

nearest gas station and purchased two five-gallon cans of kerosene.

"He's not getting my property! I'll burn it to the ground first!" the violent, out-of-control man was shouting to Claire, as they put the cans in the trunk. He had looked around first to make sure there were no witnesses. Claire was just as violently vindictive, if not more so! She would have preferred burning the property with Jake inside, if possible! They drove home to Tacoma to work out their treacherous little scheme. They tore up an old cotton sheet and wound it until it was several inches thick around the end of a long broomstick, and Ed loaded up his pockets with matches. They would come back after dark and douse the restaurant and attached house with kerosene, light it with their homemade torch, run with the empty cans back to the car, dispose of them somewhere in a deserted area, then drive south into Oregon. They would return in a couple of weeks with the pretense of having gone on a vacation, and presumably no one would be the wiser. The building had simply burned down while they were gone!

They were sure that at that time of night no one would be watching an empty restaurant and vacant house, and since the street light was a little further down the street, there wasn't too much possibility they would be seen. They would have to use their brains on this one and act quickly!

"This will take care of Miller and his crooked little scheme to take over MY property," Ed snarled. "He knew exactly what he was doing - playing up to that old woman so she'd leave him everything. It's not his. It belongs to me!!"

Of course Claire all too heartily agreed with him. They were both jumpy, irritable and filled with hatred as they waited for darkness before they drove back to Seattle to carry out their vicious plan. At precisely ten-thirty that night they went back to the restaurant, parked the car off to the side, but not too far away, as they would have to make a speedy retreat. Each carrying a kerosene can they walked briskly toward the restaurant, then tossed the contents on the lower part of the buildings, in the back so there was less chance of someone spotting them from the street. Claire emptied the contents of her can on the restaurant while Ed quickly doused the back of the house, then poured the remainder of the contents of his can on the torch. He struck a match and held it next to the saturated cloth and was totally unprepared for what happened next! The instantaneous flame, before he had a chance to throw it on the kerosene-covered building, caught a back draft and leaped toward him, burning his arms and clothing. Throwing the torch down quickly on the grass, he screamed in agonizing pain, as the flames continued up his chest and onto his face and hair. He started to run, then fell on the ground, totally immersed in flames, rolling and screaming! Claire was frozen in terror! She ran over to him but the intensity of the flames and heat drove her back. This was not supposed to happen! Her husband was being burned to a crisp while she watched helplessly! She ran into the street and began to scream, "Help! Fire! My husband's on fire!!" over and over again. The street consisted mainly of businesses, and they were all closed for the day. But there was one lone man, living above his shoe repair business, who heard their screams and immediately called the fire department. They were there in minutes and trained their hoses on the man, who by this time lay almost totally charred and motionless on the ground. He was rushed to the hospital by an ambulance that had also arrived on the scene at the same time as the fire trucks. Claire, wild-eyed and in a state of panic, nervously followed in their car. She cried all the way to the hospital, partly over Ed's obvious extremely critical condition, but mostly over the fact that she knew they were in deep, deep trouble.

It didn't take long for the firemen to discover the empty kerosene cans that had been dropped on the ground in full view, and since they were empty they correctly assumed the contents had been thrown on the buildings. They knew this was a situation for the police, and at eleven PM that night they were called in to investigate. It was the proverbial open and shut case! The burned torch on the ground, the empty kerosene cans covered with fingerprints, the kerosene-soaked buildings in the back, and the man burned nearly beyond recognition, led to only one conclusion. They had been caught red-handed! The firemen thoroughly hosed down both buildings from top to bottom with a solution attached to their hoses that eliminated any kerosene that had been thrown on them.

The police walked into the hospital at eleven forty-five to arrest the couple responsible. But they only arrested one, Ed had been dead on arrival and Claire knew there was no use denying anything, she still smelled of kerosene. In a complete state of shock she took one last look at her barely recognizable husband, then sobbing bitterly, held out her hands for the handcuffs and was led away.

A few blocks away, Jake was sleeping soundly. He had left Sandy's at about nine and had gone to bed immediately. The excitement of the day had worked like a sleeping pill. He thought he had heard sirens at one point, but since it wasn't near his street he quickly went back to sleep. He would have to take a little more time off work to attend to getting his new property listed on the market. He knew Mr. Daniels would advise him on how to go about legally getting the owner's name changed with the realtor. It was all like a dream, the last thing he had ever anticipated, but it was real, and the reality of it all left him with mixed feelings he couldn't quite comprehend.

CHAPTER EIGHTEEN (1957)

Jake heard about Ed's violent death the next morning shortly after he arrived at the hospital. Frieda, a nurse, told him about a burned man, name of Matthews, dead on arrival, that had been brought in during the night. There was talk around that he had tried to burn down a building but had fatally torched himself instead. Jake knew instantly, without any more information, the building he had attempted to burn down belonged to him.

"What agony that poor man must have gone through! And why would he want to burn down his mother's restaurant? For the insurance maybe? And look what happened, it backfired! I heard when they brought him in he was burned to a crisp - almost - !" Frieda said sadly, shuddering.

"Oh, No! - that's terrible!!" Jake gasped, both surprised and shocked, but not letting on that he knew the people or that he had any connection whatsoever to the entire incident. He was sincerely sorry that it had gone that for. He found it hard to believe that anyone could be that vindictive, but he had seen Claire and Ed in action and he knew, with them, it was possible. In a way he almost felt responsible for Ed's death; for had he never appeared on the scene, the property would have gone to them without question. But he knew it was none of his doing, he certainly hadn't asked for or expected anything, it had been Nell's final wish. He was told Claire had been whisked away by the police, probably being held as an accomplice. Didn't they realize they would be suspects even if they had managed to get away? Their wild hatred had gained them absolutely nothing, but their loss had been tremendous!

Jake was genuinely upset by the news and as soon as he could get to a phone, he checked with the police to get the entire story. A couple other people on his floor mentioned the tragedy to him, thinking he might not have heard about it, but Jake was sure that no one knew the intended target was his property, since he had so recently acquired it and it wasn't public knowledge yet.

'Poor Nell,' he was thinking, *'Her own son died attempting to burn down her restaurant, and just a short while after her death at that!'* Again he vehemently wished there had never been a codicil to the will, and although he knew he had done nothing wrong, he somehow felt like a party to the horrific events of the night before. He almost felt he should pay his respects to Ed, who was still in the morgue, but only out of respect for Nell - it was her son after all, and she would be shattered if she knew all that had transpired. He decided against it, but took a few minutes and kneeled in the nearby hospital chapel and said a prayer for both Nell and her son. He felt somehow relieved after that and went back to his duties.

A day or two later Mr. Daniels took care of all the legalities of Jake's newly acquired property. He assured him that he would see to the ownership change with the realtor, but he advised him to make an appointment with the realtor as soon as possible to discuss the selling price. Jake knew the Matthews had set a price at seventy-five thousand, but he decided to come down a little. It seemed a little high to him and he was interested in a quick sale, if possible. He met with the realtor two days later and made all the necessary changes. All he had to do now was just sit tight and hope for some interested buyers on his property.

CHAPTER NINETEEN (SEPTEMBER 1957)

Now that he was gainfully employed and a property owner on top of it, he and Sandy continued making their wedding plans. They had to move the date to a little later, the last Saturday in September, since so many precarious things had happened in the past couple of weeks. Moving the date to three weeks later would give them time to catch their breaths and allow things to calm down a bit. He knew that his recently acquired property was a heaven-sent windfall, but he would not count on any money from it until it sold. There had not been any bidders on the restaurant and house as yet, but it had only been on the market a couple of weeks under his ownership. It would take time.

Right now the most important thing on either of their minds was becoming man and wife. They had agreed upon just a small wedding with a few friends and Sandy's relatives in attendance. Small as it was going to be, it was still a busy time for them, making all of the various arrangements. Unbeknownst to Sandy, her mother had hired a caterer to take care of the food preparation and serving. Sometime earlier Sandy and her mother had gone wedding gown shopping and after a few defunct try-ons Sandy had decided upon a champagne ballerina-length gown with lots of lace, a tight bodice and a full, flowing skirt. In a size four, it looked like it had been made for her petite, slim figure, and it complimented her long blonde hair and beautiful hazel eyes.

"Believe it or not, this is exactly what I was looking for!" Sandy declared excitedly as she gazed at herself in the long mirror. "And I just love this color. I really didn't want to wear white again, since I wore it before. Oh! I hope Jake will like it!"

"It will take us half a day to get those buttons buttoned in the back, we'll have to start as soon as you wake up on your wedding day!" Her mother laughed. "Now, lets check for the veil and shoes, I believe they're over here," she said as she walked to the opposite side of the bridal shop.

"I want the veil to be fairly short, I guess I want everything to be just the opposite of what it was the last time - maybe it's the bad luck thing, I don't know -." The happy smile left her face for a moment as she thought of her last wedding day.

"I really don't think it has anything to do with bad luck, Sandy," her mother said as she quietly understood. "This is a new beginning for you, and I'm sure you'll both have a great life together!" Sandy reached over and gave her mother a quick hug and the mood became happy again.

As previously planned, they were to have the wedding in her mother's backyard flower garden, weather permitting. Since the weather could be so inclement in Seattle much of the time, they decided they should have an alternative place, like the living room, in case of rain. Even though the garden didn't need much in the way of decoration, the flowers and the rose trellis made it presentable enough. Sandy and her mother decided to suspend bells and balloons from the trees and put huge white bows on the first chair at the ends of the aisles to give it that wedding day touch. The living room would get the same treatment in preparation for the reception, so for a day or two before the wedding, Sandy and her mother were happily busying themselves with decorating inside and out.

Jake had found a tuxedo rental shop and tried on several before he decided on a white dinner jacket with black trousers and a white bow tie. For just a split second he visualized trying on a tuxedo once before, but it was just a quick flash, and he dismissed it as the possibility that he might have been in someone's wedding, or just possibly, could it have been his own? He quickly brushed the thought aside and continued straightening his bow tie and adjusting his shirt sleeves. He was too exuberant about his impending marriage to Sandy to let any disturbing invasive thoughts get to him. He looked at himself in the long mirror and was very satisfied with what he saw. He knew Sandy would be surprised and delighted, especially since he had told her he would probably just wear his best suit.

The night before the wedding, as Jake lay on his bed, he couldn't help but think of his obscure past. He kept trying unsuccessfully to clear his mind, to let it go. The nagging thoughts were relentless, convincing him that he should be able to remember something, - anything - but it seems that time had served to dull his memory even more, and the only link to his life before arriving in Seattle was still that picture of the beautiful lady and little child. He gazed at it one last time before turning out the light. Was there a possibility he was already married? Could that quick flashback he had when he was trying on his tuxedo have meant he still was or had been married? Could the woman in the picture be his wife and the little boy his child? Anyway he couldn't remember, and if his former life was ever revealed to him, he and Sandy would have to decide how to act on the revelation together. He was starting a new life - that's all that mattered now, and he would have to let his ambiguous past fade into oblivion for once and for all.

The morning of the wedding couldn't have been more perfect in every way, the warm sun shone brightly, the sky was a cloudless baby blue, and the late September air was at a just-right temperature. Jake, handsome in his tuxedo, kept his promise and went to the closest florist. He knew pink was Sandy's favorite color.

"I need a bouquet of your prettiest pink roses, and if you could, would you please fix them in some sort of a bouquet, with ribbons and all. They're for my bride!" he proudly stated. "And a couple of long stemmed pink roses, also," he added, remembering Sandy's mother and attendant.

The young girl behind the counter was delightfully taken aback at the sight of the good-looking man in the tuxedo. "Getting married, are you?" she smiled at him. "My congratulations, and I certainly will be very happy to fix a bouquet for your lucky bride to carry!" Giving Jake one more quick smile she opened the door of the cooler and pointed to the large pink roses resting in a green vase.

"Will these do?"

"They're perfect, maybe about six or eight of them," Jake said, "and could you cut the stems, and make sure you get all the thorns off?"

The young girl laughed, "I certainly will - we wouldn't want her getting snagged by thorns on her wedding day, now would we?" She quickly took out eight of the pink roses, cut them, and skillfully proceeded to create a beautiful bouquet, complete with baby's breath, and pink and white satin ribbons hanging about a foot. When she was finished she held it up for Jake's approval.

"You do a fantastic job, maam - it's beautiful!"

Seeing Jake's pleased reaction made her day. *'How lucky can one girl get!'* she thought to herself, *'to get such a thoughtful, considerate husband, and such a handsome one at that!'* Carefully she wrapped the bouquet in green tissue paper, so only the roses were showing at the top. She fashioned a lacy pink bow on each of the long-stemmed roses, after carefully making sure they were also de-thorned.

"Have a wonderful day!" she said, secretly wishing she were the lucky bride.

"Thanks so much," Jake smiled as he paid her, then gathered up the roses and walked out of the store to his car. He knew he didn't want to be late for his own wedding, which he had been told would be held promptly at eleven, so he drove directly to Sandy's mother's house.

Jake arrived at the same time as the minister. Not sure whether he should go in the house or wait outside until the appropriate time, he decided upon the latter. He didn't want to spoil anything for Sandy so he thought it best if he waited till he was cued.

"You couldn't have picked a nicer day," the minister remarked with a warm smile. "My wife and I were married in September, too, on a day much like this."

Reaching to shake the minister's hand, Jake replied, "I'm so glad it's not raining or overcast, this is just the weather we were hoping for, since we're having the wedding outdoors," Jake replied, as he straightened his bow tie and brushed a piece of lint from his pants. "I can't wait to see Sandy, I know she'll be beautiful!"

"She is a beautiful young lady, my heart went out to her when her husband died so abruptly, they were married such a short time. But she's very strong and came through it fine. I'm so glad she's found happiness again. I wish you both the very best!" the minister said with all sincerity.

"I couldn't be luckier!" Jake smiled, thinking of his bride-to-be.

A few more minutes of friendly conversing went by before Sandy's mother came to the front door and told them both to come in. She assured them both that Sandy was all ready and out of sight and Jake knew he wouldn't see her until she walked to meet him by the rose trellis in the garden. He handed her mother the roses, informing her the long ones were for her and Sandy's attendant, then walked through the house and out into the garden with the minister. His best man, Sandy's brother, Jimmy, was waiting on the back porch. About forty people were seated in the several rows of rented white chairs. He had only invited five people that he had become very friendly with at the restaurant, so the rest were either Sandy's friends or relatives. Some he had met and some he had only heard about. All eyes were on him as he walked around to the side so as not to step on the white carpet that had just been rolled out for Sandy to walk on. Everything was so beautiful! He was also amazed at the transformation in the garden, Sandy and her mother had done a fantastic job with their paper bells, streamers, and balloons. Even the late summer flowers were cooperating, and the gold, orange and deep crimson blended in beautifully with the awesome scenario. He took his place by the minister and waited anxiously for his bride.

Suddenly there was another surprise that Sandy had not told him about. She had asked her cousin, a violinist, to play 'Here Comes the Bride'. Jake glanced toward the violinist when the beautiful strains began, then turned to look immediately down the short aisle where he saw his bride approaching. He couldn't believe his eyes! She was unbelievably beautiful in her champagne gown and short veil and the pink rose corsage she carried matched the happy blush of her cheeks as she walked toward him.

"You're beautiful!" Jake whispered as she got to his side.

"You're not so bad yourself!, - love your tux!" She was beaming, clearly surprised and happy that he had bothered to rent it. Tearing their gaze away from each other, they turned toward the minister as he chatted happily with them for a minute or two. Sandy was giddy with excitement and every time she turned to look at Jake she couldn't believe her good fortune. She was actually going to be marrying this handsome, wonderful man! They both repeated the traditional vows after the minister and then they turned to face each other as they slipped the rings on each other's fingers. The short ceremony went off without a hitch, they both said 'I do' and sealed it with a kiss. As they turned to walk down the aisle the small crowd broke out in applause. The violinist echoed the joy of the couple as he played the 'Wedding March' while they walked together down the white carpet.

"I can't believe it - can you believe it? We're married!" Sandy was radiant when they had finished their walk and the smiling crowd was walking toward them. The happy couple hugged and accepted congratulations from their guests as they stood together by the back porch.

All the trepidation of the past few years faded completely away as Jake looked at his new bride and realized he couldn't remember ever being as thoroughly exhilarated as he was at that moment. He knew Sandy would be his life from now on and nothing else mattered as long as they were together.

After the last of the guests had given their congratulations,

Jake put his arm around her waist and gave her a lingering kiss.

"I feel like the luckiest man in the world today, honey, you have made me so happy!"

"The feeling is mutual - I just can't believe this is happening! I love you so much, Jake!" Sandy said with love in her eyes as a tear rolled down her cheek They would have both liked to have made their departure right then, but they knew they couldn't leave yet. There was still the reception.

Little by little the crowd drifted into the dining room and a sumptuous catered buffet lunch was served. There was hot roast beef, shrimp arranged carefully on platters of ice with small dishes of cocktail sauce in the middle, caesar salad with chunky bleu cheese, crab cakes and stuffed mushrooms, prosciutto and melon, fruit bundles in endive, ambrosia salad, crescent rolls, fancy cookies and more. Shiny silver wine decanters were at the end of the table holding white or rose wine. Everything had been placed on a treasured white lace tablecloth that had belonged to Sandy's late grandmother. Intermingled among the dishes and decanters were more real roses of various shades of pink. The cameras were almost as busy photographing the beautiful wedding table as they were photographing the bride and groom. Both Jake and Sandy were too excited to eat anything, and besides they were still very busy greeting their guests and accepting more congratulations.

Most of the guests mingled in the large living room which had been decorated very attractively with pink and white balloons, pink and white roses, both artificial and real, and the winding staircase was wound with artificial rose garlands. It was a pink and white extravaganza! Some of the guests went outside to talk and enjoy the beautiful September weather, and some just couldn't get enough of watching the handsome groom and his beautiful bride together. The violinist was standing in one of the charmingly decorated ends of the living room and continued to play beautiful strains from Bach and Beethoven and some popular music as well. Jake and Sandy danced to "I Love You Truly" and "Unforgettable" much to the delight and applause of the guests.

In another corner on a small table sat the four-tiered wedding cake with the bride and groom on the top. About two hours into the reception Sandy whispered to Jake that it was probably time to cut the cake.

"It seems a shame to cut into it," she said, "It's a real work of art!" Jake couldn't help but agree. Someone had worked very diligently to create a masterpiece for their special day.

The two of them admired the cake for another brief moment, then Jake picked up the silver cake knife and Sandy put her hand over his. As the crowd gathered around them they made the first cut and the caterer took over from there and served the guests.

The reception ended about three in the afternoon and the newlyweds were finally able to leave. It wasn't going to be much of a honeymoon, just an extended weekend in the Cascades, but to the two of them it was as exciting as a week in Europe. They both had to be back at their respective jobs on Tuesday morning, but just the thought of being away together for two whole days was exhilarating. Their happiness beamed in their eyes and smiles as they drove away in Jake's car complete with dragging tin cans and "Just Married" signs in the windows as the remaining guests filed out of the house and surrounded the car to wave goodbye to the happy couple! As soon as they rounded the corner, they glanced happily at each other and Jake reached over for her hand. They just knew that life would be great from now on!

CHAPTER TWENTY (1960)

With a brand new decade in progress, Mr. and Mrs. Miller were enjoying life to its fullest. The property that had been left to Jake a few years back had sold for sixty-eight thousand dollars which, needless to say, had made a healthy change in their lifestyle. They had bought a beautiful little house overlooking Redondo Beach on Puget Sound a year and a half after they were married. It had a spacious front deck that provided a breathtaking view of the Sound and was surrounded by spectacular flowering bushes of every variety and beautiful peony bushes, in all shades of pinks and white, that had been planted there by one of its previous owners. They had done a few remodeling jobs, like installing new walnut cabinets in the kitchen and bathroom, putting new tile on the floors that resembled slate, re-carpeting the living room and bedrooms, and of course painting throughout. They had agreed on antique white for the walls of the living and dining rooms, and soft pastels for the bedrooms. They were having the time of their lives with their decorating projects, but eventually there was nothing else to decorate and they were able to sit back and enjoy the fruits of their labor. They loved to sit on their deck in the evenings and watch the rippling waters of the Sound far below them as they told each other about their day.

"This has got to be the most beautiful place in the world!" Sandy would smile and say as she nestled in Jake's arms. "Only heaven could be more beautiful!".

"Sorry that I have to go in today, but I'll try to get off as soon as I can. Helen has covered for me a couple of times, so I couldn't really refuse her," Jake said as he shut off the alarm one morning and started to get out of bed. He bent over and kissed Sandy good morning, then sat up and started to put his socks on.

"Well it's good that you can cover for each other. I don't

know how Helen does it with three small children at home, so I'm glad you're giving her a break."

It was Saturday morning and Jake didn't usually work on Saturdays and Sandy never had to. They wouldn't have time for their leisurely Saturday morning breakfast today, but once in a while it couldn't be helped.

"Don't worry, I can keep very busy," Sandy smiled, "In fact I think I'll paint those closets I've been procrastinating over. Then the whole house will have a completely new coat of paint."

"Just don't work too hard, and, if you would like I'll even take you to dinner tonight! OK?" Jake said as he started toward the bathroom door.

"Sounds great to me!" Sandy squealed as she jumped from the bed, stopped him abruptly and hugged him. She gave him a happy smile as she said, "I'll go make some coffee."

"No, don't bother, I'll grab a cup at work. I'll just shave and be on my way." In half an hour's time he was showered, dressed, and out the door.

"Don't forget about our date tonight!" he shouted back at Sandy standing in the doorway as he walked to the car.

"Don't worry, I'll hold you to it!" she smiled, waving back.

As soon as he drove away, Sandy busied herself with getting the paint and brushes together, and then she started to empty out their bedroom closet. She never realized they had so many clothes! She laid them all carefully on the bed, with the hangers intact so she could re-hang them easily. About the last item to come out of the closet was a white lab jacket. She momentarily wondered when and where Jake had worn it. She had casually spotted it hanging at the very end of his side of the closet but had never given much thought to it. She knew he wore that sort of jacket in the hospital, but she had never seen him in any color but drab green when she had visited him there, and he always left them there when his shift was over and they were washed with the hospital laundry. She had never known him to wear one home. As she started to lay it on the bed, she heard a slight crackle noise and noticed a raised area in one of the pockets. Curiosity got the best of her and as she reached into the pocket she was amazed to discover a photo of a young woman and a little child. She stared at it for a few moments, not quite knowing what to think.

'I wonder who they are - I remember him telling me he had no brothers or sisters, so it can't be a sister and niece or nephew, and it sounded like he wasn't especially close to whatever family members he did have,' she thought to herself as she continued to gaze at the picture. *'Of course it could be just a friend and her child, someone he used to know - or - no it couldn't be! - is it possible he was married before and this is his wife and child? I suppose that's possible - maybe they died - but wouldn't he have told me? Come to think of it he has been pretty quiet about his past. NO - I'm not going to jump to any conclusions - I'll just very calmly ask him who they are. There's a very logical explanation, I'm sure!'* She suddenly felt as though she was an intruder, possibly discovering something she shouldn't have. Quickly she put the picture back in the pocket and sat down on the bed for some time, deep in thought. After a few moments she shrugged and laughed at herself as she thought, *'What am I getting myself all worked up over? I'm sure there's a very logical explanation and I know when I ask Jake he'll tell me right away who they are.'*

Attempting to turn her thoughts to the project at hand she opened the can of paint, put plastic on the floor of the closet, and started painting the back wall of the closet. But try as she may, she found she couldn't get those two faces out of her mind. She could hardly wait till her husband came home to ask him about them.

At precisely 3:35 PM he walked in the door, his shift finished. He looked tired, but he managed to greet Sandy with his usual enthusiasm. She could see from the look on his face that the day had been unusually stressful, and she was right.

"Mr. Graves went into cardiac arrest shortly after I got there today, and then we had two critical admissions about the same time. It was pretty rough for awhile, but we finally got everyone settled down," Jake said as he crashed in the nearest chair. He looked up at Sandy with a smile as he remembered. "Hey - we're going out to dinner tonight, I haven't forgotten, that may be just the tonic I need!"

"Are you sure you're not too tired?" Sandy asked with concern as she started to rub his back.

"No, just give me a few minutes and I'll be as good as new!"

She knew this was no time to bring up the subject of the photo. It would have to wait until the stress of the day had diminished and they were both in a more relaxed mood.

They were seated at a table in the back of the restaurant. It was an ideal spot for privacy, only two other couples were seated at tables several yards from them. There was a small vase in the middle of the table with three real yellow roses in it. They were obviously fresh as the fragrance was very apparent as they sat down.

"I don't know about you, honey, but I'm hungry!" Jake stated as he picked up the menu the waitress had just left for him. They started to scan the menu and decided quickly on chicken marsala. "How about some white zinfandel, to go with it?"

"Sounds great, but just a glass for me though," Sandy said, hoping she sounded enthusiastic.

Jake motioned for the waitress, ordered the wine and the meals and settled contentedly back in his chair.

"Did you get the closets painted today, I totally forgot to ask when I got home," Jake said apologetically.

"Well, yes I did, and - I have something to ask you." Since he had brought up the subject this was a good time to approach him about the photo.

"There was this white lab jacket hanging at the end of the closet, yours, I imagine, I just never saw you wearing it. Anyway when I laid it on the bed I discovered a picture of a woman and child in the pocket. I was wondering who they were, you said you have no close relatives so I assumed it wasn't family." She hesitated a moment when she saw the surprised look on Jake's face. "Are they people you used to know? I was just curious, I guess." She suddenly began to feel very intrusive, as if she was interfering with something that didn't concern her.

Jake was taken aback and didn't quite know what to say. In his contented new life he had almost forgotten about that picture. He just hadn't given any thought to the prospect that she might discover it when she cleaned out the closet. He had kept it in hopes of at least a partial recall some day, but it had never happened and now he had to explain it to Sandy.

"To tell you the truth, I really don't know," he said very sincerely, and Sandy, though a little surprised, wanted to believe that he was telling the truth.

"Then why is that picture in your lab coat, I don't understand -"

"It's a long story," he stammered, "I know I never told you and I realize I should have, but time just went by, and somehow it seemed like it was better left unsaid."

Sandy sat bewildered, anxiously awaiting and fearing the long story at the same time. This man she thought she knew had apparently kept a huge secret from her, and she almost hated to hear what he would say next.

"I might as well tell you everything, as much as I know, that is. Please, Sandy, don't hate me for not telling you before, please try to understand."

He looked across the table into her trusting eyes, took both her hands in his, and began. "It all started a few years ago, before I ever met you. I remember taking a plane out of Albany, New York and heading for Seattle. I didn't know why I was on the plane, I don't even remember going to the airport, I was in some sort of daze.

While I was looking for my wallet, I discovered that picture in my pocket. I remember staring at it for a long time, but for the life of me I had no idea who they were. I also discovered I had on that white lab jacket, so I have always believed that I must have worked in a health-related profession of some kind, and somehow came to the airport right from work. My airline ticket had a strange name on it, Timothy Rogers to be exact, with a destination of Seattle, and I assumed that must be me and that I was supposed to get on that plane and come here. I guess I assumed I was coming home but I really didn't know which end of the country my home was in."

He could feel the tension building and he knew his heart was racing. He had to tell the entire story to his wife in order for it to make any sense at all. The look on her face worried him, but he knew there was no stopping now. He took a deep breath and continued. "When I arrived here in Seattle I had no idea where to go or what to do. I had mistakenly thought my memory would come back to me on the trip out, but it never did, and still hasn't. I had discovered while I was still in the air that I had no money or identification whatsoever on me. I knew something terrible had happened, but I had no idea what it was. In my fear I threw away the ticket. Believe it or not, I was actually afraid I may had committed a crime of some sort and I thought until I got my memory back, it would be best not to have identification on me. Right or wrong, that was my way of dealing with it."

With a deep sigh he lowered his head, then raised it and looked at Sandy, desperately hoping that she was believing what he was telling her.

Sandy reached over and put her hand on his. She could tell he was going through a deep inner turmoil and she certainly did not want to add to it.. She was going through a little inner turmoil herself and although she was filled with questions she let him continue.

Jake was getting a little emotional as he continued on, "As I was walking from the airport I saw Nell's coffee shop sign and I believe now that I was drawn to it. I needed a place to stop and think and gather my wits about me. When I walked in and asked for a free cup of coffee, she unquestionably not only gave me coffee but food to go with it. Then she offered me a job - and - well, you know the rest of the story. I don't know what I would have done if I hadn't met that wonderful lady right then. Understand I had no money, no identification, no place to go. I was the proverbial 'man without a country.' I decided to go by another name, and the first name that I had already chosen was Jake. A little later I added Miller, and after a while I did go to a lawyer. I told him I had amnesia, had no recollection of my past, had no identification of any kind, and for a hundred dollars he told me I could legally use that name."

Sandy's eyes were moist with sympathy for the man she loved so much. She could only imagine what he had been going through the past few years. But at the same time she was beginning to feel a little insecure and mistrustful. Why had he never confided in her? She was his wife, after all, she certainly had a right to know something as important as this! She hated to ask the question, but she knew she had to - she had to know.

"Since you don't remember anything, is there the possibility that could be a picture of your wife and child?" Sandy could hardly trust her voice as she quietly asked the question.

Jake didn't answer, so she continued. "There must have been a way - couldn't you have checked with the local authorities to see if you lived in the Seattle area - or - why didn't you take a trip back to Albany and check there?"

"Sandy, like I said, I was afraid to check with the authorities in case I was in some kind of trouble - I know that sounds like an excuse, maybe even a very cowardly excuse, but I knew that something very traumatic had to have happened to make me lose my memory. I even thought several times about calling the Missing Persons Bureau, but I always changed my mind, because what would I say when I got them on the phone? Whatever I said they would be bound to follow up on and investigate. But I did check several Rogers in both Seattle and Albany phone books and came up with nothing. I was either told that person was deceased, or moved, or they would abruptly hang up on me. Then I met you - and as much as I still wanted to know about my past, somehow it didn't matter as much any more. That's what took me so long to ask you to marry me, I wanted to get my life in order first. But it's been eight long years since I arrived here and no one has come looking for me, so it's quite probable that no one ever will!"

Sandy sat quietly for a moment, then a tear started to roll down her cheek. "You realize, of course, that you could have a wife and child somewhere! Exactly where does that leave me? On top of that all of a sudden I find out I'm not Mrs. Miller at all but I'm Mrs. - was it Rogers? - that is, if I'm a Mrs. at all!" She was starting to become very upset and the tears were flowing freely now.

Their dinners had been placed in front of them, but neither one of them felt like eating now. Sandy was getting more and more upset by the minute. Jake decided to ask for the bill and motioned for the waitress. He told her that there had been a change of plans and they had to leave and she gave him the bill, without question, for just the wine she had already served them.

"You should have told me - right in the beginning! We could have decided what to do then. I believe you when you say you don't know who the people in the picture are, but that doesn't make them non-existent. Your loss of memory doesn't make them less real. Who else could it be but your wife and child? What if she suddenly appears, then where does that leave me?" she repeated.

Jake started to take her arm but she pulled quickly away. They walked out the door and to the car. Sandy had never meant for it to go this far. She had planned to ask him about the picture in a very calm and loving way. But somehow it had gotten out of hand and she found herself wishing she had never brought up the entire subject.

They drove home quietly, Jake silently wishing he had cut up that photo long ago, and Sandy sadly wondering if she was the real wife in this case, or if there was another woman out there with more of a rightful claim to the man beside her.

For several days after that things were rather tense in the Miller household. They both went about their daily routine, came home from their respective jobs each night, and had dinner together as usual. They were polite to each other, talked casually about their day, the weather and their home. Sandy decided she wasn't angry with him, just very upset that he would keep the fact of his unfortunate loss of memory from her. She knew it had to have been very difficult for him all these years, but she was saddest over the fact that he had not shared it with her. A time or two she even thought of calling Albany and Seattle authorities and actually asking them if they had any information about a Timothy Rogers. She could pretend she was a long-lost friend and was just interested in finding out if they had discovered his whereabouts. She even picked up the phone once, stared at the dial, and quickly put it back in its cradle. How could she even think of such a thing? It would be an unthinkable act of betrayal! How could she do anything like that behind his back? And - what if they followed up on her call and in the end he really was in some sort of trouble, or even worse, really had a wife and child somewhere. But if he did have a wife and child - what about them? What must they be feeling all these years? They probably thought he was dead by now or he would have come home. She knew her hands were tied, if she did anything at all it could possibly put them in a very precarious situation with a heartbreaking resolution. He had to do it - it had to be his decision, and she could see he wasn't about to do anything. She knew him to be a very honest and forthright man, but after all, he was human. Through no fault of his own his past didn't really exist for him anymore, and in spite of the inner confusion she knew he was carrying around, he obviously was content to let sleeping dogs lie, at least for the time being.

Over their usual after-dinner coffee one evening, Jake couldn't tolerate the troubling look in his wife's eyes any longer, even though she had made every attempt to smile and appear as cheerful as she possibly could.

Reaching across the table, he took her hand in his. "Sandy, honey, I know what you must think of me, and I certainly don't blame you, but eventually there will be a revelation of my past, I'm sure of it, and when the time comes, I'll just have to deal with it, good or bad. I just hate putting you through this, it's not fair that you should be caught up in the middle of my problem. I promise you that when that revelation happens, I will do everything in my power to set the record straight, whatever it may be. I just need to know that you love me and will stand beside me through this," he said as he looked lovingly at his wife, hoping against all hope that she would not tire of the whole ordeal and decide to leave him.

She could feel fresh tears starting as she got out of her chair, put her arms around him and nestled her head against his shoulder, "You know I'll always be here with you, Jake, right where I belong, this is our dilemma now, not just yours anymore. I feel in my heart that everything's going to work out fine, but if it doesn't I'll still be here for you in whatever decision you make. Please don't ever think for one minute that I would turn my back on you - I love you, honey, for better or worse, remember?"

"And I love you, more than you'll ever know, and I can't tell you how much I appreciate your standing by me, but I honestly wouldn't blame you if you didn't. How did I ever deserve anyone like you?"

"Just lucky I guess!" Sandy said jokingly as they both smiled through their tears and caressed again. Jake knew he was a lucky man to have a wife like Sandy, determined to stand by his side and accept whatever outcome there might possibly be. He hoped he would always be worthy of her love and unyielding support.

Later that evening, while Sandy was busy in the kitchen, Jake walked into their bedroom, quietly took the lab coat off its hanger, folded it up neatly and packed it away in a large shoe box. He then put the box way back in the corner of the top shelf of the closet. He somehow could not dispose of it altogether, but at least he could put it out of their range of vision. He would just pack away his past and hopefully, he and Sandy could put this incident behind them and move on happily to the future.

The tension of the past week slowly started to dissipate, and the love they had for each other had won out in the end. Somehow they were brought closer together by this distressing situation, and as Sandy had said it was their problem now and they would deal with it together. Jake realized he was relieved to have everything out in the open now and he believed Sandy when she said she would be at his side, no matter what! He knew he was a lucky man!

CHAPTER TWENTY-ONE (1961)

She couldn't wait to tell Jake! He would be as ecstatic with excitement as she was! They had hoped and prayed for four long years now, and their prayers were finally going to be answered! She was going to have a baby! She had suspected as much but hadn't said a word to Jake. She wanted to be sure first, she didn't want either of them to be disappointed. As she left the doctor's office her heart and mind were overflowing. She was deliriously happy and she was wracking her brain to think of some unique and awesome way to tell Jake. It would be an event, a moment they would always cherish!

As she was driving home she couldn't help but think about how fortunate they were. There was still that shadow of a skeleton in the closet concerning Jake's past, but they, for the most part, had gotten beyond it. He had lived in the Seattle area for nine years now and nothing had come of it, no return of his memory but there hadn't been anyone looking for him either. It was almost like they could tuck it away and forget about it altogether. They had each other, all the comforts life could offer and now - a baby! Good fortune had certainly been smiling on them in every aspect of their lives. They were enjoying their home, and there was a lovely little room just off their bedroom that would be perfect for the new little bundle of joy!

As she drove by the florist, she had an idea. She would purchase a bouquet of pink and blue flowers, enough for a good-sized bouquet, and arrange them in a vase in the middle of the table with lots of the blue and pink petals scattered around the tabletop. It was a little difficult to find blue flowers with petals like she wanted so she settled for dyed blue carnations. Then she picked out eight roses in a beautiful shade of pink. Together they gave the delicate and enchanting 'we're going to have a baby' effect she was looking for. She could hardly contain her happiness as she paid the clerk and left the store. On the way home she stopped at the five and dime and bought baby blue napkins and pink and blue balloons. It didn't matter that she was leaning slightly toward the boy color, because she knew in her heart that either sex would be overwhelmingly welcomed by the both of them. It seemed like perfect planning, and that spare room, just perfect for a nursery, was impatiently waiting to be filled. God willing - it would be filled with their precious little baby in just a few short months!

She had taken a few hours off from work because of her appointment, so she had plenty of time after she got home to make everything just perfect. Jake wouldn't be coming for almost two hours, she would have time to bake a small cake and frost it in pink, if only she could think of some blue food to serve! She laughed to herself at the thought of it, then decided the flowers, balloons, napkins and cake should take care of the decorative portion of her plan.

She had found a clear vase, intermingled the roses and carnations in it and sat it on an open blue napkin. She seemed to fly with sheer joy as she made lemon pork chops, twice-baked potatoes and a broccoli and cheese casserole. Everything had to be Jake's favorite, and it had to be perfect! She tied thin pink ribbons around two of the blue napkins and put them by their plates. It certainly wouldn't take a genius to figure out the happy message she was trying to convey!

Five-thirty came - and no Jake! It wasn't like him to be late. Occasionally he was held up at the hospital though, and she realized she would have thought nothing of it any other time, but tonight was so special and she was so anxious to tell him their good news.

He walked in the back door at six-thirty, tired as usual, after an intense day of dealing with his multi-faceted duties. She met him there and after a quick embrace, excitedly led him into the kitchen where the table was set in blue and pink splendor.

He gave a quick glance, turned away, then quickly turned his surprised gaze toward the table again. He had never come home to this color combination before - could this mean? He looked at Sandy with happy expectation in his eyes, while she was trying desperately to keep the give-away smile off her face, but to no avail.

"I - Sandy! - what's this? - does this mean what I think it means - are we having a baby?" His voice accelerated with each word, as the excitement mounted within him.

"I went to the doctor's today. I didn't want to tell you, I wanted to be sure first! Yes!! - we're having a baby! In about six months, the end of December or beginning of January, it'll be our baby new year of 1962!"

Jake quickly took her in his arms and with tears in his eyes, looked at her as if she had just announced the most spectacular accomplishment ever, and to them it was! They would finally have their long-dreamed of baby - a baby all their own!

"Hey - that means we've got to start looking for a crib, a carriage, diapers, what else does a baby need? Whatever he needs, he'll get! Our kid is going to have it all!", Jake blurted out between hugs and laughter.

"Yes, I know, and we're going to spoil him rotten, Oh, I can't wait!" Sandy squealed, "or maybe it'll be a little girl, and we'll dress her up in those frilly little dresses with a pink bow in her hair and take her everywhere to show her off !"

Just then Jake pulled a carnation out of the vase, broke off the flower, and put it Sandy's long blonde hair. "For the mother of my little girl - may she be lucky enough to be as beautiful as you!"

Sandy returned the compliment, "And if it's a boy I hope he grows up to be tall and handsome like his daddy! I am so happy! I do believe this is about the most exciting day of my life, what about you?"

"It's what we've been praying for for years now, honey, and I couldn't be happier, you know that!" Jake smiled as he embraced his tearful wife again.

"You know what? Supper's getting cold while we stand here like two excited kids at Christmas!" Sandy said as she remembered the specially prepared food waiting on the counter, ready to be set on the table.

"Sure smells great, and you went to an awful lot of work for this occasion, didn't you?" Jake laughed.

"It was such fun - and I wanted to make it special! I tried to equalize the pink and blue, I didn't want to show favorites, how'd I do?"

"I think it's spectacular, and either pick or blue will suit me just fine, honey!"

With another happy laugh they both sat down at the table in preparation for their colorful banquet. Only the amazing thing was that neither one of them were able to eat, they nibbled a little because it was there, but they were both already filled to capacity with joy and anticipation and that was far better than food any day!

They had visited almost every specialty shop and department store in the city, or at least their end of the city. The little white bassinette had been purchased and Sandy had spent hours fashioning a white organdy skirt around it. She had put a big yellow bow on the front of it just to be on the safe side. She could change the color later if she wanted to. They had purchased the crib, too, but had left it in the box as they knew it wouldn't be needed for a while. There were dozens of little footed rompers, in various pale-colored stretchy fabric, just perfect to keep a newborn winter baby cozy and warm. Diapers by the dozen were piled in the white dresser-dressing table combination, along with baby powder and lotion, white shirts, bath towels and booties. They had spent a whole weekend painting the spare room in a very pale blue and halfway up the wall they had put a wide border of very delicately-colored teddy bears frolicking happily in mid-air. They had the hardwood floor carpeted in a thick plush white. The lingering scent of the Mennen baby lotion, along with the baby powder, gave the entire room an enchanting newborn-baby fragrance which aromatically completed the picture. When they were all finished they stood back, admired their work, congratulated each other with a hug, and were sure their little son or daughter would be very pleased with the results.

Almost three weeks had gone by before Sandy had her next appointment with Dr. Moore. She walked happily into his office, pleased with herself that she had kept her weight down as he had instructed. Hoping to hear the latest updates on the baby's development she was informed that everything was progressing normally, and she was told to continue with the exercises he had shown her, take her vitamins, and continue to eat properly. She and the baby were both doing great and in a little over five months she would hold her child in her arms!

That evening, filled with excitement and anticipation, she wandered into the baby's room, walked over to the little white bassinet and fluffed up the big yellow bow on the end. She imagined her own precious baby sleeping there, and knew that when that became a reality it would be the happiest time of her life. She pulled open a drawer beneath the dressing table and took out a few of the tiny rompers. Holding them up, she couldn't imagine anyone being small enough to fit into them. There were several blue, a few light green or yellow and one very delicate pink with a little lace collar. She couldn't resist buying at least one in pink, even though she knew if the baby was a boy he certainly would never wear it. But, if it's a girl she would buy her lots of dainty pink outfits, and lots of adorable little dresses, and lots of frilly little bonnets. But she knew in her heart it really didn't matter, she would be happy with either sex.

Just then Jake walked into the room. He stood quietly for a minute, smiling to himself, as he watched her unfolding and then refolding the baby's clothes. He knew how excited she was over the impending blessed event, and for a moment he didn't want to interrupt her private world of daydreaming.

"I thought I heard you come in," she turned with a smile.

"Jake, I can't wait! I just can't wait! But I guess I have to, don't I?"

"Five months isn't so long, it'll be here before we know it, honey! Then we'll be walking the floor at night, washing dirty diapers, possibly dealing with colic, what have you. But you know what, I'll enjoy it just as much as you do, I promise!" Jake grinned as he walked over and hugged his wife.

"Now just remember that you said that after the first hundred dirty diapers, and the first few weeks of sleepless nights, OK!", Sandy joked as they switched off the light and walked from the room.

That night she sat up in her bed, propped against her pillows, and read for a short while as Jake slept contentedly beside her. As she reached over to turn out the light, she felt a sudden, sharp pain in her abdomen. It was probably just from overeating, she assumed. She had eaten a little more than normal at dinner that night. She would have to watch it from now on. As she stretched out on the bed she felt it again - and again! It was somewhere between a pain and a cramp and it was getting a little more intense each time. After about the fifth pain she started to get a little frightened and she nudged Jake.

"I don't know what this means, but I'm having pains in my stomach and they're getting harder. If it was five months from now I'd swear I was in labor! Ooooh! there's another one!"

"I'm going to call the doctor right now!" Jake said excitedly as he jumped out of the bed and ran into the living room to the phone. He quickly explained the problem, and Dr. Moore's answering service said they would have the doctor call him back immediately. It was several sharp pains later when Dr. Moore called and told Jake to take her to the Emergency Room immediately and he would meet them there.

Getting Sandy to the car was no easy chore. She was doubled over when she tried to walk and Jake half-carried her as he put her in the passenger's seat. She was trying so hard to be brave but it wasn't hard to figure out what this meant, she knew there was the strong possibility she was losing the baby! Jake, of course, was fully aware of what was happening but he made every effort to encourage and comfort her on the drive to the hospital. Maybe they could still do something to save the baby, Sandy silently prayed between pains, while Jake drove as quickly and carefully as he could. He knew she didn't need any unnecessary jarring at this point.

"But Dr. Moore said everything looked fine - just today he told me that - how could this have happened?" she cried between the pains, looking sadly at her husband, as he attempted to maneuver through the late evening traffic. It was a short distance, but to them it felt like an eternity before they reached the hospital.

"Honey, we just have to pray that everything will be alright. Try not to worry, I know Dr. Moore will know what to do," Jake said nervously, attempting to sound as convincing as possible. Glancing at Sandy with her face contorted in pain told him things did not look so good; that unless Dr. Moore was also a magician, that tiny being didn't have much chance of survival.

The good doctor was there waiting for them when they arrived. She was quickly put on a stretcher and wheeled into the ER. Upon examination, he could tell there was nothing that could be done to save the baby, everything had happened so fast! There had been profuse and rapid bleeding as soon as they had put her on the stretcher and the baby was lost.

"I'm so sorry! Miscarriages occur quite often in the early weeks, most of the time we never really know what causes them, but there has to be something that's not quite right. And believe me there was nothing that you did that caused this, so don't ever blame yourselves, these things happen. Hard to explain, maybe, but nevertheless, inevitable in some cases," he very quietly said as he met the saddened gaze of the distraught couple. Sandy was sobbing bitterly and Jake held her as he attempted to stay as composed as possible for Sandy's sake.

"I know it's not much comfort right now, honey, but this certainly has to be easier than if he had been born and we lost him then. And, now at least we know, if we did it once we can do it again!" Jake said in an effort to cheer her up, and Sandy did manage a little smile for the man she loved so much.

"I suppose you're right - but it's so hard - to know that I carried him all these months, and then, to have this happen. I was just so looking forward to our little baby, but maybe God had a reason," she said as she tried to wipe away the tears streaming down her face.

"That's the way we have to look at it, God had a reason, and when the time is right we'll have our beautiful, healthy baby. It'll happen - just you wait and see!" Jake kissed her and she smiled at him again, as tired as she was, there would be no way that she would be able to sleep, her heart was aching too much. Jake sat in the lounge chair beside her bed, determined not to leave her. They talked softly for hours, then he watched as Sandy lay back on the pillow and closed her eyes. As soon as he saw she had drifted off to sleep, he leaned back in the lounge chair and began to come to terms with his own sense of loss. Thankful as he was that this had happened sooner than later, he couldn't help but think of what might have been had this baby been allowed to fully develop and be born. Anyway he looked at it he knew they had lost something very precious tonight..

CHAPTER TWENTY-TWO (1962)

It was a warm, balmy, late spring Friday in early June. River Valley was in full bloom, extra warm for this early in summer, and as usual the humidity was starting to get the best of most everyone. Mary and Joe were sitting on their back deck, Mary fanning herself, Joe just sitting in the shade reading the paper and trying his best to keep cool. They had added the back deck a few years ago, put a roof over it and screened it in. They spent the good share of their time out there during the warm weather. Mary had made it very cozy with white wicker furniture and beautiful hanging plants all the way around the inside of the roof. They loved this time of year, as everyone did, except for the humidity. At least polio with all its dreadful implications had for the most part disappeared, as long as the shots were administered faithfully. Mary decided at that moment that what they both needed was some ice cold lemonade, and she walked back through the patio doors into the kitchen to make some.

Just as she took the ice cube trays out of the freezer, she heard the front door open, then Jack's voice as he walked into the kitchen. School was over for the day and the twelve-year old seventh grader always came home immediately after school.

"Mom!, if that's lemonade you're making I'll have some too! Boy, is it hot!" he said in the inconsistent voice of a boy becoming a young man. He quickly wiped his hand across his forehead, then dashed over and gave his mother a quick kiss on the cheek.

"Where's Dad?"

"On the deck, here take this out to him," she said as she handed him a glass of lemonade.

He rushed out the patio doors to the deck and excitedly burst out with, "Hey, Dad, you know those rocks we found in that old quarry last week? I took them to Science class today and we broke them apart and they're filled with something like crystals. We were analyzing them under the microscope - the whole class!"

"Probably quartz," the elder man said, "glad everyone enjoyed them, and what about the ones with gold glitters in them?"

"Oh, we looked at them a couple of days ago. They were interesting too, Mr. Simms said it was fool's gold, whatever that is - and - get this! - he announced today he's planning a field trip for the class to go to Treasure Mountain next Friday and he would like one parent of each kid to come along if they can. How about it Dad, could you make it - huh?"

Jack, the science and nature lover was still bubbling - actually he loved anything to do with the world around him, including people. At his tender age he was toying with the prospects of either becoming a scientist, a veterinarian, or a doctor. Every few days he came to a different conclusion, but he knew it had to be one of the three.

"Sure, I'll take the day off and go with you - should be quite invigorating - climbing a mountain. Haven't done anything like that in a long time, sign me up!"

"Great! He said he'll probably split us up into small groups, or we can just go by ourselves if we want to, as long as we're with an adult and as long as we meet back at the bus at a certain time." Jack was grinning his happiest grin.

"Sounds good to me! Now go get your lemonade and sit down and cool off for a while - it's too hot to get too excited!" Joe laughed as he went back to his paper.

Jack still had a slight limp from his childhood polio, and he maintained a slight frame all through his youth, but he was very healthy and the pride and joy of his parents. The adoption had come through years ago when it was legally determined that enough time had elapsed without his biological father's return.

He had two best friends, Bill and Mike, they lived just a few houses down the street from him, close enough to spend a lot of time at each other's houses. They were both very much like him, scientifically-minded, not particularly interested in the competitive sports, and not caring to follow the crowd in that respect.

But Jack's very best friend was his adoptive father, whose company he enjoyed immensely. When he was very little, he spent many hours on Joe's lap as his devoted dad read to him. He would sit quietly and Joe could tell he was devouring every word, really taking it all in. He collected rocks by the dozens and was fascinated by bugs and insects, forever examining them under the inexpensive microscope he had received one Christmas. He breezed through the grades with all A's, with only occasionally a B, and he loved school and actually disliked to see vacations and summer come. This was quite difficult for his friends Bill and Mike to understand, as they couldn't wait for the vacations from school. They loved to tease him about it but Jack knew the teasing was all in fun. As studious as he was he never lacked for friends and was very popular with all the kids in his class.

Mary watched with pride as the two men in her life chatted together happily and she silently thanked God for sending this young boy to them to be entrusted in their care. She couldn't have loved him more if he had been biologically hers and she knew Joe felt the same way. At times she was saddened when she thought of Ellen and Tim and how the joy she felt should have been theirs. But she was sure they would have approved of her and Joe raising their son and loving him like he was their own.

Friday finally came. Mary packed bagels and thermos bottles and cookies and fruit, actually more than they would need for the day. She wanted to make sure her boys didn't go hungry! Jack and his father put on their most comfortable sweats and hiking boots and after packing the necessary gear and lunch into their backpacks, they gave Mary a quick kiss and were out the door. The other parents and students were arriving at the school at approximately the same time to catch the bus. There were not as many students as Jack had expected taking the trip, even his two best friends had been told by their parents to go to school instead. Altogether there were only five boys and one girl from the science class of seventeen that were able to go, and of course there was one parent each. Apparently most parents were against the idea, or one of them was unable to accompany their son or daughter on the trip so they apparently felt insecure about letting them go. But for Jack it was an exciting excursion and he was very glad his father had gone along with it.

They boarded the bus at about eight A.M. and Mr. Simms stood up in front and briefed the students on what they would be doing when they reached the mountain. It was sort of like a contest to see who could come back with the most variety of nature items. He had told them earlier in class that they were to find as many different species of trees or rocks, or anything to do with nature, as they could. They were to identify different trees and collect their leaves, and do the same with every other facet of nature they encountered. There were no trails to follow so they were on their own, but he said he wasn't concerned about anyone getting lost because all they had to do was walk back down the mountain from wherever they were and they would come upon the highway. He said everyone should be back to get on the bus by four in the afternoon.

The fourteen people on the bus thoroughly enjoyed the scenery on the twenty-five mile trip due north up into the Adirondacks. It was the time of year when all nature was at its most beautiful, fresh and new. The songs *The Bear Went Over the Mountain* and *Row, Row, Row Your Boat* really got a workout, the kids singing them over and over, while the parents grimaced to themselves each time they heard them start up anew.

They arrived at their drop-off point in just under an hour, and the driver waited to make sure everyone had taken off everything they had brought with them, and Mr. Simms had reminded him again as to when to return to pick them up. There was no formal building where they signed in, but there were bathroom facilities, and the children were reminded they were there for their use. It was a huge mountain, not so much in height as in width, it was about two thousand feet above sea level and encompassed hundreds of acres. Everyone listened as Mr. Simms issued instructions and handed each parent a topical map of the mountain which showed precise locations of particularly interesting areas. He made sure each parent had a compass on them, if not, he had brought along spares to hand out. They were told to be back where they were standing by three forty-five to board the bus, for the departure time of four o'clock.

Two sets of four started up the mountain, branching off as they climbed, and the father and daughter accompanied Mr. Simms more or less to the left side of the mountain. Jack and his father opted to go by themselves off to the right of the mountain. This was not unfamiliar territory to Joe Lauren, in his younger years he had done quite a bit of hunting and fishing in these areas. Now, nearing fifty, it has been a few years since he had wandered around in the mountains, but he was still looking forward to it.

The two of them walked in a half-horizontal, half-vertical fashion for a while, stopping often to inspect something and gather a sample to put in Jack's plastic bag. There was every variety of tree intermingled with the pines and evergreens and in some cases walking could become a little difficult. But neither one of them minded, they made a game out of climbing over fallen trees. Jack enjoyed walking on the top of them to see how long he could keep his balance, much to the concern of his father.

"Keep your eyes out for anything unusual, Dad," Jack reminded his father. "And you can help me identify some of the trees I'm not sure of, OK?"

Joe smiled to himself at his son's enthusiasm and assured him he would help. He was quite knowledgeable in the different species of plants and trees and was eager to share that knowledge with his son.

"Just make sure you stay close by, now, I don't want to be looking for you, it's pretty dense here," he said as he adjusted the backpack to make it more comfortable.

Jack almost stumbled, then looked down at the ground at a stump that had been the culprit and said, "Hey, look, someone must have just cut down this tree. Look at the rings, Dad, it was pretty old. Wish I could take that stump back with me." Counting the rings he found the tree to be at least a hundred years old, which was comparatively young for most of the trees in this forest. Using a saw they had brought along, Joe cut halfway into the trunk and sectioned off a piece so that it showed most of the rings and Jack happily tucked it in his bag.

They had been walking and collecting for the better part of two hours when Joe decided he needed a rest. He sat down on a weathered tree trunk that looked like it had been there for many years refusing to decay.

"What do you say we have a little snack, let's see what your mother put in here," he said as he unzipped the side of his backpack with the lunch in it. "Bagels and cream cheese - sounds good right about now!"

"Wow! I guess I'm a little hungry, too - we both love bagels, don't we Dad? Mom sure knew what two hungry mountain-climbing men would want for lunch!" he laughed as he came quickly from a few feet away at the mention of food. He had been peeling off a section of white bark from a birch tree, which he put quickly in his bag, and dashed to the tree trunk his father was already sitting on. Full of energy and not the least bit tired, he nevertheless sat down to eat his bagel.

Joe was pleased at how much his son was enjoying their mountain excursion together. He silently vowed he would try to do more things with Jack, he had been pretty absorbed in his work at the bank as of late.

As they leisurely drank from their thermoses and ate cookies and fruit, Joe remembered a mountain stream that he said should be nearby. He said the water was very clear and clean and he used to drink from it when he used to come up this way.

"Maybe we'll run across it, should be nearby." He gazed around him as if reminiscing about earlier days when he was young and full of pep like Jack was now. "Well, if you're done maybe we should keep moving if we plan to reach the top. It's already noon, and we have to go all the way back down, you know."

"Yes, but Dad, we can run all the way down, that'll only take us half as long," Jack laughed flippantly. Then quietly he said, "I'm so glad you came with me today, Dad. Thanks for bothering."

"It was no bother, Jack, I've enjoyed it too, something different from interviewing people wanting loans and mortgages all day. Maybe we should do this more often, or something that would include your mother, too," the elder man said as they both put their backpacks back on.

"Yeah, I know Mom wouldn't care for this," Jack laughed. "She's afraid of bugs and she doesn't like getting all sweaty and dirty either."

"Well, that's your mother. She never cared about backpacking and walking through the woods, she likes to sew and cook and clean house, but I know she does like to travel. We'll have to take a nice trip one of these days."

"Where could we go, Dad? How about to California or somewhere on the west coast so we could see the Pacific Ocean? I've seen the Atlantic, now I'd like to see the Pacific."

"Sounds like a good idea for the future. We'll have to think about it. But right now lets concentrate on the trip at hand. Maybe we can make it to the top in another hour." Jack nodded his agreement as they started trudging up the mountain. The twigs underneath their feet snapped and by this time their boots were pretty muddy, at least they didn't leak. Occasionally an evergreen branch would snap back into one of their faces but it was all part of the game and they didn't seem to mind. They started walking in a more straightforward direction slowly and carefully so as not to miss anything Jack could add to his already quite full plastic bag.

They had only been walking about half an hour when Joe knew he had to sit and rest again. There was a pain in his left arm which seemed to be moving to his throat and chest. It had come on him very suddenly and it frightened him to think that possibly it was the beginning of a heart attack. He was deep in the woods with no help available within miles and only his twelve-year old son to help him. He sat very quietly hoping the pain would disappear before Jack had a chance to notice.

"That's an unusual looking flower up on that branch, I'm going to climb up to get it, OK, Dad?" Jack excitedly said as he started to climb the tree. "OK, Dad?"

When there was no answer he turned and looked in the direction of his father. It wasn't like his father to just sit there and not answer him. Joe had his back to him so his son wouldn't see the pain etched on his face but Jack ran immediately over to him sensing something was wrong.

"Just a little pain, son, it'll go away in a minute," he said softly as he gripped his chest. But somehow he knew it wouldn't. This was no place to have a full-blown heart attack! It must have been the climbing, he just wasn't used to it anymore. But he had never had any heart trouble or any indication that he had a problem. He had just had a physical and the doctor had congratulated him on having the body of a twenty-five year old. But even twenty-five year olds could have heart attacks!

"Dad, are you going to be OK? What'll I do? Shall I run for help and try to find someone? We should have stayed with them! I'm sorry, I made you do this -" Jack was becoming very frightened as he watched his father in such apparent misery.

"I'll be OK," he was struggling with his breathing, "help me lean against this stump, and get me -" he paused grasping his chest again, "water-"

Jack gently helped prop him against the stump and quickly opened the thermos and put it to his father's mouth. He took a very short sip and motioned for Jack to take it away.

"Dad, I'm going for help - they can't be too far away." Then as an afterthought he knew he didn't want to leave his father alone so he started to shout.

"Help!! Somebody!! Mr. Simms! My father is sick! Can anyone hear me?" He was yelling as loud as he could but there was no response, apparently they had wandered too far away from the rest of the group. He yelled again and again but to no avail!

He thought again about running for help but to where? He could run to the bottom of the mountain - it would take a while - but there would probably be no one there when he got there, they didn't have to be there until almost four o'clock! He could try running across the mountain to where some of the others might be but chances of just accidentally running into any of them were probably pretty slim! And then what if he found someone. What would they be able to do? And regardless of what he did it would mean he would have to leave his father. He knew he needed to get to a hospital. And besides, if he left his father here in search of help would he know where to find him when he brought someone back? He decided the only thing he could do was to stay within sight of his father, maybe walk a little way in each direction and yell at the top of his lungs, and just possibly someone in the group would hear him and a couple of the men could carry his father out. Oh! if only they could hear him!

He could tell his father was losing his color and getting quite gray and Jack knew that meant he was getting worse. He covered him with a jacket as best he could and tried to comfort him.

"I'm not going to leave you, Dad." Glancing at his watch he said, " It's nearly two now, and everyone has to be back at the bus before four. When we're not there they'll start looking for us, and they'll find us, Dad, don't worry. Just hang on, you'll be OK! I'm going to stay nearby and just hope someone hears me shouting!"

His father's breathing was labored but at least he didn't seem to be grabbing his chest anymore in pain. He seemed to pass in and out of consciousness or he was just dozing on and off, Jack really didn't know which. But Jack was mature enough to know that his father needed immediate medical attention or he might not survive.

The young boy continued to run several yards in each direction and shouted as loudly as he could in hope of attracting someone's attention. After approximately two hours had passed he tearfully sat down on the ground beside his father. The elder man was still having difficulty in breathing and was very gray but Jack held his hand, hoping to give him even the slightest amount of comfort. They would just have to sit and wait, at least they knew they were expected to be at the bus and when they didn't show up, something would certainly be done about it. Either the men from the bus would come looking for them or they would alert a search party. It wasn't as if Jack and his father had wandered into the mountainous woods alone with no one knowing they were there. It was very comforting to know they would be missed at the bus boarding, and that there were several others that knew they were still somewhere on the mountain.

"They should be all meeting the bus about now, Dad, and when we're not there they sure won't leave without us. Everything's going to be alright - I just know it is. Are you warm enough?" Jack was very frightened but was determined not to show it if he could help it. He decided he was going to calm himself down and just pour all his energy into keeping his father alive. Joe looked toward his son with very tired eyes and nodded to let him know he was warm enough.

Again his father's hand moved slowly to his chest and by the contortion of his face Jack knew he was having another very sharp pain. He had been hoping possibly the worst was over but it seemed it was still very much ongoing.

In his mind Jack was thinking, *"Oh, why did I talk him into doing this? It's all my fault! I wish I had never mentioned anything about this darn field trip! I should have gone to school just like Bill and Mike did, then this would never have happened!"* He looked hopelessly about him, thinking how unimportant were all the nature items he had collected in his plastic bag, how unimportant everything was at that moment except getting help for his father.

Five o'clock, then six, and no one had even come close to finding them yet. Were they even looking? Maybe the bus just left without them and they'd be here all night in the cold and darkness and maybe - maybe his father would die! Jack started to panic at the thought, but caught himself. He knew he had to be the man in this situation, his father was unable to function in that capacity.

They had brought matches in his father's bag. He would gather up some twigs before it got dark and possibly he could start a fire. That might keep them warm in the cool night air and even send forth smoke enough to help someone find them, if anyone was looking for them. He gathered up all the dry twigs he could find, put them in a pile and started to search for larger pieces of limbs that were dried out. They were quite close to a small clearing, just a few feet wide in any direction, but big enough to start a campfire without danger to nearby trees and underbrush. He didn't dare attempt to start a fire near where his father lay as there was too much danger of it spreading, but he knew he could contain it in this little clearing. He wished he could get his father over closer to the clearing but he wasn't going to attempt to move him in his condition.

He cleared a circular area about five feet in diameter, pushed together a small pile of dried leaves, lit them, and while they smoldered he put a couple of twigs on top. He saw a tiny flicker of a red flame and put a few more dried twigs on top. Soon he had a campfire, it wasn't going to help much as far as heat was concerned, but somehow he felt better as he watched the smoke circling up into the air over the tops of the trees. Someone could pinpoint exactly where they were if they saw the smoke. It gave Jack his first real ray of hope! He kept refueling it when it started to die down, first with more twigs, then with larger pieces that weren't completely dried out knowing those would cause more smoke, and heighten the chances of their location being discovered. Between gathering wood, keeping the fire going and continuously checking on his father, Jack was kept very busy. He was keeping his hopes up that they would be found before darkness had set in, but the sun was going down and Jack was becoming increasingly worried.

He heard his father mumbling and rushed to his side. The elder man looked up at Jack and whispered, "Promise me - if something should happen to me and I don't make it - out of here - that you'll be strong and take care of your mother - you're being real brave now and - I'm proud of you - and don't worry - we'll make it-". His voice trailed off so that it was hardly audible.

Jack put his arm around his father's shoulder and said with staunch determination, "We'll both make it, Dad. They're probably looking for us right now, don't you worry about anything, I'll take care of it. You just sit here and rest, and don't try to talk, OK?"

As darkness approached, and the cool night air was really setting in, Jack wondered how he would keep his father warm. They hadn't brought any blankets, they hadn't anticipated anything like this happening, all they had were their jackets. He decided to take his own jacket over by the fire, try to warm it, then bring it back and put it over his father, then do likewise with his father's jacket. Switching from one jacket to the other should keep his father warm enough. He knew he would be able to just stand by the fire to warm up as often as he needed to.

'Hope there aren't any wild animals around,' Jack thought to himself, suddenly thinking what easy prey they would be for a bear or wolf or coyote. *'Maybe the fire will keep them away, I think I've read that that's what you're supposed to do.'*

For the first time he thought of his mother. *'She must be worried sick. She wasn't too thrilled about us coming in the first place. Oh, I wish we'd never done this!'*

Approximately three more hours passed and after refueling the fire and returning to his father with a warmed jacket for about the twentieth time, he heard in the distance what he thought sounded like a dog barking. He heard it only once, than decided he must have been mistaken. He only hoped it wasn't a wild animal prowling nearby. Then after a few minutes - Wait! There it goes again! Yes, it is a dog barking! Could it be possible that there was a search party with a canine helper searching for them? He knew a dog would pick up their scent and lead the searchers right to them. He was jubilant with hope as he stood up and looked in the direction of the barking. It was getting closer, with each bark it was a little closer, and Jack stood up and shouted, " Over here! We're over here!!" as loudly as he could.

He knew it would have to be rough walking in the dark over already rough terrain, and it would take a while for any searchers to reach them, but he decided to keep shouting to try to keep them steered in the right direction.

Another quarter hour passed, was that the glint of a light in the distance? Jack gave one loud whoop and shouted. "Over here, we're over here - thank God!"

"We hear you! We'll be right there!" came the shout in return.

A moment later he heard the crackling of twigs underfoot and the swooshing of trees as a big dog ran up to him wagging his tail profusely, ecstatic that he had accomplished his mission. Shortly behind him were four men, Jack knew them all, and as they all approached him he quickly motioned to his father, by now nearly comatose, and the men rushed to his side.

They were all ambulance attendants, and as always, thoroughly prepared. They had brought along a collapsible litter, and they immediately started carefully transferring Joe onto it. One of them put an oxygen mask over his face, while another was monitoring vital signs. They wrapped a blanket around his body and tied him onto the litter.

Jack could feel hot tears of relief running down his cheeks, and he hoped the men couldn't see him in the darkness. "You can't imagine how happy I am to see you guys! I'm so worried about my father, I think he had a heart attack!"

"That's what it looks like!' one of the men said. "We came just as soon as we got the word that you guys didn't meet the bus. Your teacher called us as soon as he could get to a phone, and we had to take the dog to your house to pick up your scents. Anyway, son, everything will be alright, just got to get back down this mountain and get your father to a hospital!"

Two very bright lights were held by two of the men to light the way as they gently started to carry Joe out of the forest and down the mountain. They moved as quickly as they could taking extra precaution not to cause unnecessary trauma to the man on the stretcher.

Putting his arm across Jack's shoulder and giving him an understanding smile, one of the men added, "You did good, son, we're proud of you, and we did see your smoke - that was good thinking!"

"I was hoping someone would see it, and how's my mother, did you see her? Was she awfully worried, huh?"

"She was, but we assured her we've found people in these mountains before and we knew we'd find you two - especially with Roger to help us!" Jack was sure he had never been as happy in all his young life as he was at that moment and he thanked his rescuers over and over again. He stroked the back of the bravest one of all - Roger, the K9 rescue dog, and Roger wagged his tail again in appreciation.

"Will he be OK? Can you tell?," Jack asked the men quietly.

"He seems to be resting fairly comfortably, but we don't know for sure what's happening without a complete evaluation, but he doesn't seem to be in much pain right now, so we'll just hope for the best," one of the attendants volunteered.

It was slow walking down the mountain even with the lights and it took upward to an hour to reach the ambulance parked on the road below. The men had to be extra careful carrying the litter, they could have tripped or fallen easily, and they certainly didn't want to add to the problem. Jack walked behind them carrying the two backpacks. He had left his plastic bag with all the nature items he had accumulated behind - he didn't even want it now! This trip had caused him to have the worst experience of his life and he didn't want anything to remind him of what he had put his father through. All he wanted was his father back, healthy and well like he had been before today!

They reached the bottom finally, loaded Joe into the ambulance, still monitoring his pulse and blood pressure and oxygen intake. An attendant sat by his side and motioned for Jack to sit on the opposite side of his father. They were heading for the nearest hospital, which was about ten miles away in Williamsville. It would save them an extra fifteen miles of traveling by going there instead of back to River Valley, and Joe needed medical attention as quickly as possible.

The hospital was informed of the patient's condition, vital signs, and estimated time of arrival in plenty of time in advance, and when they drove up to the emergency center a doctor and two nurses were awaiting their arrival. Joe was quickly assessed and hooked up to a heart monitor. Jack sat by his bed, nervously awaiting the arrival of his mother, still very frightened over his father's condition but extremely relieved to be off that mountain.

Mary had been called and a neighbor had driven her the fifteen miles to the Williamsville hospital. Not knowing the seriousness of her husband's condition and not even knowing for sure just what had happened on the mountain, she was an emotional wreck by the time she reached the hospital. She immediately ran to Jack and hugged him when she saw him coming toward her just inside the emergency room.

"What happened? Is your father going to be OK? Oh, I've been so worried about both of you. It must have been terrible for you, seeing him like that and being all alone!" Tears were streaming down her face and she hugged her son again and looked into his sad face. "But I'm so proud of you, you stayed by him, and took care of him. I'm sure he's very proud of you, too!"

With tears of relief at seeing his mother he said, "He's doing better, Mom, he'll be alright, I know he will - don't cry!" He put his arm around her as he led her back to the corner area where Joe gave them both a weak smile when they pulled back the curtain. Mary was in understandable shock to see him lying there helpless when this morning he had seemed in the peak of health. She stroked his hand and told him she loved him and little by little her fears started to subside as she noticed his color returning and his breathing becoming more normal.

"He's doing much better now, he's resting comfortably, and you both should try to get some rest. There's a room just outside of the door where you can stretch out. I'll bring a couple of pillows and blankets," said the attractive blonde nurse that was attending to Joe.

It was close to midnight and there was nothing that either of them could do at this time. Joe was sleeping so they decided to take the nurse's advice and at least try to rest and unwind for a few hours. Jack, although still very worried, but extremely tired from the day's mountain climbing and totally stressed out from the dreadful experience he had just been through, fell asleep almost immediately. His mother on the other hand, stayed awake as if to stand guard, so she would be ready at a moment's notice if her husband needed her.

She walked into the room in the early morning hours, around five to be exact, and found Joe sitting up in a chair. He was still hooked to the machines, but he looked one hundred percent better than he had the night before. When he saw her approaching he broke out in a big smile.

"Hope I didn't scare anyone too much," he said apologetically. Mary hugged her husband and kissed his cheek and said quickly, "You scared us to death! Are you feeling better now? What did the doctor say? They let you sit up? Are you sure that's OK?"

Joe smiled at her series of questions. "Yes, they got me up about an hour ago, said it's the best thing for me, and I feel good, stop worrying!" He turned and looked toward the door and asked, "And where's that boy of mine? You should have seen him, what a brave kid!"

Just then Jack walked in the door, rather slowly at first, still feeling the pangs of guilt for having dragged his father up on the mountain in the first place.

Joe saw him immediately and reached out his arms, "Come here, son. I'm so proud of you, you saved my life!" They embraced each other for a long moment as tears flowed freely and unashamedly. Mary watched with pride as she witnessed the love between the two men in her life.

"I made you go up that mountain, Dad, I should never have talked you into it," Jack sobbed as all the tension of the last twenty-four hours was suddenly released.

"You didn't talk me into it, remember, I went on my own free will, I wanted to go, I wanted us to spend some time together, neither of us knew it would turn out the way it did. What happened to me could have happened anywhere, don't you ever feel guilty about anything, do you understand? And, by the way, thanks for saving my life!"

Jack beamed at the last comment and gave his father another quick hug. As he sat down beside his mother, he said thoughtfully, "And thank you for being such a great dad, but you know what, I knew we'd make it out of there, although I was sure scared to death. From now on, what do you say we stick to fishing, and I don't ever want to see another mountain as long as I live!" Mary and Joe both laughed as they looked lovingly at their son.

A few days later Joe was released from the hospital. He had had a moderately severe heart attack but it had seemingly left no damaging complications. There was definitely blockage, to be sure, but he was told that as long as he avoided unnecessary stress, took his medication they had prescribed, and didn't over exert himself too much, he should be in good shape.

For four more years he was faithful to the regiment, took his pills, walked regularly, he even took an early retirement from the bank, so he could lead a less stressful, more relaxing life. The family traveled a bit, never quite making it to the west coast, but they did go to Canada, the New England states, Florida, and as far west as Texas. Then one day in late November 1966, when Jack was sixteen, his father collapsed and died in the living room of their home. Both Jack and his mother were at his side in a moment but death had been instantaneous. Mother and son had lost their husband, father and dearest friend. It would take both of them a long time to deal with their loss, but they knew they still had each other.

CHAPTER TWENTY-THREE (1966)

It was a slow and painful recovery but Sandy eventually rallied from her loss and slowly became her usual bubbly, happy self, or so it appeared on the surface. Inside she was always wondering what their child would look like now! When she lay in bed at night she would think about him, he or she would be starting kindergarten this year, five years old already! Each time she saw a child that would be about the same age she could feel her heart ache a little and her eyes grow a little moist. Why was it that other women could have three, four, five and more children and she couldn't even have one? Try as they may she had not been able to get pregnant again for those five long years.

She had gone back to the doctor again about a year after her miscarriage, and the doctor assured her there was no reason why she couldn't conceive again. She knew she had been stubborn about adoption but she wanted so much to have their own child. It wasn't that she was against raising someone else's child, she just wanted a baby that was part of her and Jake. "Just relax and let nature take its course," the doctor had told her, but that did very little to relieve her anxiety. She was beginning to think it was hopeless, she was starting to accept the fact she would never be a mother biologically and she was beginning to agree with Jake about possible adoption. So, shortly after that visit to the doctor's they made an appointment with an adoption agency and filled out all the paperwork to request a newborn baby, boy or girl, that way it would feel more like their own right from the start. As much as Jake wanted a child too, he knew it was imperative that Sandy have a shot at motherhood for the sake of her sanity. She was becoming more and more obsessed with mothering a child as time went by.

They were told there was a long waiting list for newborns - it could take years! Nevertheless they put their name on the list hoping for a miracle, maybe some impatient couples would change their minds and either take their names off the list, or, even get pregnant while they were waiting. But that never seemed to happen and after five long years had gone by and after repeated checking with the agency throughout the years, their name had still not come up for the adoption of a newborn. There had been so many hopeful parents ahead of them and too few newborn babies to go around, that they were still way down on the list. They had tried other agencies, but it was always the same story.

Months went by and nearly another year had passed. They both had a vacation coming up, last two weeks in August of 1967, and they were going down into Oregon to a beautiful resort Jake had heard about at work. It would seem good to get away for two whole weeks, away from the hectic pace of their everyday living. They needed a break just to relax and spend more time with each other. Both of their jobs had been so demanding over the past few years, they had barely had time to take a vacation, at least at the same time. Maybe doing something different for a change would take their minds off their endless longing for a child. Besides, they would be having a tenth anniversary coming up soon, and this getaway could be an early celebration of that fact.

The Oregon coastline was breathtaking this time of year and they ate incredible amounts of delectable food, danced every night, went sight-seeing and spent every magnificent minute together. Their motel room overlooked the beach and the sky was so clear most days that it seemed as if you could see all the way to Hawaii. It was like a second honeymoon! It turned out to be wonderful therapy for both of them and when they returned home at the end of the second week, they felt refreshed and ready to conquer the world all over again.

The next Monday morning they were ready to go back to their jobs again, but Sandy had almost decided not to go in. She was feeling rather queasy and decided she must have caught something on vacation, or maybe all that food she wasn't accustomed to was getting the best of her. She went in anyway, thinking she would most likely feel much better in an hour or so, but that was not the case. As noon approached she knew she had to go home and lie down. She called Jake, and he left the hospital immediately to pick her up.

"I hope it's not contagious," she said as she laid her head back on the headrest, "maybe just a case of delayed food poisoning. Anyway, it'll pass, I'm sure, but I hope it's soon!"

"Just take it easy and rest, but if you don't feel better, call me again and I'll take you to the emergency room," Jake said as they walked into their living room. Almost immediately Sandy made a quick dash for the bathroom, and although the door was shut Jake could hear her being sick. When she came out her face was flushed and wet, and he was not so sure whether he should go back to work or not, but she finally convinced him she was feeling much better.

When he came home that night she was her usual contented self and seemed to be feeling great. It must have been just a passing bug that was going around and she had caught it. The next morning Jake awoke to the sound of someone gagging. Sandy was hanging over the toilet bowl, and when she came back to bed she looked flushed again and very exhausted. She pulled the blankets up under her chin and didn't move for a few minutes, afraid that if she did she would have to throw up again.

"Think you should see a doctor?" Jake was a little concerned.

"No, I'll be alright, whatever it is, it'll go away soon, I hope ."

Without bringing up the subject, the possibility of pregnancy had entered each of their minds. But it was too soon, too soon to hope, and have their hopes shattered again! Neither one of them dared to mention it that morning, and Jake made sure she was comfortable, told her to stay in bed and rest and he would call her often. He dressed, kissed her goodbye and went off to the hospital.

She slept most of the day, and once again was feeling her old self when Jake came home from work that night. They even went out to dinner that night, but the next morning was a repetition of the morning before and as sick as she felt she was inwardly rejoicing because she knew it probably meant she was pregnant again. She hadn't remembered too much morning sickness the first time, but she knew each time could be different. It was a little too soon to be confirmed by her doctor, but she made an appointment that day for about two weeks in the future. Every morning was the same, and she welcomed it, in fact was elated over it, that wonderful morning sickness that lasted at least two hours after she got out of bed! She couldn't keep anything down, even water. She was able to drink ginger ale occasionally, but sometimes she had trouble retaining that also. It was hard getting ready for work each day, but she managed somehow, and that familiar and happy feeling of anticipation was returning to the both of them. They tried as best they could to keep a low profile on their excitement, just in case.

Dr. Moore confirmed the fact that she was indeed pregnant and the baby would be due the beginning of June. Although they were both quite sure at this point, she would just simply pass on the confirmation to Jake this time, no balloons or flowers, nothing in pink or blue, she didn't want to jinx anything. They had decided to wait till the very end to get the room ready again. The walls were still the pale blue, with the romping bears in the border just waiting for company. They had packed away the crib, bassinet and dressing table and Sandy had even given away all the baby clothes and diapers they had purchased, it just seemed inappropriate to keep them for another baby, like bad luck, or something. In fact, everything was toned down with the exception of their inner excitement, that was stronger than ever! Each night they prayed that this baby would survive and be brought into the world full-term and healthy.

"I've decided to take a leave of absence from the bank," Sandy told Jake one evening, "I want to be able to rest when I feel like it and really take good care of myself and my baby." She was about six months long and had planned on working up until six weeks before the baby was due, then going back afterwards, but being so tired all the time, she found she was dragging most of the day. There was no more nausea in the morning, at least that had stopped.

"I was hoping you'd decide that you would quit entirely," Jake surprised her by saying. "We can get by fine without you working, and I know it would be best for the baby when it gets here, you don't really want to hire someone to take care of our baby, do you?"

"No, but if you think we can afford it, I'll be more than happy to retire!," Sandy beamed. "I can always go back when our child goes to school. Great idea! I'm so glad you feel that way! I'll put in my two-weeks notice tomorrow!"

That she did! The next day. And all the girls she worked closely with in the bank immediately started planning a baby shower as a going-away party.

She was going to be getting through that Friday and was happily anticipating the baby shower that the girls had been so meticulously planning for the past two weeks. She could tell they were going all out from all the little tidbits she heard here and there. She knew she would miss seeing all her friends every day, after all she had worked there fourteen years. But she knew she could always go back many years later, when her child was in school. Now, at thirty-three she was retiring to start her new career, motherhood! And she couldn't have been happier!

She had just put the last dish back in the cupboard after Thursday night's dinner when she felt a sudden, severe cramp in her abdomen. She said nothing at the time, Jake was in the living room watching the news and she didn't want to alarm him needlessly. But then it happened again about five minutes later, just as hard. She remembered the last time she had had these kind of pains and immediately became frightened.

'Oh - no! This is too early for labor pains - please! - please don't let there be anything wrong!' she pleaded silently to herself. But instead of stopping, the cramps were intensifying. She knew she had to tell Jake, much as she hated to worry him.

They didn't waste any time calling the doctor, Jake rushed

her to the emergency room as fast as the car could take her. He knew the doctor was somewhere in the hospital and could be paged to come to the ER. Sandy sat uncomfortably doubled up on the short ride to the hospital, and Jake ran into the inner entrance and grabbed a wheelchair for her and wheeled her into the emergency room. Dr. Moore came immediately upon being paged.

"I'm not quite seven months, doctor, could I be in labor?" Sandy nearly cried in pain as she looked up at him. "Will my baby be alright? Has he had enough time to grow? Owwww!" The pains were coming much harder and closer now.

Dr. Moore quickly examined her and confirmed her suspicions. "Yes, maam, you are certainly in labor and it looks like this one is going to be quick!"

"But it's so early - will he be OK? - will he, doctor?"

"As far as I can see everything is progressing fine right now - it's a little early - but premature babies have a much better chance of making it today then they did a few years ago. Try not to worry, we'll take good care of both you and your baby." He smiled as he touched her hand as if to offer encouragement, but she was in too much pain to be consoled. She reached for Jake and he brushed back her hair and wiped the perspiration from her forehead. He didn't look so good either! She thought he looked like he was ready to pass out.

"Is it alright if I stay with her, doctor?" he was asking, but keeping his eyes fixed on Sandy. .

"Yes Jake, you certainly can, but we better be moving !"

She was quickly wheeled to the delivery room, and as she saw the walls swirling past her, she felt dizzy and nauseous. It seemed to be almost one continuous excruciating pain now. There were white uniforms everywhere telling her not to push. Someone was putting a cup over her nose and told her to count backwards from ten. She got as far as eight and the last person she saw was Jake as he kissed her. Then she seemed to be spiraling downward into a peaceful sleep and the harrowing pains stopped!

The tiny three pound, two ounce, foot long baby girl was born at 10:05 PM on the tenth of March, 1968 within fifteen minutes after her mother arrived in the delivery room. Her labor hadn't lasted that long but it had consisted of intense contractions very close together. The umbilical cord was wrapped tightly around the baby's neck, but the doctor was able to loosen it quickly. It took a minute for that first cry and Jake held his breath as he watched the doctor hold the baby by its heels. Suddenly, there was that first weak cry - very weak - but it was there! Sandy was still too groggy to be too aware of what was going on but she did hear the baby cry as she was coming in and out of the anesthetic-induced sleep and was awake enough to see her baby's tiny face when they held her close to her for just a minute. She was completely and perfectly formed by all outward appearances at least, but, being a preemie, was taken and placed immediately in an incubator in an adjoining room.

"You did it, honey! I'm so proud of you. She's beautiful, isn't she," Jake was beaming as he looked at his wife and kissed her again on the forehead. He didn't tell her about the short lapse of time before the baby cried, or about the umbilical cord. She didn't have to know about that right now. She only needed to know that her baby was here, and although very premature, seemed to be doing well.

She beamed with joy as she said, "Yes she is, and I love her so much already. When do you think I can see her again? I saw her for just a second, I didn't have time to see the color of her eyes and hair, did you?"

Jake laughed and said "Would you settle for no hair at all, and blue eyes, I think, they were so tiny and barely opened, but I think they were blue."

"Oh, I'm just so happy that she's alright," Sandy said happily as she kissed her husband back. They were both ecstatic as they hugged each other and thanked God for the precious little bundle they had been given. Tears were running freely down both of their faces and they were bubbling over with pure happiness.

"I can't believe it, she's so tiny, but - she made it!" an elated Sandy said as she lay back on her pillow and smiled. "She was worth a billion pains. I'm sorry if I carried on, but I sure am glad it's over!"

Dr. Moore had finished with Sandy and was conversing with the nurse on the far side of the room. He walked back to the happy new parents and with a big smile shook Jake's hand, congratulated them both and told Sandy she had been a model patient.

"At this point everything seems alright, but we'll be keeping a close eye on your baby for the next few weeks. I don't want to alarm you, but babies born with this low birth weight have about a 50% chance of survival. There could be complications that don't show up for a day or two, such as interior organs not formed enough to sustain life, sudden drops in blood pressure, and possible respiratory difficulties. As I said before this is not to alarm or upset you but to make you aware of what we're dealing with. From what I see right now I would say we are within the 50% survival class - but time will tell. I have taken the liberty of assigning Dr. Mike Laselli, an excellent pediatrician, to your case. He should be contacting you shortly."

The doctor's words were like a suddenly dropped bombshell neither one of them had anticipated. Fifty percent chance of survival? That meant it could go either way, their baby could live or die. Their state of ecstatic joy diminished very suddenly. They were aware there could be problems, but did Dr. Moore need to put it so bluntly?

"And if there are going to be any complications, they should start to show up fairly soon, right?" Jake asked, although he knew it was an redundant question.

"It would probably be very soon, if it was anything serious. Regardless, she will have to be monitored twenty-four hours a day until we know we're completely out of the woods." Dr. Moore had a reputation for not mincing words. "You can be sure Dr. Laselli will keep you informed around the clock." With that assurance he left the room.

Sandy and Jake looked at each other for a long moment. Unanswered questions and unexpected fears were apparent in their eyes. Everything had seemed so wonderful a short time ago, how could such a beautiful moment suddenly become so filled with apprehension and uncertainties? But it was best not to jump to conclusions, they just had to believe their baby girl would be okay.

Just then the nurse came into the room and told Jake he could come to see his daughter in the incubator if he wanted to. She told Sandy she could visit her later, it was best if she didn't move around right now.

"I'll wait - we'll see her together," Jake smiled at the nurse and she quietly understood and walked away. "We're a family now and if I know my daughter she'll want to see both her mommy and daddy!"

"Oh, Jake will she be alright? We can't lose her now, now that she's here and we've seen her and - she's all ours -" Sandy's voice broke as tears welled up in her eyes again.

"Let's try to think positively and keep the faith. That's all we can do," Jake hugged his wife and wiped away a tear. Sandy couldn't help but smile. This man she had married had so much tenderness and strength. Much more strength than she had, that was for sure!

"A name - we have to name her," Sandy said after a few moments. "I know we never really decided on a girl's name - but I was thinking - how about Elena Marie, after my grandmother? Do you like that name? Or would you like to name her after your mother or grandmother?" Sandy realized she had misspoken the moment she said it, she had momentarily forgotten that he didn't remember his family.

Jake thought for a minute, he had no idea what his mother's or grandmother's name was. He had absolutely no memory of his ancestral background, and now he had a child that he would not be able to relate any of his family history to.

"No, I like Elena Marie - it's a beautiful name. Elena Marie it is!" and he smiled happily as he gave her another kiss.

Early the next morning Sandy was told she could walk across the hall and visit her new baby girl. Jake had stopped by her room before he went to work and they were both very elated as he helped her out of the bed and walked with her to the room where their baby girl was in an incubator. As they gazed at her they were overwhelmed again by how very little she was; she seemed to take up a very small space in the incubator. It looked like there would have been room for three more babies her size in there with her. Her skin was not as pink as Jake would have liked, but he said nothing to Sandy. She moved her tiny arms and legs once or twice as they watched her and Sandy thought she looked just like a little baby doll she had gotten once for Christmas when she was a little girl. Her miniature face contorted as she started to cry, a cry so weak it could not be heard outside of the incubator. She wanted so much to hold her and cuddle her in her arms, but she knew that would have to wait.

She instinctively reached her hand through the hole in the side and touched her baby's hand. A tiny little finger curled over hers and for the two of them there was immediate bonding. She hated to let go, but she wanted Jake to have the same contact with his little daughter. He reached in and the same tiny finger wrapped itself around his and he looked at Sandy with smiling moist eyes.

"Looks like we're a family!" he said, looking lovingly at the two girls in his life.

"And young lady, did I tell you you have a name. It's Elena Marie, remember that, you'll be using it many times in your life!"

"I'm a little concerned about the formation of some of her vital organs, her heart and lungs in particular. She does show signs of an arrhythmia, that is, a slight deviation from the normal rhythm of her heart, which in all probability is due to the fact that there is more development needed there. And there could be a pulmonary dysfunction, her lungs are not as formed as I would like them to be, which, of course, is due to the fact that she's premature," Dr. Laselli was explaining to the Miller's that morning shortly after they had visited their baby. "Try not to worry, she is being very closely monitored and if any situation develops we'll be on top of it immediately. Meanwhile, just stay close and spend as much time beside her as possible. I really believe they know by instinct when their parents are close by."

"Oh, I wish she could have had another month at least before she was born," Sandy said sadly as she put her head in her hands, and Jake reached over and put his arm around her. "I feel like a failure as a mother!"

"It is unfortunate, but no need to blame yourself, it was nothing you caused. Right now she's holding her own, lets hope and pray it stays that way," Dr. Laselli said as he headed toward the door.

Sandy turned her head on the pillow as the doctor walked away, and as Jake looked down at her he knew she was trying not to cry. He would stay with her for awhile before he went back upstairs. He held her hand and they both were quiet, each praying silently in their own way for the life of their precious baby girl.

Sandy was allowed to go home in four days, but she hated the thought of leaving her newborn daughter behind, although she knew she could come and visit her as often as she wanted to. Jake was able to stop in at any time too, since his floor was just above obstetrics and pediatrics. Only in the late hours of the night was little Elena Marie without one or both of her parents with her. She was gaining, but just an ounce after a week, and her tiny eyes were more opened and seemed to be fixed on her parents when they were beside her. But her skin just didn't seem to have that healthy pink glow that newborn babies usually had and it constantly worried them both.

Dr. Laselli didn't help much in the encouragement department either, he never gave them any false hope, he told it exactly as it was. He said her condition was not getting any worse, but it wasn't improving as quickly as he thought it should either. It was a wait and see situation, and time would be needed to develop those vital organs. But the question was, would she be allowed that much time?

Elena Marie was six days old when Sandy was told she could hold her baby for the first time. It was determined she was much too fragile to be out of the incubator before that. The tiny baby was swaddled and placed in the eager arms of her mother and Sandy was so excited that she asked that Jake be called down to enjoy this event with her. When the nurse on the fourth floor paged him, he wasted no time, in fact he ran down the stairs instead of waiting for the elevator. Sandy handed the fragile bundle to him and as tiny little blue eyes looked up at him, he found it difficult to hold back the tears. It was so wonderful to know they finally had their baby - after all these years!

When Elena was about seven days old, Sandy couldn't help but notice what appeared to her to be a decline in the baby's activity. She was sleeping more than before, cried less, and seemed more listless when she was awake. Dr. Laselli stood with them beside the incubator that afternoon and hesitantly told them their baby was not responding to any treatment they were able to give her.

"I'm sorry to say her heart and lungs are not developing as well as they should have by this time. I was sure there would be more improvement, but it seems there has been a slight decline in her progression. You can be sure we are using every procedure known to modern medical science to help her, but, just so you'll be prepared, it's more or less up to God now," he very sadly informed them as he put his hand on Sandy's shoulder.

Sandy cried out and clung to Jake. "Up to God? Does that mean she's going to - die?" She wailed as she looked down lovingly at her tiny daughter.

"I'm afraid that's within the realm of possibility. At this point it doesn't look too promising, just continue to stay by her side. She needs you now more than ever."

The doctor's words faded into oblivion. Sandy and Jake

were so deeply lost in their emotions, that for a moment they heard or saw nothing around them, only the tiny bundle of life that may not be theirs for much longer lying there in the incubator. They both refused to leave their daughter the rest of the day and all throughout the night. Sandy would not leave even for a moment. Jake, at one point, went to the cafeteria and brought them both coffee and a sandwich which went completely uneaten. They huddled together and held the tiny fingers and talked constantly to their baby; her little head was turned to face them and they were sure she heard their voices.

At about seven-thirty the next morning, Sandy closed her eyes and from sheer stress and exhaustion soon drifted off into a restless sleep, still holding the tiny fingers through the hole in the incubator. Jake, seeing she was asleep at least for the moment, decided to run up to his floor to let them know his whereabouts. The nurses at the desk assured him they would call down if he was really needed, but they very adamantly encouraged him to stay with Sandy and the baby. He was not to worry about work.

He had been sitting there about an hour, Sandy was still dozing, when he noticed on the monitor that there had been a noticeable drop in the baby's blood pressure and her breathing was more labored. The stand-by nurse had already notified the doctor who rushed into the room a few seconds later. Sandy, hearing the confusion, woke with a start and reached for Jake, instinctively knowing something was terribly wrong.

"It might be better if you folks left the room," the doctor quietly said.

"No! We're not leaving her!" Sandy cried.

They stood holding each other next to the wall as the doctor and nurses did what they could to help their child, but it was to no avail. The line on the monitor went flat, and the doctor turned toward the couple with moist eyes.

"I'm so sorry, but there was nothing more that could be done. Your little angel is with God now. It was a combination of respiratory and heart failure, she just couldn't sustain life on organs that just wouldn't develop."

"Please, can I hold her just one more time - please, just for a moment?" Sandy was crying as she pleaded.

"Honey, do you think it's wise?" Jake tearfully said.

Without another word the doctor opened the incubator, wrapped the tiny bundle in the blanket underneath her and placed her in Sandy's arms. He had been around bereaved parents long enough to know they needed closure and a final goodbye. They both cried as they held her and kissed her several times on her tiny forehead.

"Your mommy and daddy love you so much Elena Marie, but God will take care of you now until we see you again." Sandy sobbed as she looked lovingly down at the tiny little face for a few moments before she reluctantly handed her back to a waiting nurse.

They decided on just a very quiet service in their church and Jake called the minister and scheduled it for the following day. They picked out a little white casket with embossed lambs on each side and lined with pink satin. Jake bought a tiny pink teddy bear and they requested that it be put beside her. They hardly noticed the rows of friends and co-workers that had come to pay their respects and nearly filled the little church. Before the casket was closed, Sandy lovingly broke off a pink rose from their floral arrangement, kissed it and placed it beside her little girl. She and Jake held each other and neither one of them could barely see through their tears.

The minister gave a brief but beautiful eulogy on the promise of eternal life, and how their little girl would be waiting for them with open arms. He told them she would never leave them; as long as she was in their hearts she would be with them always. Their hearts were filled with gratitude as they accepted hugs and condolences from their friends. Somehow it helped to ease the pain a little.

Their little angel was buried in the church cemetery under

a tall evergreen with wide spreading branches, and all the many floral tributes were spread on top of the freshly overturned dirt. Jake and Sandy stayed after everyone had left and held each other tightly. Sandy, who had successfully tried to keep her composure throughout the funeral and grave-side services could stand it no longer. She kneeled down in the dirt and cried bitterly, her tears falling on the pink roses with the banner that read, *'We love you - Mommy and Daddy'*. Jake knelt beside her, put his arm around her and just let her cry. He knew that was the best therapy for her right now. After a few moments they got to their feet and solemnly walked away leaving their baby daughter in God's hands.

CHAPTER TWENTY-FOUR (SPRING 1971)

Time has a way of moving on. They had been married a little over four months short of fourteen years. Sandy had been reinstated at her bank, and Jake had earned high respect and credibility at the hospital. He had been promoted, with a substantial raise in salary, to head of a department where he had constant interaction with both the patients and the medical staff and it seemed that even the doctors were asking his opinion on cases, and constantly telling him he should go to medical school, that he was a natural. He was doing far more than his job description dictated, but he really enjoyed every minute of it. The patients loved him, recognized his ability to communicate with them on their level, and enjoyed the way he treated them with respect and kindness. He couldn't have been more contented with his job, and he decided to himself that if he never accomplished anything more, career-wise, in his life, he could be very happy here doing just what he did every day. The hospital recognized his worth and was paying him very well now.

The two of them would sit on their deck overlooking Puget Sound in the evening and watch the golden waves ripple as the sun set over the water. Some evenings they would take long walks along the shoreline and chat about what had occurred that day at their respective jobs. Or they would talk about their lost baby, little Elena Marie who would have been slightly over two now. Sandy could almost picture her, walking between them, holding their hands and skipping along, chattering happily in two-year old fashion. They knew they would never forget her, she was part of them and sometimes they felt as if they could feel her presence -- even though she had only been with them for eight short days.

On weekends they would take little jaunts to nearby places, like downtown Seattle and Pike's Market, or ferry over to Bainbridge Island, or just visit the little shops scattered throughout the city. They were happy together, for the most part, except for that emptiness that continually haunted them, which was, of course, the absence of a baby in their lives. After the disappointment of the miscarriage and then the heartbreak of losing Elena Marie two years ago, it had been a while before they had seriously attempted to try again. The sadness was so intense when their baby died that they had become almost terrified that it would happen for a second time and break their hearts all over again. But as time went on with it's healing effect, the parental yearning, which had never really been quelled, became rekindled anew and now, just for the last few months, they had resumed visiting several doctors and different clinics in an attempt to find out why Sandy couldn't conceive again. They always came away from every visit with the same conclusion - there was absolutely no medical reason why she couldn't become pregnant again.

"How do you want your eggs this mornings, scrambled or over-easy?" she asked her sleepy-eyed husband as she bent over the bed to kiss him good morning.

Jake sat up quickly, suddenly realizing he had promised to cook breakfast this morning. "Sorry, guess I overslept, I meant to cook you your favorite breakfast but I guess I flubbed it again," he laughed.

"That's perfectly OK," Sandy laughed back, "Coffee's ready and bacon's frying, so everything's under control, and don't tell me you aren't glad! After fourteen years I guess I know you pretty well!!"

"Well, if you insist on pampering me, I'll have my eggs scrambled, and the toast nice and brown, and make sure the bacon is real crisp, and bring it to me on that black tray, and don't forget the little vase with the fresh flowers in it - and -"

"You're pretty darn particular this morning, aren't you, Mr. Miller?" Sandy laughed, as she grabbed a pillow. He pulled the blanket over his head in an attempt to avoid the blow that he knew was coming, but she was too fast for him.

"OK, I suppose I can come to the table," he laughed as he

watched her turn and walk toward the kitchen. Picking up the same pillow, he quickly threw it at her and with a squeal of delight she turned and pounced on the bed and an all-out pillow fight ensued. Jake appeared to be winning the battle so at the first opportunity Sandy hopped from the bed and ran to the kitchen again. She turned in the doorway and gave him a playful smirk, making sure she was out of range of another flying pillow.

A few minutes later Jake, still pajama-clad, walked to the table thinking how lucky they were to have found each other. Sandy was a wonderful wife and a great cook. She loved domesticity and keeping him happy. They had a lot of good times together, too. They usually went out to dinner once a week, and they both enjoyed the movies and caught nearly every new one that came out. They had purchased a nineteen-inch television which was their entertainment on week nights, but Sandy was a stickler for getting her eight hours of sleep each night, and some nights would leave Jake watching the TV by himself so she could accomplish that. But for the most part they were inseparable, and loved every minute of being together.

They were just finishing breakfast when Sandy said, "I have to hurry, I have that appointment with Dr. Simons at nine this morning." She bit off a piece of toast and glanced up at the clock. "I certainly don't want to be late for that, that's so important to us." She said thoughtfully. Maybe with today's test, there might be something uncovered that had been previously overlooked for they knew that medical science had advanced rapidly over the past few years. They were getting desperate now, for after all, Sandy's biological clock was ticking away. Jake was already forty-seven. and she was nine years younger at thirty-eight. She couldn't help but think she could have had children almost ready for high school by this time. It bothered Sandy immensely, she felt very inadequate, but she tried to console herself with the fact that they had a very happy marriage and were fortunate otherwise.

"I sure hope they find something positive this time," Jake

said thoughtfully, as he reached for her hand. "I'll drop you off this morning, since his office is right next to the hospital, and when you're done give me a call and I'll skip out and take you to work, or home if it's not okay for you to go to work." He finished his last sip of coffee.

"That's good, I'm almost ready, just give me five minutes," Sandy answered as she and Jake picked up the dirty dishes and set them in the sink.

Sandy grabbed a sweater in case it was a little chilly, and they rushed to the parked car in the driveway. It was late May but it could still be a little cool in Seattle in the mornings. Before getting out of the car at the doctor's office fifteen minutes later, Sandy bent over and kissed him on the cheek. "See you later," she smiled. "I'll call when I'm done."

"The doctor will be right with you, Mrs. Miller," the peppy receptionist said as Sandy walked into the waiting room. "Help yourself to the coffee over there, I just made a fresh pot."

"I could do with a second cup," Sandy smiled back. "Maybe it will calm my nerves." After pouring a cup she picked up the latest Reader's Digest and made herself comfortable.

Ten minutes later the receptionist ushered her into the doctor's office. Dr. Simons had taken the liberty of bringing in a fertility specialist, a Dr. Willis, whom he promptly introduced to Sandy and the three of them sat down.

"I need to warn you, I plan on doing some quite extensive tests," Dr. Willis smiled, "so we may be here awhile. I'd like to start with a complete examination to make sure you're in top-notch physical condition. Shall we get started?"

If Sandy had been nervous earlier, all her fears were calmed by this kind yet very serious white-haired gentleman. She was ready to submit to almost anything if it gave her even the slightest chance of carrying a child again.

It took nearly an hour and a half for the completion of the examination and tests and the kind doctors told her she could leave, they'd call her at home with results.

It was a tense four days for both of them waiting for the results. On the fourth day Sandy could stand it no longer and she decided to call the doctor's office.

"Yes, we have the results of your tests, Mrs. Miller, they just came back this morning. Is it possible for you and your husband to stop in at two this afternoon?"

"My husband, too? I'll have to call him to see if he can get away."

"It's quite important that your husband be here," the nurse added.

Sandy was elated. Happily she thought, *'It must be good news, why else would Jake have to be there? They want to tell us the great news together! There must be something they can do to help us - maybe a new pill or procedure, - or something!'* She quickly dialed the hospital's fourth floor desk's number and asked for Jake.

"They've got the test results back, I just called," an elated Sandy nearly shouted into the phone. "They want us both to come to the doctor's office this afternoon. Both of us, you know what that must mean!"

"Now don't get your hopes up, honey, just in case, it may not be what you're hoping for."

"Oh, I know its good news, its got to be, its just got to be!" Sandy nearly dropped the phone in her excitement. "Will you be able to pick me up here about one-thirty?"

"I'll be there, but calm down, I don't want to see you get disappointed, understand?"

"I'll try, see you later," she said as she hung up and turned to see a client waiting to talk to her. She invited him to have a seat and, a little begrudgingly, eased herself back into the world of finance and banking.

Jake picked her up at one-thirty as promised and they drove back to Dr. Simon's office. Hand-in-hand they walked into the outer office.

"He'll see you right away," the receptionist said as ushered them into the doctor's office. Dr. Simon was looking at papers on his desk and didn't look up when they walked in. He motioned for them to sit in the two chairs in front of his desk.

"I called you both in because there seems to be a problem we have to discuss," Dr. Simon began in his fatherly, compassionate voice.

Jake and Sandy looked at each other, curious as to the problem, but also as to why Dr. Simon had not lifted his head to look at them.

Suddenly he looked up with a grim face and quietly started. "Folks, I hate passing on this kind of information, but I'm going to come right to the point. Sandy, the tests show that you have a tumor on your uterus and upon further evaluation we discovered it is malignant and your only real option at this time is a total hysterectomy."

The room suddenly became a hall of horrors as they both stared in disbelief at this bearer of bad news. How could this be, this wasn't supposed to happen!

"You mean - I have cancer! But I feel fine, nothing hurts me! Are you sure, doctor?" Sandy blurted out as tears started to stream down her cheeks. Jake put his arm around her in an attempt to comfort her, but he was also so stunned by this bitter piece of news he could feel his body shaking.

"A total hysterectomy, doctor? Will that take care of it?" Jake found enough composure to ask. "She'll be alright afterwards, right?"

"Hopefully so, but I'm afraid that's our only alternative. I'm so sorry, with luck we can catch it before it metastasizes. It may have been there for some time, I'm afraid. I don't understand why it wasn't discovered sooner." He paused for a moment, looking at both of them thoughtfully. "I've taken the liberty of contacting an excellent surgeon, Dr. John O'Leary. He's the head gynecological surgeon in Seattle and has a remarkable reputation, and after discussing your case with him he wants to see you right away - today if possible. I can call him right now and set up an appointment. I know he will want to operate within the next day or two. I'm sorry, folks. I know this is a lot to swallow all at once," he said as he got up from his chair and reached for her hand. He would rather have been anywhere in the world than in this room at this moment. He always felt so intensely involved with his patients, especially when he had to pass on bad news, but he knew there was no point in beating around the bush, he always gave any news, good or bad, point blank to his patients.

"But, that means I'll never, never have another baby," Sandy sobbed.

"There's always adoption, there are always babies needing good parents," Dr. Simon said in an unsuccessful attempt to comfort her.

Still stunned, Jake said, "I feel terrible about this too, honey, but right now my main concern is you. Let's get that appointment set up and get this taken care of. I don't want anything to happen to you."

The appointment was set for the next afternoon and the saddened couple, exhausted from disappointment coupled with such bad news, decided not to go back to work but to go home and just be together. Jake told her he was familiar with Dr. O'Leary, he had had the opportunity to associate with him several times at the hospital, and he knew he had a very commendable reputation as a surgeon. The fact that Jake knew him didn't do much to ease the disappointment Sandy was feeling. She was sure the surgeon would do the best he could, but this operation meant she was going to be losing the ability to ever become a mother again. Not only would all possibility of having another child be taken away, but Sandy's life was on the line now and they both knew it, even though they could not admit it to themselves or each other.

Jake made a fresh pot of coffee, the warmth of which somehow seemed comforting in the wake of bad news, and they took their cups out on their deck and gazed silently at the ocean waves coming into the sound. In the matter of a few hours they knew their lives had changed forever. But they would try to be strong and optimistic and, with God's help, they would get through this together.

CHAPTER TWENTY-FIVE

The next afternoon came almost too soon. Red-eyed and exhausted, the weary couple walked into Dr. O'Leary's office, trying real hard to keep their frazzled nerves at bay. The kindly doctor paused momentarily, as if studying something on his desk, then rose to greet them. He reached out with a warm smile and shook their hands and motioned for them to sit in the two seats in front of his desk. He quietly discussed the procedure with them, and asked if they had questions.

"Does it have to be a total hysterectomy, Doctor. Is there anyway you can just get the tumor and leave everything else intact?" Sandy tearfully implored him. "I want so much to have a child again - if only there were some way."

"I'm sorry, I know it's hard to accept, but we don't have any options here. We have to take out the uterus, and hopefully it hasn't spread beyond. The x-rays show that the tumor sort of disguised itself and that's why it wasn't discovered sooner. I'd give anything to be able to give you good news, but I'm afraid I can't offer much better than that. Believe me, we'll do our very best," Dr. O'Leary said as he took both of Sandy's small hands in his as a means of reassurance. "Believe me, I've had worst cases!" he added with that same warm smile.

As soon as Dr. O'Leary examined Sandy he knew he had to operate immediately. He scheduled her for the next morning at eight o'clock. He had to move another surgery that wasn't life-threatening so he could fit Sandy in as his first operation of the morning.

She was very tired and depressed, she had slept fitfully and had cried most of the night. When Jake brought her into the hospital she looked and felt like a zombie and he wasn't in much better shape, but he knew he had to be the strong one.

"I guess I never thought this could possibly happen to us. It all seems like a terrible dream - a nightmare. There'll never be a chance for another baby, do you realize that? I'll never have a baby now!" she wailed.

"I know, I know, honey, but I just want you well, and we can always try again for adoption, like Dr. Simon said," Jake reassured her again as they walked to the admitting office.

Sandy seemed unconvinced as she hugged her husband just before a nurse came to take her to a preparation room. Jake helped her into the wheel chair and walked beside her as she was whisked away to a small room surrounded by curtains. As he gazed lovingly at his wife he found himself wondering what was in store for them next. He stayed beside her, trying desperately to comfort her, until a gurney was wheeled up to take her into the OR. Sitting in the waiting room, he couldn't concentrate on anything but Sandy and their shared heartbreak. The minutes seemed like hours but he knew he had to retain his composure, Sandy would need him. After consuming several cups of black coffee, he realized that maybe if he went up to his floor and attempted to resume his usual duties, that that might make the time go faster and also help to keep his mind occupied. He left a number where he could be reached with the desk and asked that he be called immediately when the doctor came out of the operating room. The fourth floor staff was surprised to see him as he stepped off the elevator and walked over to the nurse's desk.

"Is the operation over?" the surprised nurses, Nancy and Joan, said in unison.

"No, she's still in the OR, but I'd like to keep busy up here, they'll let me know as soon as there is anything. Please get hold of me right away," his voice trailed off.

Nancy gave him an understanding look and said, "Well, Mrs. Riley in 412 is getting hard to manage again. You seem to have a way with women, why don't you see what you can do. She insists on getting out of bed to go shopping, you know- the usual," Nancy said quietly, as she nodded towards the patient's door. She was very fond of Jake and she knew the senile old woman could keep his mind off his personal problems if anyone could. The young nurse had noticed that Jake seemed to have a calming effect on her, as he did on most all of the patients. Jake, with his kind approach and convincing ways was eventually able to convince the old lady to stay in bed and then he gently talked her to sleep. When he saw she was in deep slumber and breathing deeply he went back to the nurse's station. He met Nancy just as he stepped out into the hall.

"Just coming to get you. Dr. O'Leary called, says he'll see you in the waiting room."

Jake was on the elevator before she could finish the sentence. Dr. O'Leary was waiting, still in operating room garb minus the mask and gloves. The look on his face was not what Jake wanted to see - it was much too somber..

"We did a total hysterectomy." the doctor began, then hesitated.

"Yes, I know, that's what you said before. Is anything wrong, is she alright?" Jake could tell things had not gone as well as they could have, the doctor's voice and face gave testimony to that.

"It was a fairly large tumor, larger than I had previously thought. We'll be sending tissue to the lab for further examination, then we'll know more for sure whether the cancer has metastasized or not - hopefully we got it all. I wish I could tell you that in the affirmative, but we'll know more when we get the report back from the lab."

Jake felt his legs go weak and his head was swimming. She had to be alright! Nothing was going to happen to her - not Sandy - not his beautiful, young, energetic Sandy!

"You can see her now, she should be in room 131. If all goes well she'll probably be able to go home in about a week to ten days. Please don't mention anything to her at this point. I promise I'll inform you the minute we hear anything."

After giving Jake a sincere handshake, the doctor walked over to the station. He never relished the job of giving bad or potentially bad news to a patient's family member, but it all went with the territory. And he knew things did not look so good at this point. He had done this sort of operation many times before but this one was definitely a worst case scenario.

Jake made sure he gave Sandy the biggest smile he was able to conjure up as he walked into her hospital room. She was still very groggy from the anesthetic as he bent to kiss her, and he could tell all she really wanted to do was sleep. She was able to squeeze his hand and squeaked out a barely audible "How did I do?"

"Honey, I'm sure you were the best patient Dr. O'Leary ever had!" He tried to sound light-hearted as if he didn't have a worry on his mind.

"Did he say anything? Did he say everything's going to be alright, you know, did he get all of the - the cancer?" She could hardly bring herself to say the word. She was so groggy the words were barely audible.

"I'm sure the worst is over, honey, he just told me it's going to be examined in the lab, then we'll know more. You look exhausted, why don't you try to rest and I'll sit right here. Don't worry, I won't leave. You did great, I'm proud of you!"

He could see she couldn't keep her eyes open, so he tiptoed over to the overstuffed chair on the opposite side of her bed and put his head back. Though his mind was crowded with worry, exhaustion soon took over and he started to doze fitfully. Before long a nurse came into the room to check on her patient. Although she had tried to be as quiet as possible, Jake sat up with a start and the painful reality returned.

A while later, after the anesthetic had finally worn off, Sandy opened her eyes and smiled at her husband. He had pulled the chair up close to the bed and had been holding her hands while she slept.

"It's over, isn't it?" she asked sadly as she attempted to keep her eyes open.

"Yes, honey, it's over, and you'll be fine now."

"I mean - everything - no more babies - it's all over," she cried, as fresh tears welled up in her eyes.

Jake couldn't answer her, he found he was getting too choked up. He hated seeing his wife, who wanted children so badly, in such a sad state. Why, he thought, was Sandy denied motherhood when it was what she wanted more than anything in the world. All he could do was hold her and tell her how much he loved her. Sandy, of course, was convinced that the worst was behind them, when Dr. O'Leary walked into the room to check out his patient. He said very little, was brief with his examination and soon left them alone again.

She lay her head back on the pillow and silently stared straight ahead for a few moments. Then, suddenly quite alert, she grabbed Jake's hand and with quiet determination said, "Let's start the adoption process just as soon as I get out of here. Please - I don't want to wait any longer, OK, honey? There's probably a long waiting list like before, but I'm willing to wait, now I know for sure." She turned her head toward the wall, hoping Jake wouldn't see the tears in her eyes.

"We will, I promise, when I know you're strong enough," Jake answered, holding her hand as he silently prayed they would get through this new hurdle that had just been handed to them.

They didn't have to wait long. Just after lunch the next afternoon, Dr. O'Leary stopped in the doorway, hesitated slightly, then proceeded to walk to Sandy's bed. Jake was there, trying to keep the conversation as light-hearted as possible. Sandy was eagerly trying to discuss adoption, and Jake was agreeing with her that it didn't matter whether they got a boy or a girl, but hopefully a newborn, so it would be theirs practically from birth.

The good doctor tried to keep a calm, non-assuming look on his face as he observed the apprehensive couple in front of him.

He shook Jake's hand and put his hand on Sandy's shoulder as he asked how she was feeling today.

"I feel fine, doctor, better than I thought I would, how soon before you think I can go home?"

"Let's not rush it, Mrs. Miller. I'm afraid I don't have the best of news." He hesitated before he went on. "I'm sorry to tell you both that the lab tests have confirmed that the cancer has spread outside of the uterus. Now we have to determine if additional surgery is an option. We're going to run more tests."

"Oh, my God!!," cried Sandy as tears began to well up in her eyes. Jake put his arms around her as he tried desperately to keep his composure. Was there no end to bad news?

"How bad is it, doctor?" Sandy was able to ask through her tears.

"I won't give you false hope. We know it has metastasized into the lymph nodes, and very possibly into some vital organs." Dr. O'Leary paused as he looked compassionately at both of them. "I know this is a tremendous blow, but I can assure you that everything possible will be done to see you through this. Have faith, that works wonders many times when medicine doesn't!"

After one last reassuring handclasp the doctor walked slowly from the room. Jake and Sandy were stunned and left to contemplate the terrible news they had just received.

"Maybe they got the tests mixed up. It's possible, isn't it? Maybe it's not as bad as it sounds!" a desperate Sandy cried as tears rolled down her face. All Jake could do was to hold her and fight back his own tears. "It'll be alright, honey, it'll be alright," he blurted out in an attempt to reassure her.

The rest of the afternoon was spent consoling each other, running the gamut between bitter tears and moments of deep faith. Finally, Sandy fell into a deep sleep and Jake crept from her bedside and went down to the cafeteria for a much-needed cup of black coffee. He sat there alone in deep thought, nearly unaware of the cafeteria personnel clearing off tables all around him. Wasn't losing their baby girl two years ago sorrow enough? And now this! Why did this have to happen to his beloved Sandy? And would more surgery help her or cause the cancer to spread further? Would they ever get the chance to adopt the baby Sandy so desperately wanted, and why had they waited so long? He put his head in his hands and stared into his cup but no answers came to him.

CHAPTER TWENTY-SIX   (SEPTEMBER 1971)

Time had taken its toll on the once-beautiful cancer patient, her hair was gone now and she had lost a lot of weight. Nearly four months had passed since her initial operation and Jake had stayed at her side as much as possible. When her hair was coming out in bunches Jake had brought her several brightly colored scarves to tie around her head but she didn't seem to care anymore whether she wore them or not. The small golden hairpiece he had bought when her hair was completely gone, which at first she had seemed very delighted about, had also fallen by the wayside. At first she was very conscious of her bare head, but the chemotherapy made her so tired and sick that the only thing she seemed to be interested in was seeing Jake at her bedside, and she always managed a smile when she saw him come through the door. He knew she was going downhill fast. It was late September 1971 and their fourteenth anniversary had been the day before and she barely noticed the red roses he had brought her. She was terminal now, just a matter of time. He stayed with her most of the time, only leaving her bedside when she drifted off to sleep, which was more and more often now. Then he would go up to the fourth floor and make an attempt at his duties there. His fellow workers could not have been more compassionate and understanding. The nurses watched over him like old mother hens, making sure he ate something occasionally, and reassuring him he had total freedom to spend as much time as possible with Sandy. Everyone was eager to help by doubling up a little on the duties to lighten his load.

He was at his usual place one Saturday afternoon, watching her as she intermittently dozed, ghastly white and very quiet. She suddenly become very aroused and reached for his hand. All at once he knew something was terribly wrong. Her emaciated body was trembling and she was gasping as she clutched at her heart with her other hand and he knew instinctively she was going into cardiac arrest. He quickly pushed the call button on her bed while at the same time caressing her hair.

"It's alright, honey, I'm here and it will be alright, just hang on, I'll never leave you, I promise!" Jake tried to keep his voice steady, although he was seized with sudden panic. He was sure she was slipping away.

A team of white uniforms swiftly invaded the room and rushed to the patient's side. Jake moved away quickly to make room for them to gather around Sandy's bed. His head was reeling as he watched anxiously. He heard their controlled voices, watched them moving quickly around his wife, and couldn't believe this was really happening. Was this it? Was Sandy's battle coming to an end?

"Flat line! Stand back!" he heard one of the doctor's practically shout. Immediately, he put the paddles on her chest and Sandy's body lurched. No response on the monitor. "One more time!" he said as he repeated the process. She lurched again, then seemed to rest peacefully back on her bed. Vertical lines were appearing on the monitor and the medical team seemed to breath a collective sigh of relief. "She's back!" the doctor said as he watched the monitor.

After it was all over everyone left the room except for the young doctor who had seemed to be in command of the situation. He walked slowly over to Jake, put his hand on his shoulder for a moment, spoke to him about what had just happened, and then quietly left the room. Without actually saying the words, it was as if he was telling Jake that this had been just one more chapter taking Sandy closer to the final episode. But Jake already knew that.

A nurse whisked into the room, checked the patient's vital signs, and tried to make her as comfortable as possible. Looking compassionately at Jake she said, "I'll bring you a cup of coffee, there's a fresh pot brewing" Before Jake could tell her he really didn't care for any, she had dashed out of the room again.

Jake was staring at his beloved Sandy as the nurse handed

him the cup of black coffee. He took it, thanked her, and sat it down on the night stand. He was relieved when the nurse left the room once more - he wanted to be alone with his wife.

Suddenly, as if she knew he was there, Sandy opened her eyes. Those eyes that had been so dull and lifeless a short time before now seemed to hold a radiance that Jake could only remember seeing once before - the day they were married! They were shining with happiness as she tried, with some effort, to talk to her husband. She seemed extremely excited and he knew she was desperately trying to convey something to him so he bent down closer to her face and listened intently as she spoke.

"Oh, Jake!" she whispered, "It was so beautiful - so beautiful - I can't explain - a long tunnel, a light - so bright and so warm. I felt such happiness. And then I was there - and I saw her! Elena! I saw her! Our baby! I saw her! She smiled at me and then I reached for her and she seemed to be coming toward me," Sandy paused for a brief second to catch her breath, "and then I heard a voice say I had to come back, I couldn't stay there! I said please, please let me stay, but then I was back here and I heard the doctor say "she's back!" But I wanted to stay so bad! Oh - I didn't want to leave you - but - it was so beautiful!! You do believe me don't you?"

"Honey, just judging from the way you look, you look so radiant, something wonderful had to have happened!" Jake replied as he stared in awe at Sandy. She looked so different, like she was glowing from within! She was still thin and very sick, but she somehow had taken on a remarkable transformation. She was suddenly very alert and excited, eager to talk, and Jake could tell she had been through an overwhelming experience. He couldn't wait to talk to the doctor later about it, perhaps he would say it was the drugs she was taking, or hallucination on her part. Or, perhaps it was an NDE, (near-death experience) the reporting of which was becoming more widespread in the medical community, but, unfortunately with much reservation. Dozens of books with hundreds of documented cases had been written on the subject by very reputable sources, and the hesitancy of the patient to talk about the experience was slowly disappearing. Jake had heard of this phenomena being discussed before and suddenly it was taking on new meaning. Could this have happened to Sandy? He knew something incredible had happened while the doctors were attempting to get her heart beating again, he could tell by the radiant look on her face. And that beautiful smile, that a few moments before had been totally nonexistent, confirmed it to him. He knew suddenly, in her extremely ill state, that she could not have, on her own, conjured up this miraculous account without divine intervention! She said she had seen their baby and he was convinced that she had!

"Honey, if you say you saw her then I believe you," Jake said, as he held her close and kissed her. She was deliriously happy and couldn't stop talking about her miraculous experience!

"I really saw her! I really did! And she was so beautiful and happy and she's waiting for me. Oh, Jake, you really do believe me don't you? I mean, really? It was as if she were right here and I could almost touch her. Please! Please believe me!"

"I do believe you, honey, I honestly do. If you could just see the glow on your face right now! It leaves little doubt to me that something wonderful happened, and I am so happy about it!" Jake said very tenderly, becoming almost as excited as Sandy.

He couldn't believe the sudden and amazing transformation in her from just a very short time ago. She was breathless as she continued on, "Oh - I almost forgot! A lady, a very pretty lady, said to tell you she loves you, and was so sorry she had to leave you. She told me to tell you that! She said everything happened so quickly she never had time to tell you goodbye! And she said you would know- you would know who she was!"

Jake was momentarily stunned. Who could this lady be? There seemed to be no doubt but that Sandy had had a fleeting encounter with heaven! And their baby - she had seen their baby girl!

Something wonderful had certainly happened to her during that short time the flat line on the monitor indicated that she was clinically dead!

No one else had to believe it! He believed in Sandy's faith and honesty, and he knew she was entirely sincere and would never conjure up anything like this. She was still elated when she said, "Oh, Jake, if that's what it's like to die, I'll never be afraid again. I just want you to know that - it was like passing into another beautiful world!" As she blissfully looked up at him and her frail, thin fingers grasped his hand he could tell that all fear and trepidation had been lifted from her heart and had been replaced with an undeniable joy. What a marvelous gift God had given them!

For a few days immediately after her miraculous encounter, she was so much more contented, much more accepting of her condition. She smiled more, actually seemed happy most of the time, and when Jake was with her they laughed together and talked about their past happy times. She was like a new person, and Jake was hopeful that it meant remission, but he was told by the doctor that the cancer was still continuing its invasion of her frail body. He was gratefully hanging on to each moment they had together, for he knew, in spite of what seemed like improvement in her condition it was actually going the other way.

It was a bright, sunny morning in late October, just three weeks after their fourteenth anniversary. Jake had just spent a couple of hours at Sandy's side, attempting to optimistically talk about the future, the future which they both knew was not going to exist for them together. They talked about Elena Marie and how lucky they were to have had her, however brief. Sandy turned suddenly to look at Jake, then with a very confident, almost blissful smile said, "I'll be seeing her again soon, won't I?"

Jake was too choked up to answer so he nodded his head.

She was facing the inevitable with a quiet, almost joyful acceptance and for that he was thankful. Her temporary recovery was short-lived, however, and in the matter of a few days the strength and energy she had received after her life-threatening experience was starting to disappear. She was becoming listless and extremely tired again, and one afternoon when Jake kissed her to go upstairs, she almost willingly let go of his hand and told him in a very weak voice to 'get to work'. She smiled as he waved to her from the doorway. Then she closed her eyes and drifted off to sleep again. With a heavy heart he got on the elevator.

He knew the end was very near. He had been informed that the cancer had metastasized to the majority of her vital organs and there was no way to stop its spreading. He couldn't help but notice that a gentle peace had enveloped Sandy. She seemed to be almost anticipating death. Her peacefulness somehow transmitted itself to Jake and he couldn't help but feel relieved that she was able to acquire that peace. He hated to leave her now, even for a moment, but the glowing serenity shining in her eyes told him it was alright. He stepped off the elevator and walked to the desk.

"Jake, surprised to see you! How's Sandy today?" said Nancy with her usual concern.

"No improvement, I'm afraid. She's sleeping now so I decided to come up and keep my mind busy. What's going on up here?"

"Well, for one thing Mr. Wilson has been calling for you, Jake. Seems he won't let anyone else help him today, he says you're the only one that can move him without hurting him," Nancy answered.

"I'll see him right away ," he said quietly as he walked away with a heavy heart. After he had made Mr. Wilson comfortable, he went to the elevator and decided to take a quick check on Sandy to see if she was still asleep. As he approached her door he heard voices and confusion and upon entering the room he saw a sea of white uniforms surrounding her bed. Dr. Simon spotted him and immediately walked over to him. When he got to his side the doctor gestured toward the flat line on the monitor.

"I'm so sorry, Jake. She went into cardiac arrest a few moments ago. This time we couldn't bring her back. Believe it or not, this was the best way. Her pain would have only gotten more intense and we both knew her time was quickly running out. I know it's still a shock, even though we knew it was inevitable. Are you alright?"

Jake let himself collapse into a nearby chair, he knew his legs were about to give out under him. He had only been away from her side for a few minutes, and now she was gone. His eyes welled up with tears as he listened to the doctor. "But I just left her not ten minutes ago and she was asleep. I should have stayed - why did I leave?"

"We always think we could have done something different, but believe me this was the best way. She actually went very quickly and nothing you could have done would have made any difference. It was probably best that you weren't here, you'll remember her at peace, and I'm sure that's the way she would like you to remember her."

Jake nodded, he knew the kind doctor was right. "I'm sure you did everything you could, And since she couldn't get better I guess I'm happy she's at peace now."

He walked over to the bedside and gently kissed his dead wife and buried his head on her chest. "We will meet again, sweetheart, I just know we will! I love you so much!" he uttered through his tears. He sobbed quietly for a moment or two until Dr. Simon put his hand on his shoulder and led him out of the room.

"I'll start making the funeral arrangements," he told the doctor as he started to regain his composure. He stopped at the desk, gave them the name of the funeral parlor, and walked out the front door to his car. He would stop at the funeral parlor, make all the required arrangements, then go home. Home to an empty, lonely house without Sandy.

The next afternoon and evening were spent greeting friends from their church, the hospital and Sandy's bank. They came up to Jake as he stood by Sandy's casket, some with hugs and some with just sincere handshakes, all professing their condolences. He was amazed at the number of people that had come. It gave him such comfort to know so many cared.

She was dressed in a white chiffon dress and her makeup was impeccable and for all intent and purposes she looked very elegant. The baby blue of the satin lining seemed to emphasize the splendor of the small blonde wig that exactly matched the color and texture of her real hair. Several people commented on how young and beautiful she still looked. Jake kept his eyes on her as much as possible, as if to engrave on his memory her every feature.

He was amazed at himself, he somehow didn't feel the overpowering sorrow he had expected at this time. Thank God for the wonderful abiding faith they had both shared! As he looked at her he saw only peacefulness and contentment, her face seemed to glow with it. He somehow knew deep inside that she was with their baby girl, that now she finally had her child and that they would never be separated again. He knew her lifelong wish in life was being fulfilled in death, and suddenly he couldn't help but inwardly rejoice! He kissed her several times and before they closed the lid he pulled a pink rose from a bouquet, kissed it and put it in her hand - to match the one she had given Elena Marie over two years earlier. Then her casket was put back into the hearse and driven over to the cemetery where she was buried close beside their baby. Jake stayed with his wife and daughter long after everyone else had left, and silently prayed for their happiness together in heaven. He walked away from her grave side with a heavy heart that late October day. He knew he had to go on alone, but his faith was unfaltering and he had no doubt but that he would see them both again. Sandy had unquestionably convinced him of that!

CHAPTER TWENTY-SEVEN (APRIL 1972)

He was alone now, completely alone! Sure he had friends at the hospital, a few others he had met when he worked at the restaurant, but they all had their own lives, and he had nothing but a lonely house and a million memories. He found that long walks seemed to help, so every night after he came home from work he would walk a mile or two. Other times he would take his newspaper to the nearby park and attempt to read it amid the happy sounds and laughter of the children on the playground equipment. It made him sad to think that he and Sandy could have had children playing there, instead, here he was alone - all alone with no one.

It was the beginning of April. Sandy had been gone now for a little over seven months, and although he was contented with his job at the hospital, there was still an emptiness that he couldn't seem to overcome. He went through the motions every day, tending to sick patients and their families, and helping people cope with their individual problems. He was still being encouraged by the entire staff to go to medical school, but at forty-eight he felt he was too old to embark on a project that would continue for at least eight to ten years. He had procrastinated for so long, and it was too late now. Besides, he seemed to have lost any motivation that he might have had earlier to further his medical knowledge. He missed Sandy very much. Just what was he going to do with the rest of his life?

One evening he decided to try something different. He drove back to the restaurant where he had worked for Nell those first few years after he arrived in Seattle. He and Sandy had come there together once, just for old times sake, about two years into their marriage. At that time, the new buyers, a man and his wife, had kept the place pretty much as it was when Jake was there, and business seemed to be quite good. But now, approximately fifteen years later,

Jake was astonished at what he found. He wasn't sure whether Nell would be happy or sad at what had been done to her cozy little restaurant. The new owners had added on a huge beautifully-decorated dining room, which encompassed Jake's former living quarters, plus a lot more, and there was a large circular bar now in what had been the former restaurant area. In one corner of the dining room, a combo was playing soft dinner music to a full house, and the bar, not to be outdone, was crowded with patrons of all ages. Jake had to admit it really was a thriving, fine-looking establishment now, so different from the fifties when he was there. But he had come there this evening hoping to recapture a little touch of the past, to possibly sit at the counter in the seat that Sandy used to occupy every morning, and imagine himself and Nell behind that counter busily waiting on their customers. He laughed at himself - what had made him think it would still all be the same? There wasn't even a hint of the old days, everything had changed, life had moved on, and he suddenly knew he had to move on too!

He was several doorways down the hall when he heard the call over the intercom.

"Attention! Dr. Lawrence and all available staff to elevator two, STAT."

This was not an unfamiliar call, it happened at least two to three times a day. It meant the ER was sending up a critical case ready for admittance, or they simply were overloaded and didn't have enough doctors to handle the emergency room traffic..

Jake found himself rushing to the elevator to be of assistance if necessary. He had seen all kinds of horrific accident cases with gaping wounds and blood-covered bodies, but his heart sank when he saw that this patient was a little child, probably about four. The entire body was burned, skin was hanging everywhere, and many parts of the body were charred black. Thankfully, the child was unconscious, and if he lived through this it would be a miracle. An explosion, he was told, a gas leak. His mother was brought in too, but was dead on arrival. They had called his father and he was on his way. What a horrific scenario that poor man had to face!

Jake helped pull the gurney into the Burn Center. All the time he couldn't get his eyes off the pathetic little child lying there, so still. How terribly painful and horrifying this must have been for him! It would probably be better if he didn't make it. He guessed that approximately ninety percent of his body was burned.

He walked out of the Burn Center and collapsed on the nearest bench. Suddenly, he felt tears streaming down his face, and a lump in his throat that was nearly choking him. In his years at the hospital he had seen probably hundreds of critical cases, sometimes little children hurt badly, but he had never been so affected as he was this time. Something was different this time - terribly different!

He couldn't seem to control the sobs, and realized he should probably step out of sight until he could regain his professionalism. He was amazed by his reaction, it wasn't like him to fall apart this way. Trauma wasn't a new thing to him. Why was this affecting him so strongly?

Suddenly a bright flash passed in front of him. Another person - body wrapped in a cloth, on a litter - an ambulance - firemen everywhere! What was this? Who was this? Another flash! He saw a house aflame and water all over the ground. There were people everywhere just watching. The flashing lights of the ambulance were almost hurting his eyes, they were so real! Still another flash! An attendant telling him the person lying there was dead! His heart was racing now. There had to be a connection to him because he was suddenly feeling such deep remorse. It had to be someone he knew - but who? Why couldn't he remember? The white jacket - the man in the white jacket - could it be? - why yes - that was HIM! He was there and the burned person was - it couldn't be! - but it was! He couldn't believe the images passing through his mind!

'ELLIE, my wife, ELLIE! Oh, No! Now I remember! That was Ellie lying there - Ellie - my wife! Why did I run away? What was wrong with me?'

He was shaking now as the memories came flooding back. He laid his head against the wall and put his hands to his face. Then another vision - a little boy - I had a little boy - just a baby - Oh, no, not my little boy, Jackie! - I didn't see him anywhere! Where was he? Was he wrapped in the cloth with Ellie or was he still in the burning house? Oh, God, he was only two, my baby - and what did I do? I ran away!

Pieces of his past were coming clear to him now. It had taken the sight of this burned child to activate the initial attempts at restoring his memory. His head was reeling from all the new information buzzing around inside of it. He didn't know how he was going to step back into the hall to resume his duties. He felt like a fool and certainly didn't want any of his co-workers to see him in this state, but at the same time he also felt tremendous relief. It was like a huge weight had been lifted from him.

'The picture - the woman and little boy - that's them - Ellie and Jackie! Oh, why didn't I know that? All these years - why didn't it come to me sooner? Neither one of them must have survived or I would have been notified. But then, how could I have been notified, no one knew where I was! And my name, I had changed it, how could they have found me? Now I remember, I remember being Tim Rogers - Dr. Timothy Rogers, and I worked at the hospital in - River Valley, - yes - River Valley! I remember - I was called to come home immediately. I wonder, did the authorities think I was implicated in any way? I remember seeing the fire - my house in flames - the ambulance. I even watched them loading Ellie. Could it be I thought I was somehow partially responsible, is that why I ran like I did? Was I afraid of something? Did they bother to look for me? How was I able to block everything from my memory for twenty years?'

Jake allowed his newly-recollected memories to wash over

him for a few more minutes. He finally regained his composure enough to go back into the hallway. He walked directly to the desk and saw Nancy bending over a file drawer. He knew he couldn't finish out the day, it was only a half-hour to quitting time anyway.

"I'm leaving a little early today, Nancy," he said quickly and turned to walk away before she could see him.

Nancy stood up and said, "OK, Jake, see you tomorrow," then sensing he was acting differently, she added, "Is anything wrong?"

Jake heard her but didn't answer, he was too deep in thought. He was anxious to hurry home and remove that long-forgotten picture from his white medical jacket pocket in the far corner of the closet and just gaze at the faces of the two people from his other life that he had once loved very much.

As soon as he got home he went to the closet in his bedroom. It took a little searching but on a high shelf in the very back, there it was, the white lab coat still neatly folded in the shoe box, just as he had left it years ago. He was glad he had never discarded it, he had always known it had to be a link to his past. The photo had to be there too, in one of the pockets. He reached in and pulled it out and stared at it, this time with full recognition of the two beloved faces. The longer he gazed at the photo the faster the memories returned. He recalled how Ellie had kissed him goodbye that fateful morning and asked him to come home for lunch, she'd make something special. She had said she had to take Jackie to the library for his reading group, but would be home in time for lunch.

He recalled more now - there were neighbors, Mary and Joe, they were good friends, would they be able to tell him more about that day? Should he try to contact them, or possibly contact the River Valley authorities? Wouldn't they wonder why, after twenty years, he was suddenly interested? And what would he say to them, *"Hello - I'm Dr. Tim Rogers, I left town immediately after the fire that killed my wife, but I've decided to come home, does anyone remember me?"* No, he decided, calling the authorities would just open up a can of worms and there would be endless questions. Maybe at this point, he should just limit the investigating to what he was able to do himself but that might be a little hard to do at this end of the country, so far removed from the scene.

He couldn't take his eyes off the picture. What should he do now, now that he knew why he had had amnesia for all these years? Should he return and attempt to salvage part of his old life, if possible? He knew that would mean leaving behind the part of his life that he and Sandy had shared together - but that was only a memory now anyway - and he knew he would never forget his second family whatever part of the country he was in. It was so hard to comprehend. He had had two wives, two children, two families, in the less than half a century he had lived, and now he had nothing! But, maybe he still had a son! Maybe Jackie was still alive. Possibly there might be some remnant of family left on the opposite coast if he dared to return and check into it.

He thought long and hard all through the evening and came to the only logical conclusion. He would go back - back to River Valley - and then possibly he could summon up enough courage to visit Mary and Joe and confront them with his identity. He would try to find his son! He certainly had nothing to keep him here in Seattle. Everything he had ever loved was gone. There was no money problem, Sandy and he had saved their whole marriage and he had quite an impressive bank account now. He struggled with the idea of taking a leave of absence from the hospital or just resigning completely. Maybe he would want to come back. But then maybe a new start would be the best thing for him. A new start with an old life, that's what it would be! Possibly a new start with his son, his long-lost son if by some fortunate chance he had survived the fire and was still alive! After a little consideration, he decided he would resign from the hospital and just wait to see what River Valley held in store for him.

He put in his two weeks notice the following day. He told

them the truth, but not quite the whole truth, that he was going back to where he had originally came from, that he had friends and relatives there that had encouraged him to return. He didn't want to go into any lengthy explanations, besides without the complete story, no one would understand. The nurses hugged him, the doctors shook his hand and wished him well and the comradeship he felt with his co-workers almost made him change his mind. But his desire to connect with his past was too strong to ignore. He walked out of the hospital on his last day with a healthy optimism that even he couldn't explain. He was going home to try to find his son and solve a great mystery - the mystery of his past!

Packing up his memories of Sandy didn't come that easy. He had not disposed of any of her personal items. He knew he should have as they were just a constant reminder, but he had always put it off. As he was going through her clothes and jewelry he felt a knot in his stomach that just wouldn't go away. He kept just a very few of her favorite things and packed up the rest to drop off at Good Will. He advertised in the paper to sell some of the better pieces of furniture and the rest he left for the Salvation Army truck to pick up.

He knew his 1965 Chevy would probably make it to the east without a problem, but he decided he preferred to fly - so he put it up for sale and had a buyer within two days. He knew he wanted to make a clean sweep. He felt that his life here in Seattle was over, there wasn't one thing left to keep him here. Possibly back east he could start putting the pieces of his long-forgotten life back together. He couldn't help but think what he would have done if the revelation of his former life had come to him while Sandy was still alive. Being the understanding kind of person she was, he knew they would have investigated it together. She would have been with him all the way.

With a tug at his heartstrings he put his beautiful Puget Sound house up for sale. He knew the price was more than reasonable and the realtor brought over several couples within the first week it was on the market. The third couple to see it fell in love with it at first sight and put in a purchase offer of the full price requested. It was sold that day and the affluent couple paid in cash. That made short work of the whole procedure and within three weeks the house was empty, he had closed his bank accounts, and tended to any other necessary paper work. Before he left the house for the last time he took one long last look at the room painted blue with the dancing bears in the border. Sandy and he had spent so many happy hours decorating that room in anticipation for the first baby that miscarried, and then for Elena Marie who never got to occupy it. All of a sudden he couldn't leave fast enough. There had been too much sorrow connected with that house and he knew he had to put the past behind him. He decided to keep his assumed identity until he knew what was in store for him in the east. He would continue to be Mr. Jacob Miller until the time was right to do otherwise.

CHAPTER TWENTY-EIGHT   (1972)

The flight back east seemed much shorter than when he had flown out twenty years earlier. He realized times had changed, the whole world had sped up in those twenty years. There was a stop in Chicago to change planes, then he continued on to the Albany airport. He felt sad leaving Seattle and all his happy memories behind but he knew it was for the best. Life had been so empty without Sandy that perhaps a change was just what he needed. If nothing was ever finalized as a result of his return to River Valley, at least he knew he would be no lonelier there then he would have been in Seattle. He decided he wasn't going to force the issue and whatever was meant to happen would become the blueprint for the rest of his life.

The plane landed and he rented a car at the Albany airport and drove north. He had forgotten how beautiful the foothills of the Adirondacks were. Seattle had the tall, jagged snow-covered peaks of the Cascades nearby, stunningly beautiful in their own right, but here the hills and mountains were worn down and tree-covered and seemed to offer an invitation to explore. He felt a uplifting sense of peace as he rounded each corner of the highway on this beautiful, sunlit day in late May of 1972. The physical landscape had changed. Large office buildings and gas stations, parks and golf courses now shared the sides of the highway. It seemed to him there had been a lot of undeveloped land in this area when he lived around here twenty years before.

He spotted the sign up ahead of him - **River Valley, 3 miles**. Suddenly he noticed that he was getting nervous, his heart was starting to race, and his feelings were somewhere between excitement and apprehension.

The little town wasn't so little anymore. It had grown considerably in twenty years. He drove by the hospital he had once worked in and continued on approximately five more blocks, then made a left-hand turn and drove three more blocks to Linden Street where he and Ellie and Jackie had once lived. He knew the house wouldn't be there, after all it had burned down, but he wasn't prepared for what he confronted. A huge shopping center stood where his former home and many other homes had once stood. The parking lot alone took up a block and there was a minimum of a couple of dozen stores, some large and some smaller. Somehow he had expected some things to remain exactly as he had remembered them, but he also knew nothing would stand in the way of progress, and this certainly seemed to be a progressive town. He parked the car and walked into the drugstore to get a coke, half-hoping he might recognize someone he used to know. Then he thought better of it. Maybe he should just do some quiet exploring first, on his own.

He decided to check with the library, maybe he could get a copy of the newspaper from that day in 1952 when his home burned. It was in the same place, same old brick building just around the corner from where his home had once stood. He stopped at the librarian's desk and she very bluntly told him they kept papers only three years, but he could try the newspaper office. He turned to walk away but then an idea came to him. Perhaps she could tell him something about that day if she lived here at the time and remembered. She was a stern-looking woman in her late fifties, and she looked like the kind that kept track of everyone's business, so he ventured a try.

"Maam, I can see you're busy, but could I interrupt you for just a moment?"

She raised her glasses as if she could see better without them and gave him a cool, rather unfriendly look.

"Yes, what is it?"

"I know this was a long time ago, but is it possible that you might recall a house fire that happened in the spring of 1952 just around the corner from here on Linden Street?"

"Now, how do you expect me to remember something that happened twenty years ago? No! I don't remember!"

Jake thanked her and started toward the door.

"Just a minute - do you mean the one where the woman burned up and there was a little boy, I believe. If I remember right he survived. Oh, yes, I do remember now! They never could find the husband, he disappeared right off the face of the earth. Yes! As I remember now there was quite a ruckus about the whole thing! Story was that he had something to do with the fire. Don't know how true it was, but it looked mighty suspicious!"

"The boy survived!! Are you sure? Do you have any idea where he is now?" Jake excitedly asked.

"Look, mister, I don't know who you are and I've told you all I know. No more questions, OK?", she said as she quickly went back to her work.

"Please, if you know what happened to him would you please tell me! I was very close to the family and would appreciate any information at all!" Jake pleaded.

"If you were that close to the family you wouldn't be asking me! Go ask at the police station. They can tell you! And if you don't leave, I'll call them!"

Jake could tell he had gotten all the information he would be able to get from her. He was afraid she might make good on her threat so he thought it best if he didn't pursue the issue any more. Her words rung in his ear. So it was possible that the general assumption at the time was that he had something to do with the fire. He hardly could blame them, since he had run away while the fire was still raging and never returned to check on anyone. He walked out of the library and drove around in search of the newspaper building. After about twenty minutes of searching he found it right where it used to be but now was dwarfed behind a tall six-story building that had been built in front of it. Funny, it had seemed like such a large building years ago when he lived there.

"Do you have copies of newspapers from 1952?" Jake asked the little old withered-up man behind the information counter just inside the door.

"That's twenty years ago, mister! I don't think you'll have much luck but you can ask in the back room, I know we keep a copy for around fifteen years at least, but you can give it a try. Back wall, second door to the left," the old man said.

Jake walked back, asked permission to look through the dead newspaper files, and started his search. After about two intensive hours the oldest paper he had been able to find was June 11, 1957. Giving the front page a curious glance he spotted an article at the very bottom that surprised him. The headline read,

"DOCTOR STILL MISSING AFTER FIVE YEARS."

There is still no clue to the whereabouts of Dr. Timothy Rogers who disappeared in May of 1952 at the time of the fire that ravaged his home and killed his wife, Ellen. He was seen momentarily at the scene but vanished without a trace after that sighting.

There was an extensive search for him at the time and is still possibly ongoing, but without any success. The possibility that he might have flown to a scheduled meeting in the Seattle area was also investigated but he was found to be a no-show at the medical symposium he was supposed to attend. Authorities and friends alike clung to the possibility that he would be back to claim his young son, who had survived the fire, but so far he has not returned. If anyone has any clue to his whereabouts please notify the local authorities.

Jake sat upright in his seat. 'My son survived, the librarian was right, thank God - he survived!'

He looked again at the words - *'vanished without a trace - extensive search - still ongoing.'* Of course, this newspaper article was written after five years. This is fifteen years later, could they still be looking for him? Maybe he was under suspicion, just like he had thought. He had better keep a low profile. Maybe he shouldn't even try to find Mary and Joe. If there was a problem he didn't want to implicate them. Nevertheless, he was elated to know his son had lived through the fire. He would find him eventually - he just knew he would!

He was in excellent shape financially, but he knew he still had to find a job so that he wouldn't gradually deplete all his savings. He bought a newspaper and got a room that night in a small motel just outside of town. Scouring the ads he found a job listed for an aide in a clinic located about fifteen miles out of town. The next morning, promptly at seven-thirty, he left in his rented car to check it out.

When the lady in charge of hiring saw his application with all those years of working in a large hospital in Seattle, she knew he was the man for the job. But, as she told him, she still had to check references from the Seattle hospital just to be sure. She told him to stop by the next afternoon, that she should have all the confirmation she needed by then.

He was hired, at a very good salary, and was told to start the following Monday. Good! That would give him some time to scout around and try to attain some information on his son. Jackie would be twenty-two now, a grown man. Was he still living in River Valley or had he reached out for greener pastures in a larger city or different state? Possibly he was in college somewhere. Then a terrible thought hit him. Left without a mother or a father at two years of age he was probably put out for adoption! He could be anywhere! Maybe he would never find him! He knew he had to think positively. He would go back to the newspaper building and scour more old newspapers from as far back as he could. Maybe there would be a mention of his son's name now and then regarding scholastic or sporting achievements. He spent the next two days doing just that, but never came across his name once. Should he risk going to the police to see if they could give him any information? Maybe, when he had exhausted every other avenue. But what could they do to him after twenty years?

He also realized he had to look for some sort of permanent residence, he couldn't stay in a motel forever. He decided to drive north on a well-paved state road for several miles, then he turned east on a bumpy country road with rolling green hills and well-kept, flourishing farmland. It was just about the most tranquil and beautiful area he had ever seen. He drove up the road about a mile and a half and, as if he had planned it, spotted a cottage in rather run-down shape with a FOR SALE BY OWNER sign on it. He was in a financial position to purchase a much larger and nicer home, but there was something about this cottage that caught his eye. The surroundings were picture-perfect and it seemed to offer the kind of solitude he had been looking for. He could see the potential, so in a sudden surge of curiosity he pulled into the driveway. An elderly man emerged from the garage when he heard the car. Jake introduced himself and commented on the For Sale sign.

"Nice to meet you, I'm Clarence. Yes, we've had to put our home up for sale. I'm afraid we just aren't able to keep a house up anymore," the old man started, "Martha's in a wheel chair and I'm so crippled up I can't do much of anything. Gotta get rid of it. Our daughter outside of Albany wants us to come and live with her. Hate to give up, but I guess it's for the best." He looked a little sad as he added, "I'll give you a good price, mister, needs some fixin' up, I know, but I'll allow for that."

"Well, you see I just happen to be in the market, mind if I take a look around?"

"Look around as much as you like - oh, and there's twelve acres that goes with this property, nice fertile soil in the back yard for a garden, I might add," the eager owner said.

Jake walked around to the back of the house and surveyed a large area of green lawn surrounding the house on both sides and at least fifty to sixty yards of the same in the back. He could see where there had once been quite an expansive garden, but was now mostly weeds. Clarence was quick to point out the vastness of the width and depth of the property. There were long stretches of pine trees on each side of the property and beyond that lay a dense array of more trees, among them birch, elm, oak, and numerous members of the evergreen variety. Clarence excitedly told him about the stream several yards beyond the trees that was filled with trout, and there was a little waterfall downstream that was enchanting to look at while one just relaxed. Jake could see that the old man really loved the place and he could see why, it had a tremendous amount of appeal. This was just what he was looking for, a spacious area where he would never feel hemmed in and, preferably with no neighbors anywhere nearby that he could see; a place where he could feel comfortable, yet not isolated. He walked back with Clarence to the front of the cottage where the old man invited him in to see the interior of the house. As he ascended the steps and stepped onto the porch, he could feel the boards creaking under his weight. They certainly needed attention, he was worried with each step that one of them would break.

Martha was a sweet, little old lady with a ready smile, and after exchanging pleasantries told Jake to feel free to investigate the house at his leisure. He couldn't help but notice the place was in sad disrepair, but judging from the ages and condition of the couple he understood why Clarence had said it had been quite difficult for them to keep the place up.

The front door opened into a modest living room with two windows on either side of the door. An old stone fireplace, looking rather unused, lined one wall. The linoleum on the floor was badly worn and ripped in places and the wallpaper was faded and torn and looked like it might have graced the walls a long time. A cozy armed rocking chair sat in one corner and a small sofa on the far side of the room was covered with a khaki army blanket. There were two small but pleasant bedrooms leading from the hallway off the living room. Jake noticed a bathroom between the two bedrooms. The humble kitchen off the other end of the living room was equipped with a black wood stove and a refrigerator that would need replacing. A wide window over the kitchen sink looked out over the spacious back yard. There was the cozy aroma of something baking in the oven of that black stove, an apple pie! The baking aroma served to give the little cottage an aura of pleasant homeliness. Just at that moment, Martha wheeled herself over to the oven and opened the door. With Clarence's help she took the pie out of the oven and carried it over to the counter top.

"I'll make some coffee," she said with a smile, " and when you're through looking around you can sample my apple pie!" With that she wheeled across the floor to the tall cupboard and proceeded to make the coffee and take out dishes and silver. Meanwhile, Clarence invited Jake to check out the basement. It was messy, but that wasn't a problem. The furnace, Clarence told him, had been replaced two years ago, and the roof had leaked a while back, but he had had it repaired last fall. The entire place just needed a good overall cleaning and sprucing up which Jake knew he was capable of doing. He was very pleased with the whole scenario as he and Clarence ascended the stairs for coffee and pie. He knew he could make this into a pleasant home for himself. His biggest problem might be loneliness, something he realized he would have to contend with anywhere he lived. He didn't even want to compare it to the beautiful home he had owned in Seattle. This one was a handyman's dream and he knew he would enjoy the challenge of fixing it up to his liking, and besides it would keep his mind busy and maybe he wouldn't miss Sandy so much.

The apple pie was delicious, and as he put the last forkful in his mouth, Jake decided the time was ripe to talk business. He was seriously considering buying this place if the price was right.

"Best apple pie I've had in a long time," he said sincerely, then after a brief pause he continued. "Exactly what are you asking for your property, folks?"

"Well," Clarence started, "We know the place is pretty run-down, and we're not trying to get rich on it, so tell me, what do you think is a fair offer?"

"I really don't know what houses like this are going for in this part of the country," Jake said, "but why don't you start with a price and we'll work with it."

Clarence and Martha looked at each other, he whispered something in her ear and she nodded. "How about eleven thousand, like I told you there is twelve acres with it?" he blurted out.

"Are you sure you-"

"If that's too much we can come down -"

"No, that price is fine with me, if it's OK with both of you," Jake said. "Of course it will all have to be legalized with a deed and abstract drawn up at the county clerk's office. And there will probably have to be a land survey update and whatever else is required in the process. But I'll take care of everything that I legally can so the two of you won't have to do any extra running around."

"Then it's a deal!" said Clarence with a relieved grin. "I'm so glad you came along, we've had that sign out there for six months now and you're only the second person to look at it! I guess it's kinda out of the way. It'll be good to get out from under it." He gave Martha a quick hug and she just smiled. Jake knew he wanted this to be his home, the whole house just seemed to generate love!

CHAPTER TWENTY-NINE (1972)

Jake was actually excited about moving into his new house. As he hung his shirts, (among them the white medical jacket), and pants in his closet he couldn't help but believe that this was the place he was meant to be. He purchased gallons of paint and painted every room. It took a while to peel all the wallpaper off the walls but he had all the time in the world.

Every evening he would work diligently on it and was thoroughly enjoying the transformation. It seemed the rooms were coming to life, after having sat dormant for years. The living room became a moss green, the kitchen a light yellow and the two bedrooms and hallway a soft beige. He ripped up the linoleum in the living room and bedrooms and found hardwood floors underneath which he sanded to a fresh new beauty. The old stone fireplace spoke for itself, it really didn't need any kind of repair, just a little dusting off. He proceeded to put new tile on the kitchen and bathroom floors. Next he painted the kitchen cupboards white, the countertops just needed a good scrubbing. He purchased a new refrigerator but decided to leave the antique black wood stove, it just seemed too majestic to replace. Besides it would be great for heating purposes and there certainly was plenty of wood for burning on his acreage. He decided he could do the majority of his cooking on a hot plate. The couple had left their bed frame, so he only needed to buy a new mattress and box springs.

He bought a brown leather sofa and matching chair, and at a sale found a kitchen table and four chairs, a couple of lamps for the living room and tables to set them on. Sears had a sale on televisions, so he picked up a nineteen-inch color, that would be company for him evenings after he was through transforming the house. He decided that would be enough furniture for the time-being, he would acquire other things that he needed as time went on. He was very pleased with the results, the little house had become very cozy and inviting and he knew also that the transformation process had been therapeutic for him, it had helped him get his mind off the past for a while.

The grass in his yard was starting to come in pretty thick now; he had found a small hand mower the couple had left in the shed and the immediate lawn surrounding his house was beginning to look quite nice. There was a lot of lawn to mow, however, and he knew he would soon have to purchase a power mower, as it was slow-going with the push mower. But all in all, he was contented in his cozy new home and was glad he had had the foresight to know that this was just the right place for him.

He was also enjoying his new job. The people he worked with accepted him immediately and he found his work was every bit as fulfilling as it had been in Seattle. He quickly became a favorite with most of the patients and one nurse-receptionist in particular tried very hard to become more than just good friends. Try as she did in her attempt to develop more than a friendly relationship, Jake was just not a willing participant. He did not want to wade into a relationship at this point. He decided he was not going to allow himself to become interested in anyone, but at forty-eight he was still a very handsome man and it did not go unnoticed by any of the female employees. He realized he was every bit as contented in this hospital as he had been with his job at the hospital in Seattle, but he never stopped missing Sandy.

He would spend many a Saturday afternoon fishing in the stream behind his house, working in his garden, or gathering firewood from his twelve acres. He knew the winters could be long and deep in this part of the country and this was the time of year to stockpile what he would be burning this winter in his furnace and black antique kitchen stove. He had planted a small garden in the back yard with intentions of enlarging it a little each year. He was already starting to enjoy his fresh lettuce, carrots, spinach and beets and decided next year he would expand his planting to potatoes, tomatoes, peas and possibly corn On weekends when he wasn't fishing, gardening or mowing, or wandering around his land, he was making minor or cosmetic repairs to his home. Landscaping his front yard had also become a hobby with him, and the results were gratifying. He only wished Sandy was here to enjoy it with him, he still missed her so much, more than he dared to let himself realize. She would have loved making this place a home. He had planted six pink rose bushes in the front of the house in honor of her and they were blooming profusely now. Every time he looked at them he felt he could almost see her smile!

With every trip into River Valley to buy his weekly groceries or pay his few bills he half expected to be confronted with someone from his past. But it never happened, so much time had passed, people had grown older, moved away, everything was different, except of course, the library and newspaper office. They had remained the same On his way home from each trip he had gotten into the habit of stopping at Lorraine's Coffee Bar, a tiny establishment at the edge of town. He knew instinctively why he stopped, it reminded him of Nell, and somehow gave him a warm, comfortable feeling each time. He had become acquainted with an elderly couple, Fred and Carrie, and they would sit together and enjoy friendly chit-chat whenever they were there at the same time. They had invited him over for Sunday dinner a couple of times which he had readily accepted and he had reciprocated by inviting them to his cottage. But the friendship was destined to be short-lived, as Fred passed away suddenly one morning from a heart attack, and broken-hearted Carrie followed a short time later.

He would stop in the newspaper office occasionally and check out more newspapers in the dead file, hoping to possibly find Jack's name. He knew small towns would print almost anything, however insignificant, to fill up paper space. But he was totally unprepared one day for the small item he found on the second page of a several month's old newspaper.

UNIDENTIFIED MAN ASKS QUESTIONS ABOUT 1952 FATAL FIRE

Carrie Smith, local librarian, has told police that she was recently questioned by a middle-aged man about the 1952 fire in which Ellen Rogers, wife of Dr. Timothy Rogers, died so tragically. She said she did not ask the name of the man, only that he became very agitated when she refused to give him any more information about the incident. She said she told him to check the newspaper office which he apparently did as confirmed by Will Richards at the information desk. He said an unfamiliar middle-aged man has asked several times to check through some old newspapers. Could this be the missing Dr. Rogers who disappeared at the time of the fire and was never located, or just a big city newspaper man trying to get a scoop on how a small town operates in the aftermath and coverage of a fatal fire? But why the sudden interest now after all this time? The local police would like to know!

The words rang in his ears for a moment - *the local police would like to know* - just what did that mean, was that one more possible confirmation that he was wanted in connection with the fire? He put the newspaper back where he had gotten it, and started to walk toward the front door. He was more confused than ever. Maybe it meant nothing, simply that if they knew the absent doctor had returned, the missing persons case would be solved, and the police could wipe the case off their books. As he walked by the information desk with the white-haired man behind it obviously being Will Richards, he couldn't help but feel very uneasy. As it happened Will had his head down, very engrossed in what he was doing, and paid no attention to Jake's leaving.

For the first time Jake questioned that his return to River Valley possibly was not in his best interests. But he wanted to find his son, if he was still living around here, so he decided he would keep as low a profile as possible. He would have liked very much to have looked up Mary and Joe, but he pondered over and over in his head as to whether or not he really should. He knew there would be no possibility of them turning him in, in the event that probability even existed, but he didn't want to put them in a compromising situation either. As long as he continued to be Jake Miller from Seattle there shouldn't be any questions. He would just refrain from outwardly showing any interest in the past history of the town or its occupants for the time being. And he would not go to the library or newspaper office again.

CHAPTER THIRTY (1987)

Jenna awoke to the familiar smell of bacon and eggs frying, the aroma was unmistakable. As her feet hit the floor she pondered for a moment the events of the day before that had brought her to this strange place. She shot a quick glance at her watch and she realized she had been gone from her home for almost a full twenty-four hours now. What was her mother feeling? She knew her family must be very worried and she felt a sudden twinge of shame for the anxiety she knew she must be causing them. Slowly she walked over to the door and opened it. Tom was still on the sofa, looking like he had barely slept a wink, and he, too, got up immediately at the sight of her.

"My door was open a little, did you open it?" Jenna whispered..

"I thought I told you to lock it!"

"I must have forgotten - anyway, I wasn't worried!"

"I just decided to check on you this morning to make sure you were OK, I expected to find a locked door, but it opened easily, and since I was wide awake I left it open a little," Tom confessed with a sly grin.

"Thanks for your concern, but like I said, I'm not worried about him, and you shouldn't be either!"

"Anybody hungry?," came a sudden call from the kitchen. They were unaware that Jake had overheard their conversation and he smiled to himself at the contrast of Tom's uneasiness and Jenna's confidence in him. Jake realized he was secretly very pleased over his unexpected guests. "Rise and shine, everything's ready!" He picked up the frying pan and walked over to the table and put two over-easy eggs on each of their three plates. Taking the pan back to the stove he picked up another one and dumped a healthy helping of home fries next to the eggs. The bacon was draining on paper towels and he sat that plate on the table. Without missing a beat he poured hot coffee from a blue and white speckled coffee pot into three earthen mugs that looked like they belonged in a museum.

"Come on kids, get it while it's hot!," he said as he poked his head into the living room.

"It smells sooo good, Tom, and I'm hungry!" Jenna said with a smile. "You look hungry, too. Don't tell me any different!"

Tom tossed her one of his lop-sided grins as if to say he'd be glad to eat breakfast, but he was still going to be cautious. Jenna took his hand and they walked slowly to the kitchen, and since they had had very little to eat since they had left home, they had no trouble devouring the tasty breakfast put before them. As Jake was eating beside them he couldn't help but think how pleasant it was to have someone with him at the breakfast table and he watched contentedly as they cleaned their plates.

As they were finishing up, he looked at Tom and said, "Exactly what do you kids plan on doing now? Are you going to make the right decision and go home or just keep running?"

He looked from Tom to Jenna and back to Tom, then paused before he continued, "Don't you think that maybe your folks have worried enough?"

The scrutinizing look he was giving them made them cower slightly in their chairs, and his words made Jenna feel sad and ashamed. After another long moment he got up and walked toward the back door.

"Well, you two think about it while I take Scout out for his morning walk. I'll be back soon, and we'll talk about it some more." He took a few steps then turned around and said, "Don't forget, the phone's right over there."

After he left, Tom and Jenna looked at each other as if reading each other's minds.

"You really want to go back home, don't you?" Tom offered.

She hesitated a minute before she answered. "I'm sorry, Tom, but I'm afraid I do. I think we were wrong in running away like we did. I was just so afraid if I didn't go with you maybe I'd never see you again. I knew you were so set on leaving - and I'm so sorry about your situation at home - but I think it's best if we go back now," she said quietly. "He's right, you know, what we're doing is wrong."

Tom could tell by the look on her face that there was no point in continuing their sojourn and the guilt he was feeling was getting the best of him anyway.

"Should we leave now before he gets back, we could probably make it back by dark if we get started?"

Jenna didn't want to appear too relieved, even though she was, as she said, "I wouldn't leave without saying goodbye and thanking him. He's been good to us, you know. and there's just something - something about him."

Tom had no idea what she meant by that last statement, but he couldn't help but admit that the old man had indeed been very kind to them.

As they waited for his return, Jenna couldn't help but scan the inside of the little house. It was such a sharp contrast to the home she had always lived in. Instead of expansive rooms with bright, luxurious Persian rugs throughout, and a winding staircase that rivaled *Gone With the Wind*, she saw inexpensive scatter rugs on the floors and the entire living quarters were less than a third the size of her parent's house. Her mother's beautiful antiques and exquisite vases and glassware were on display in nearly every room and the furniture was the most expensive found anywhere. That was the home she had been brought up in but she knew not everyone had been as fortunate. Nevertheless she felt a certain aura of comfort and pleasantness in this little house.

Next to the stone fireplace she saw a high shelf with two very striking photographs in frames. On one end was a picture of a blonde woman, probably in her late thirties. It was in full color and the smiling lady was very pretty. Jenna immediately wondered what her connection was to this old man, and while she was pondering that, her eyes wandered to the other end of the shelf where a wooden frame with a small black and white picture had been placed. That woman appeared to be a little younger than the blonde lady and the small child beside her didn't look any older than two or three. Jenna decided he was probably a boy by the way he was dressed. She took it down from the shelf to see it better. Possibly this was his mother and himself, or, possibly he had had a wife at one time. The woman was very attractive, and the child clinging to her was smiling happily. She was still studying the picture when Jake and Scout walked in the door. Jenna quickly attempted to put the picture back on the shelf.

"See you've been looking around, that's OK, afraid you won't find too much to look at in this place," he said apologetically.

"Is that your mother in either one of these pictures?" Jenna said softly, as she pointed to the pictures on the shelf.

He didn't answer at first. Then very quietly he said, " No, I don't even have a picture of my mother." Another pause. "There's a long story associated with those pictures. It goes way back, long before you were born."

Jenna could tell by the sad look on his face that she had misspoken and wasn't quite sure whether she should pursue the subject or not. She waited for him to speak which, after another moment, he did.

"You see, I was married to both of those ladies at different times, and the child is my little boy." She noticed that his eyes were becoming very misty, and he didn't volunteer any additional information. The three people in the photos had to have been very near and dear to him, she thought.

"Where - where are they now?" curiosity had gotten the best of Jenna. She knew she shouldn't be quite so inquisitive but she just had to know. She was intrigued by the fact that he had been married to two such beautiful women.

"Well, I lost my last wife to cancer quite a few years ago," he said pointing to the picture of Sandy. " And the other picture, well, I lost them too."

"I'm so sorry, that must have been so hard," Jenna felt her own eyes getting moist, as she reached out to put a consoling hand on his. He put his other hand on top of hers for a moment and she could see the loneliness in his sad eyes.

"It was a long time ago," he muttered, forcing a smile, "but sometimes it seems like only yesterday." He quickly diverted his eyes from the picture and proceeded to walk toward his bedroom. Jenna decided it best not to say anything more. She knew he must have had a very sad life, and she shouldn't prod him regarding it unless he wanted to tell her.

Just at that moment Jake staggered, uttered a faint cry, and grasped his chest. He hung onto the back of the lounge chair, and Jenna and Tom, not knowing what was happening, stood frozen for a minute as the old man gasped for air.

"I think he might be having a heart attack!" Jenna whispered to Tom, and then ran over and took Jake's arm. "You have to lie down, let us help you." she said softly. He made no attempt to protest as between the two of them they led him to his bed and covered him with one of the khaki blankets. Jenna seemed to instinctively know he had to be kept warm, although the perspiration beads were standing out on his face. His hand still clutched his chest, but from the blank look on his ashen face, the two assumed the pain was either subsiding or he was near death.

"On the shelf - behind the coffee - nitro -" he uttered nearly incoherently, struggling with the words, but Jenna managed to catch the key words and jumped up quickly and ran out to the kitchen, and spotted a coffee can on a shelf above the sink. Behind it was a large, brand-name bottle of nitroglycerine pills. Very quickly she took a pill from the bottle and ran back to the distressed man on the bed. Between the two of them they raised his head up enough to put the pill under his tongue, which Tom assured her was the right thing to do. Then they gently laid him back on the pillow. After a while it looked to them that he had fallen asleep, they could tell he was still breathing, so they thought it best if they let him rest. They tiptoed back into the living room and sat down together on the sofa.

"Poor old man! I'm not leaving him!" Jenna said adamantly as she brushed her hair away from her face. "He's sick and he's all alone!" Jenna's compassionate nature was getting the best of her and she knew it. For some strange reason she was drawn to Jake, a reason she just couldn't explain. She had always missed not having a grandfather, and this man would have made a perfect grandfather, she thought to herself.

"No, of course we can't leave him like this," Tom assured her, "he needs us to stay with him for awhile. No - don't worry, we won't leave him alone."

Jenna was thankful that Tom felt the same way she did. As the two sat on the sofa, both rather tired from their life-saving ordeal, Jenna found herself thinking of home, of her mother and father, and what they must be going through wondering where she was.

"Do you think we should call home?" she said glancing at the phone.

"How would we explain? Let's just wait a while. Let's see how he feels when he wakes up, and then, maybe we'll call, or leave." Tom glanced at Jenna, feeling rather guilty, knowing he was responsible for that sad look. She'd be at home now where she belonged getting ready to go to school if he hadn't talked her into running away with him.

Jenna got up from the sofa and stood looking again at the two pictures on the shelf. "He said these two ladies were his wives, and he has a little boy somewhere. I wonder if he keeps in touch with him. I wonder if he knows his father has a health problem."

"Hard to say - but you know Jen, that's really not our problem," Tom said hoping to discourage Jenna from becoming too over-involved.

He had found a container and filled it with fresh water. They would take it with them when they left. But he realized he was starting to soften on the whole idea of running away, especially the part involving Jenna in his plan. She should be home, safe and sound, with her family. But Jenna was keeping very busy keeping close tabs on Jake; she would walk to the bedroom door and check on him every few minutes. She couldn't explain her compassion and the attachment she felt for Jake and she had no intention of leaving him until she knew he was feeling better.

About an hour later Jake woke and attempted to raise himself from the bed.

"Are you feeling O.K?" Jenna asked. "Maybe you should not try to get up yet. Just lie still and rest awhile longer, we won't leave you. I think you had some sort of attack. Is there anyone you want us to call?"

"No, there's no one," he answered weakly.

"We weren't sure what to do, so we just gave you your nitro like you said and got you to bed and let you sleep."

Although still quite disoriented, he got to his feet and walked over to the sofa. He looked at both of them for a moment and then said, "How can I thank you kids for helping me? You could have left and gone on your way. How can I repay you?"

"That's not necessary," Tom said, "You were in a bad way, and needed help, that's all."

"It was those pictures, wasn't it?" Jenna said. "I don't mean to distress you but don't you think someone should be called so they can at least know about your condition?"

"I told you - there's no one to call. I have no one around here."

After another few quiet moments he looked at both of them and said, "I guess it doesn't matter, I might as well tell someone," he began. He sighed a deep sign, and as his face took on a very dark and intense countenance, he slowly continued, "The people in the small picture were my wife and little son. He was only two years old, just had his birthday three days before. They were my whole world!" He wasn't even trying to hide the tears in his eyes as he looked deep into the photo on the shelf as if trying to lose himself in it.

"It was back in 1952. My wife and I, and our baby, we lived in River Valley. There was a fire, I was at the hospital in my first year of residency-"

"You mean - you're a doctor?" Tom interrupted.

"Yes, I was at the time. Now I can remember the day like it was yesterday, but for many years I kept it buried so deep in my mind that it couldn't come to the surface. It seems I was sitting at my desk in the hospital looking over these pictures I had just picked up that morning from the drug store. I had given them a negative that I had brought in from home and they had made me an enlargement for my desk and this small one which I intended to put in my wallet. I was also checking over my airline tickets. I had a flight late that afternoon to a medical symposium in Seattle, and I was looking through my wallet to make sure I had enough money to cover my expenses on the trip, when I was paged to come to assist in an emergency. I remember hurriedly putting the small snapshot and tickets in the white lab coat pocket I was wearing and rushing to assist. In my haste I obviously forgot to pick up my wallet. I was just finishing when I got the call to come home immediately. I was told my house was on fire! I ran to the parking lot and drove home as fast as I could, - and our house -" he paused and sighed deeply, "It was engulfed in flames - and they were just bringing my wife out on a stretcher. She had been burned so badly I barely recognized her." He grimaced as he continued, "There was no way she could have been alive, and when I saw her my mind must have flipped, because I ran away as fast as I could. I ran away, can you believe that?"

"I'm sure you were in shock. But what about your little boy? Was he burned too?" Jenna asked all wide-eyed and teary.

For the moment he evaded the question. Then he continued, "I have since learned that my child survived the fire but I have no way of knowing where he is now. I didn't remember anything until many years later. I guess I elapsed into total amnesia when I saw my wife's body. I can remember not knowing who I was, but a little later that day I noticed I had tickets in my pocket so I must have driven to the airport and boarded the plane. I guess I just assumed that that was what I was supposed to do. The name on the ticket was totally unfamiliar to me. My mind had gone completely blank and when I arrived in Seattle, I had no idea why I was there. I got a job, first in a restaurant, and then in a hospital, and I eventually remarried - to Sandy, in the other picture - and was very happy for years, but without any recollection of the past."

He paused for a moment and looked down at the floor, then slowly continued. "One day, many years later, a child was brought into the hospital where I worked. He had been in a terrible fire; his little body was so badly burned that he was barely alive. As soon as I saw him my mind started to relive the scene I had run away from twenty years earlier. Little by little I remembered things. I remembered seeing the flames leaping into the air and hearing the shrill of the sirens, and - seeing this burned body on a stretcher. It finally came to me that that body was my wife."

"I had that lab coat on when I boarded the plane and I used to spend hours looking at that picture in the pocket wondering who they were, what their connection was to me, knowing full well they must be very important people in my life."

"I shouldn't be telling you kids all this. I never intended to tell anyone, but I feel relieved getting it off my chest. But remember, it's kind of between us, OK?"

He was becoming emotional, and Jenna, not wanting a repeat performance of the attack, thought it best if he rested awhile. Surprisingly enough, he took her advice and with Tom's help he lay down on the sofa.

"That must have been a terrible ordeal, no wonder you lost your memory - you poor man!" Jenna exclaimed, as she knelt down

241

by the sofa and put her hand on his.

Although he didn't speak for a few moments, his mind was racing and finally he blurted out. "I have been so ashamed all these years for running away. I was so weak that I chose amnesia instead of coping with the situation. But my little boy, he would be all grown up now, and probably wouldn't want a thing to do with me, and I certainly couldn't blame him."

"But you didn't set the fire, - it just happened, you weren't to blame for anything." Tom offered, in an attempt to make up for his ill feeling toward the older man.

"Yes, I know that, but I still deserted the two people I loved the most."

Jenna, anxious to change the subject for fear of more anxiety on his part, said, "I don't know much about such things, but I do know that if you suffered amnesia at the time that it certainly wasn't your fault, it was just something that happened and you certainly shouldn't blame yourself for anything. And that was so long ago, I'm sorry I brought it up, I shouldn't have been snooping."

"Don't feel bad about it, as a matter of fact I feel better now, I haven't spoken to anyone about it ever, you kids are the first," he said, and he actually had a look of relief on his face.

"Can I make you a cup of tea?"

"Only if you both have one with me," he smiled.

"We will," she smiled back and went into the kitchen and filled the teakettle and set it on the hotplate. She found some teabags in the cupboard and set out three cups.

"Don't you ever get lonely out here all by yourself? Do you have any neighbors?" Tom asked.

Jake thought a moment before he answered, "No close neighbors, but I guess I keep pretty busy around the house, tending to my garden, keeping Scout in line, running into town a couple of times a week. I was still working up until about two years ago, then I decided to retire and take it easy. And yes, I really do get lonely, sometimes."

"What I don't understand is," said Jenna, bringing Jake his cup of tea, "why all these years we've never seen you around town or anywhere else. The place isn't that big, seems like I would have seen you somewhere. When did you come back from Seattle, anyway?"

"I came back in 1972 and it could be you weren't even born yet," Jake laughed.

"I'll have you know I was one year old in 1972, so there!" Jenna giggled as she went to get the other two cups of tea. They all sipped silently for a moment until Jake broke the silence.

"Oh, like I said I do go into town occasionally to stock up on what I need, pay a couple of bills, and so forth. I used to try to do some checking around concerning the past, but I've kind of given up on that, never seemed to get anywhere, and I seemed to hit an obstacle at every attempt. So you see I'm really not a total hermit. But - one thing I know for sure," Jake said, getting serious, "is that I know the consequences of running away and I hope you two don't make the same mistake. I'm sure your folks are crazy with worry! Now why don't you just hightail it on home where you belong and stop this foolishness!" he said with sincere concern.

Jenna looked at Tom. Jake didn't know they had already made the decision to go back.

"We're going home, we've decided, thanks to you. The whole thing was all my fault, I should have never dragged Jenna into this," Tom replied.

Jenna turned to the old man. "Jake, why don't you come back to River Valley with us. You know, you didn't start that fire, there was no way you could have prevented it, so you should stop feeling so guilty. Come back with us, my father's a doctor, he can make sure you get the help you need. You're not very well, don't you think you should be checked out?" She was forming an attachment to Jake that even she couldn't understand.

"No - not necessary. I'll be alright! But I'm glad to hear you two have smartened up!" Jake said with a relieved grin. "I'll drive

243

you into town. Don't worry, I feel much better now. I think I got a lot off my chest by talking to you kids, thanks for listening, I really mean it!" he said sincerely as he patted Jenna's head.

"Are you sure you feel well enough to drive us, you didn't look so good a while ago, " Jenna said, concerned.

"Oh, I have those little setbacks all the time - nothing new - they pass and I'm OK again for a while," Jake smiled, happy about her concern.

Jenna slowly picked up her sweater and she and Tom followed him out the door. His car was parked in the little garage by the cottage and they waited by the driveway as Jake went into the garage to start the car and back it out.

"Do you think you should have tried to get him to come back with us? Maybe he wants to be left alone, besides where would he get a prescription for nitro if he didn't already have a doctor?" Tom questioned.

"You're probably right, but all I know is - when I get home and after everyone has cooled down, I'm going to tell them about Jake living here all by himself with heart trouble. No one should be so alone when they're sick!" Jenna said with compassionate determination, and Tom knew she meant it.

The car plodded along on the bumpy country road, and the occupants were aware of every bump. They were relieved when it turned onto the smoothly paved state highway.

The three were quiet for the most part during the drive back to River Valley, and Tom and Jenna were both deep in thought trying to envision what their punishment would be for their overnight excursion. Maybe with a little luck everyone would be so glad to see them safe and sound that the punishment wouldn't be too harsh. They could only hope so!

"You can drop us off, we can walk from here, we live just a few blocks from here," Tom said quite apprehensively as he looked in the direction of home.

"OK, but promise me you'll go straight home, both of you, and don't try anything foolish like this again. And remember, where I live is just between the three of us, OK?"

Jenna looked up at Jake as she got out of the car, wondering for a moment why he so adamantly wanted to keep his address a secret. "I wish you'd come and meet my parents - maybe help us explain." She not only was feeling compassion for Jake but for her and Tom too, not quite sure what was awaiting them at home. If her parents could see what a good man Jake was and how well he had looked after them, it might soften the blow for them.

"Sorry, kids, you're on your own!" Jake laughed. "I think you both need to take your medicine! Just run along now where you belong, and I'll go back where I belong, so forget you ever saw me. Now, scoot! Get yourselves home to your parents, they must be crazy with worry!" He was obviously trying to cover up his feelings with forced agitation; if he acted annoyed with them they wouldn't suspect that he really hated to see them go. It was the first time in a long while that he had let himself become attached to anyone. He concluded that the sooner they got out of his sight, the better!

"Just remember, Jake, you'll always have two friends if you ever need us. My last name is Lauren and Tom's is Wilson, just look us up in the phone book when you're in town!" Jenna said as she lingered by the car, looking at Jake and feeling a strong bond that she couldn't explain.

Jake nodded and smiled at her, then reached over and shut the car door. As he backed up into a side street and started back over the highway they had just traveled on, Jenna felt a little tug at her heart. She turned slowly around and with Tom beside her started walking toward her home.

"When I tell my parents about Jake, and how sick and alone he is, I know they'll want to help him. I'm sure my father will be concerned; after all, making people well is his job," Jenna said with a look of determination on her face.

"But what about the secret he asked us to keep?" Tom said as he glanced sideways at her with a sly look on his face.

"I never promised to keep that secret, so there!" Jenna grinned.

"Well, right now, I guess I'm more worried about us. Suppose they'll do something drastic to us? Hope my old man's been drunk since yesterday, maybe with a little luck he won't even know I've been gone!" Tom said, kicking a stone from the street.

"I'm not looking forward to it, either, but I think if they punish me, it'll be more because they're relieved than anything else. I just wish we'd never ran away in the first place! But then we would have never met Jake!" With that last revelation a smile swept across Jenna's face.

Jake was nearly back to his cottage when it hit him. He had been so engrossed in thinking about what had happened in the last two days that it took a while for him to absorb Jenna's last statement.

"Lauren - Lauren, why does that sound so familiar to me? Who did I used to know named Lauren?," he said aloud to himself as he bounced along the road. Then he decided it was probably a name he had heard working at the restaurant or in the hospital, it could have been anyone. Just another name - it wasn't important!

After a few minutes of walking, Jenna and Tom leaned against a cement abutment to rest. As they were silently pondering the inevitable awaiting them, they heard a siren directly behind them. The two looked up just in time to see a police car pulling off the road just a few feet away from them, and they realized they had been spotted. Two officers emerged from the car and walked briskly over to them.

"Are you Jenna Lauren and Tom Wilson?" the tallest one asked rather brusquely.

"Yes, we are, and we're on our way home, we just stopped to rest a minute," Tom said in their defense.

"You can rest in the car. Come along, we'll take you home

personally! Do you kids have any idea of the rumpus you've caused? Your parents are just about out of their minds!" He said as he ushered them into the car with stone-faced authority.

"We're sorry - I know we really shouldn't have done it, it was a stupid thing to do," Tom stammered.

"Save your apologies for your parents," the officer interrupted. "We're just doing our job, but we're glad to see you safe, anyway!"

CHAPTER THIRTY-ONE

They were well into the second day of her daughter's disappearance, and to Bonnie Lauren it had seemed like an eternity. The initial despair was over, and now chronic anxiety and panic had overwhelmed the household. She sat with swollen eyes looking out the window, as if by doing so, Jenna would magically appear. Jack Lauren had gone to the hospital very early this morning as one of his patients had taken a turn for the worse. Being a very devoted father, he was almost glad to have another crisis enter into the picture. He could lose himself for a while in someone else's problems. As it happened his patient passed away and as soon as his duties were completed he came home as quickly as possibly.

There was no need to give the officer their addresses, he had already been to their homes the day before when they were first reported missing. He dropped Tom off first as it was on the way. He was met at the door by his father who embraced him immediately, and Jenna could see from the car that things were alright with him, at least temporarily. Then the officer drove to Jenna's home, and as she nervously walked beside him up the front walk, the door to the house suddenly opened and her mother ran out, screaming Jenna's name. Intensely relieved, she too embraced her daughter.

"Jenna - Jenna - where have you been? We were all so afraid - afraid that something bad had happened. Thank God you're home, thank God!" Her mother couldn't hug her enough and Jenna realized that she was just as happy and relieved as her mother to be back where she belonged.

Tears ran down both their faces, and Jenna, laughing and crying at the same time, said over and over, "I'm home, Mom, I'm home. I promise I won't ever do anything like that again!"

After a few moments, they looked at each other, still crying with relief.

"Why did you - where did you stay last night? Do you know

what you put us through?" Bonnie was asking questions in quick succession, not waiting for any answers.

"Mom, it's a long story. I know it was wrong to run away, but we met this old man and we stayed in his cottage."

Jack Lauren excitedly popped in the front door at that moment, interrupting Jenna's explanation.

"Daddy!" Jenna ran to him, hugging him happily. They clung to each other, one obviously as relieved as the other.

After thanking the officer, the three happy people went into the house.

"Jenna, thank God!" Jenna's grandmother nearly screamed as she appeared in the double door between the dining and living rooms. She had been in her room, but when she heard excited voices she decided to come and investigate. She hugged her granddaughter and said, "I just knew you'd come back O.K. I prayed and prayed, and now you're here. Thank God!"

Jenna was thankful that things were going so well. She thought of Tom and hoped that he was not having too bad a time with his father. After several minutes of the happy family reunion, however, the mood in the living room of the Lauren household changed. Jack Lauren knew that as happy as he was to see his daughter safe, he had to let her know he did not condone her actions.

"So tell us, young lady! Why did you do what you did? You put us all through almost two days of torture. I want a complete and thorough explanation of this whole thing, then we'll decide what your punishment will be!"

"I was just trying to tell Mom," Jenna started to cry. "I know Tom and I did wrong, but it started to get dark and we stumbled onto this cottage, and an old man lived there, and he invited us to stay the night, and -"

"Wait just a minute - not so fast. You stayed in some old man's cottage last night? Where? And who was this old man?" her father asked, frowning.

"He was a nice old man, his name was Jake. Well, at first we were a little scared, but he was good to us, then today he had some sort of attack, and he told us all about his life and how he had lost both his wives and little boy, and - Oh, Dad, he's so lonely and he's awfully sick!"

"Jenna, I'm glad to see you have compassion for your fellow man, but you just don't take up with total strangers like that, you never know what they might do!" her distraught mother interrupted.

"Mom, he's a doctor, well, he used to be. And when he was young he used to live near here, and he was called home one day from the hospital because his house was on fire and his wife died in the fire. I guess he suffered amnesia and went to the west coast and didn't know who he was for years and years."

"Wait a minute!! He told you all this? Sounds like a far-fetched line of baloney to me! I'm certainly glad you got away from him. He sounds dangerous!," the ever-cautious Bonnie said very emphatically.

Jenna's grandmother was listening intently.

"He was a doctor? And there was a fire where his wife died? What else did he say?" she gasped with total interest.

"Well, like I said, his name is Jake, and when he finally realized who he was a long time afterwards, he came back here, but he feels so guilty and sad over everything that he doesn't want anyone to know where he is! He said there's a shopping center where his house once stood. Must be the River Valley shopping center!" Jenna said.

Mary turned white as snow, and her knees felt as though they were going to buckle under her as she turned to leave the room.

"I - I think I'll warm up some soup, I feel a little hungry, you must be hungry, too, Jenna," she said as she fumbled with the words. She went into the kitchen and held on to the table for support, hoping that she wouldn't pass out. She knew the house she had lived in in the mid-1950's had been torn down and the entire block demolished to make way for the new shopping center.

Her mind was racing. The mystery man had to be Tim Rogers, the young doctor she had called home from the hospital back in the spring of 1952 when she saw flames leaping from his house next door! After thirty-five years there had been no doubt in her mind but that he was gone forever, either dead or at least never returning. He had completely dropped out of sight - until now!

She had to ponder this situation thoroughly. Forgetting all about the soup she had said she was going to warm up, she quickly went through the door off the kitchen to her room. Once there she took out from deep within her closet a small wooden box. It had not been opened in thirty years at least. As she opened it, the first thing she spotted was an envelope containing the marriage license of Timothy and Ellen Rogers. The next envelope contained a birth certificate of their son. There were also several small black and white snapshots, slightly faded with age. She couldn't resist looking at them; Tim Rogers had been a very handsome man, and Ellen had been quite beautiful. They had made such a good-looking couple. There were several baby pictures and one small snapshot of Ellen and the baby when he was about two. She spread them out on her desk to study them. Just then she heard footsteps She quickly gathered up the pictures, put them in the box and closed it. It was Jenna.

"Gram, are you alright? You look awfully pale!"

"I'm alright, Jenna, and I'm awfully glad you decided to come home without persuasion." She paused long enough to give her granddaughter another hug. "I've been thinking about that man you met. You called him Jake, you said he's sick? Maybe you're right, perhaps we should try to help him, get him to go to a doctor or something," Mary said, not wanting to appear too interested.

"Oh, Gram, I'm so glad you said that! I'm going to try to get Dad to go see him, and see if he needs some kind of medicine or something, just as soon as things calm down a bit around here," Jenna winced.

At that moment the doorbell rang, and Jenna ran down the

stairs. She somehow knew it was Tom.

He seemed to cower at the doorstep for a moment, not sure whether he should come in or not. Jack Lauren spotted him and walked over immediately, and spoke to him before Jenna had a chance to say anything.

"Was this your doing, Tom? I know Jenna went with you willingly, but I doubt if she would have done it on her own! I think you owe us all an apology and a promise not to lead my daughter astray again!," he said very firmly.

"Yes, Dr. Lauren, I take full responsibility, and I'm sorry, and I promise it will never happen again." The look on the young boy's face told Jack he seemed sincere enough. "I just came over to tell Jenna that everything's alright now, my father has promised not to touch another drop. He was crying when I got home, and I think he means it!"

"That remains to be seen, I'm sure!" Jack retorted, "but just to be on the safe side, you'll not be allowed to visit Jenna anywhere but in this house and at school, of course. And you both better go to school from now on! Don't ever put us through this again, do you understand?"

Jenna reached up and kissed her dad on the forehead. "Thanks, Dad, for the lecture. I think that's what we both needed, and don't worry, I realize now what I have right here, and it will never happen again - I promise!"

Jack patted his daughter's head and half-smiled as he walked away and left the two to talk. What more could he say? Relief at their safe return over-shadowed any anger he had harbored and Jenna certainly sounded sincere in her promise.

"I'm going to convince Dad to go and see Jake - just as soon as I dare bring it up again." Jenna said to Tom.

"I'm glad to be home. If this will make my father stop drinking for good it will all have been worth it!" Tom stated happily.

CHAPTER THIRTY-TWO

The station wagon bounced around as it traveled the bumpy road to Jake's cottage way out in the country. Jenna had succeeded in convincing her father to take a look at Jake, and she wanted Tom to go along, too, just in case she had trouble finding the cottage. Finally, after what seemed an eternity of bumps to Jack Lauren, they spotted the cottage in the distance.

Jake's car was parked in the driveway, and Jenna decided it would be best if she and Tom were to go to the door without her father. The door was unlocked and Jenna pushed it open and called. No answer. She took the liberty of walking in, and upon further investigation found that Jake wasn't there.

"Maybe he's walking the dog," Tom said. They stepped back outside, walked around to the back, and in the direction of Jake's garden Jenna thought she saw something unusual. As she got closer she discovered it was Jake, lying face down on the ground.

"Dad! - Dad! come here - quick!," she called.

Her father bent over the unconscious man and felt for a pulse. "He's still alive - just barely! I'll drive the wagon over here, and we'll put him in. This man needs to get to the hospital fast!"

The three of them managed, with quite a little effort, to get Jake into the back seat and covered him with a car robe to keep him warm. A good share of his body was covered with dirt and there was no way of knowing how long he had been lying in the garden. Jack surmised that he had had a heart attack, possibly a massive one, and as near as he could assess he was very close to death.

Jenna, nearly in tears, sat on the edge of the back seat beside him to keep him from falling on the floor during the fast, rough ride to the hospital.

"Is he going to be OK, Dad? He looks awful - I'm not sure he's still breathing - oh, Dad, hurry!" She held the unconscious man's hand all the way just to somehow let him know he wasn't alone and that he would be getting help.

After the swift ride to the hospital, Jake was quickly evaluated and admitted to the cardiac care unit and hooked up to all kinds of life support equipment. Jenna's father saw to it that the best cardiologist available was called in, and eventually Jake's heart was beating regularly and all systems were stabilized.

"I think we might have gotten to him just in time," Dr. Lauren told his daughter. "Chances are he would have died if we had found him a few minutes later. You really like this man, don't you?." Without waiting for an answer he added, "When he's feeling better I'll tell him how thankful we all are that he took such good care of you kids while you were pulling your little escapade. If he hadn't been a good man, anything could have happened - you realize that, don't you?"

"Yes, Dad, we were both being pretty stupid - that's for sure. I'm sorry about the whole thing, except the part about meeting Jake, of course," Jenna added.

It wasn't until he had rested awhile that Jenna's father allowed them to go in to see him, then only for a minute. He knew it would be important for Jake to see faces he recognized as he was gaining consciousness.

Tom and Jenna walked cautiously over to his bedside. He was lying there quietly, but when he saw the two of them you could almost see a sparkle in his eyes. He lifted a very weak arm from under the covers and put his hand on Jenna's. "We went to see you, Jake, and you were lying in your garden unconscious, so Dad and Tom and I brought you here. You must have had another attack! Anyway, don't worry, Dad's seeing to it that you get the best of care. I'm so glad I convinced him to go, so glad we found you," Jenna said tenderly.

"Thanks," Jake muttered rather weakly. "I owe you both so much." He paused for a moment, then added, "The last thing I remember is that I had decided to do a little weeding in my garden, and I must have collapsed. You folks probably came along just in time. Thank God for all of you!" The tears in the corners of his eyes revealed his sincerity.

"We're just so glad you're OK! And don't worry, we'll take good care of you. Oh - Dad's motioning for us to leave, but we'll be back as soon as we can," Jenna said as she touched his hand again and turned to walk away from the bed.

The next couple of days Tom and Jenna stopped in to see him as often as they could. Since he was still in CCU they could spend only a few minutes with him at a time. They had gone back to school and had managed to survive the teasing and taunting about having run away together. It wasn't easy to live down, but they both realized the whole episode had helped them to mature, although they knew that was really not the right way to accomplish maturity. For the most part they ignored the teasing, it was really no one's business but theirs and their parents, and they knew in time it would be forgotten. They found the less they reacted to the teasing, the sooner it stopped.

After a couple of days, Jake was assigned to a hospital room. It dawned on him as he lay there one afternoon that this was the very hospital that he had been practicing in the day of that dreadful fire. He forced himself not to dwell on that fact. Instead, this whole experience had caused him to almost miraculously take on a whole new demeanor, inside and out. His beard had been shaven off, his eyes had lost the dull, lifeless look they had had before, and the attention he was getting seemed to give him a lift, a renewed reason for living. He was still a rather handsome man. He had managed to maintain his good looks all through his life, and the addition of gray hair had only added to his charisma and charm. He was smiling a lot now, joking with the nurses, actually enjoying his new social existence.

He had been evaluated by the cardiac team and it was determined that a bypass operation was not necessary at this time, there was blockage in his right coronary artery but not enough to warrant the operation. He knew stress had been a big factor in his heart problem, it had been building up to a breaking point for many years now. He felt so much better now, this heart attack was almost like a blessing in disguise!

He was sitting up in bed when Jenna popped in one afternoon after school. Quenched in her hand was a large, beautiful bouquet of miniature pink roses and baby's breath. It tickled her to see the way Jake's eyes sparkled when she held them up in front of him.

"From my mother's greenhouse," she said, "she has so many she'll never miss these."

"Beautiful, Jenna!," he smiled, " How did you know I loved roses? How thoughtful of you to bother. I don't deserve all this attention!"

"Nonsense!" Jenna laughed, "I'm going to spoil you all I can while I have you as a captive! And, you have all those rose bushes in front of your house, remember, and I just know some of them have to be pink. At least that's my favorite color. Anyway, that's how I knew you would like them!" Then, looking around the room for a place to set them, she said flippantly, "And don't worry, I didn't forget the vase. All we need is some water and we'll be all set."

She lay the roses down as she filled the vase with water. One by one she arranged the flowers so that the roses would be intermingled just right with the baby's breath. Then she set the vase on the stand opposite Jake so he could see them as he lay in bed. She paused for a moment, making sure they were centered just right, then turned back to Jake.

"By the way, my grandmother wants to meet you. She's asked me a lot about you. Do you mind if I bring her over?"

Jake smiled, "Not at all, I'd love to meet your grandmother. Bring her over anytime. I guess I'm ready to join the human race again. Guess I kind of kept to myself for too long." He took a deep breath as he added, " I can't believe how kind everyone had been to me here. Your father has taken good care of me. You can be very proud of him, you know!"

"Oh, I am," Jenna beamed, "Everyone likes my dad, they all say what a great doctor he is."

She could see Jake looked tired, so she told him she'd come back later, probably with her grandmother. Jake told her that would be fine, maybe he'll catch a little nap in the meantime. She waved to him from the doorway, and he smiled back.

CHAPTER THIRTY-THREE

"Yes, I have to take this box with me - it's very important, you'll see," Mary Lauren was saying very emphatically, as she walked out the door with Jenna and Shiela. There had been a lot of soul-searching on her part the past few days, but she decided it best to get everything out into the open. Yes, she decided, whatever the repercussions may be she had to go through with it. It was the only thing to do at this point, now that she knew for sure!

No amount of coaxing on Mary's part could convince her daughter-in-law that she should go along with them. She saw no point in visiting some old man in the hospital she had never seen before. The rest could if they wanted to, but she had better things to do. And besides, why did her mother-in-law think it so important that she come?

Jenna was puzzled by her grandmother's interest in Jake; she knew her to be a very kind and thoughtful person, but her interest seemed to be way beyond simple compassion for a fellow human being. Nevertheless, she was pleased to have someone share her enthusiasm - but why the wooden box? Mary Lauren had suddenly become very mysterious since Jenna had returned home from her two-day escapade.

Jake was sitting in a chair beside his bed when the trio walked in. Mary could feel her heart beating rapidly in her chest as she nervously pondered the task ahead. Her eyes fell on Jake the second she walked in the door. She spotted the distinguishing features right away - the big dark eyes, the broad shoulders, and the cheekbones slightly high on his still-handsome face. Naturally he was much older, his hair was gray now, his skin drawn and dry where it had been firm and supple, but he was still a very attractive man, so Mary thought to herself. There was no mistaking his identity, this was the ambitious young doctor who had lived next door to her. The same man she had last seen standing with horror-stricken eyes as he watched the firemen place the body of his beloved young wife into the back of the ambulance. Yes, this was Tim Rogers!

"Jake, meet my grandmother, Mary; Gramma, this is Jake!" Jenna flippantly made the introductions, then watched attentively as the two eyed each other. Jenna then introduced her younger sister, who made no bones of her disinterest in the whole affair. She had only come along to please her grandmother.

Mary reached over and took Jake's hand, and he politely returned the clasp. After a few pleasantries, Jenna pulled a chair up for her grandmother and couldn't help but notice they had taken to each other immediately. She rather casually thought this might develop into something in spite of the age difference.

Just then Dr. Lauren walked into the room to check on his patient. His mother had suggested that he drop in to see Jake about 7PM if possible, but, of course, she didn't tell him why. He was surprised to see three members of his family around Jake, where it was usually just Jenna. He smiled to think how his daughter had won them all over; coerced them all to come to visit the old gentleman she had become so attached to.

"Well, Jake, I guess you've just about met my entire family," he laughed. "I didn't realize you were going to have all these visitors -"

"Sit down, Jack!" Mary interrupted, and when she used that tone of voice even now, Jack listened. " I have something very important to tell all of you! I only hope you can all forgive me!"

Not a sound could be heard in the room. Everyone was staring wide-eyed at Mary. Forgive what? She had been a model mother and grandmother, what could she possibly had done that would require forgiving? They could tell by the look on her face that she was about to bring up a very important issue. She looked briefly from Jack to Jake. They all watched her not knowing quite what to expect. She got up from her chair and with trembling hands she set the wooden box on the end of the bed and proceeded to force open the cover. All at once the cover bounced open with a sudden snap, and two of the snapshots flew out onto the floor. One of those photos was of a woman and a small child. Jenna, standing next to her grandmother, immediately bent over to pick it up. It had landed right-side up directly in front of her.

"Gramma! Jake!," she screamed, "It's that picture, the same one - the very same one you have in your cottage!" She immediately looked up at her grandmother, her eyes filled with bewilderment. "Gramma, where did you get that picture?"

"That's exactly why I'm here," Mary said slowly, as she took the picture from Jenna and handed it to Jake.

. "That's the same picture you have in your house, Jake, isn't it? How did it get here?" Jenna asked wide-eyed.

"You're right, Jenna. That's a copy of the picture I have at home. But where -??" Jake was extremely surprised and puzzled.

"Thanks, Jenna, you've made it much easier for me," Mary said, now much calmer. She smiled in relief, took a deep breath and proceeded with what she knew she had to do.

"Jake, - Tim - I know you don't recognize me now, it was so long ago, but I lived next door to you and Ellen.-"

Suddenly recognition shone in Jake's eyes. As shaken as he was by that fact he smiled broadly as he said, "I knew there was something vaguely familiar about you. Mary, it's so good to see you again - after all these years!"

"Wait, Tim, let me finish. I was there the day of the fire. I tried desperately to keep Ellen from going back into that burning house to salvage what she thought was important. She threw this wooden box out the window, then apparently succumbed to the smoke before she could get back out. Luckily, she had brought the baby out and handed him to me before she went back in."

"The baby, my little boy, where is he now? Does anyone know where he is?" Jake gasped as he bolted upright in his chair. Dr. Lauren immediately moved to his patient's side and gently maneuvered him back to a resting position.

"Mom, this may be too much -" the good doctor said to his mother, as he gave her a 'that's enough' look.

"I have to finish - please don't stop me now! If I stop now I'll never finish!"

Even Shiela, with her heretofore disinterest, was suddenly wide-eyed and awestruck. Jenna, needless to say, was totally speechless, totally engrossed in her grandmother's enlightening words.

"Mary, God bless you, then you know what happened to my son, tell me please!" There was no way to calm Jake down now. He looked at Mary, excitement showing in his dark eyes. He had to know!

Mary swallowed hard and said, "Tim, your son is right beside you! He's been taking care of you the past few days. He's my adopted son, but he's your real son. Ellen made sure he was safe with me before she rushed back into the house. I saw you briefly at the fire, but then you just seemed to disappear before I could get to you. Joe and I thought you'd be back, but after a few years when you didn't return, we adopted Jack," She paused for a minute, then continued before any of the stunned people in the room could say anything.

With moist eyes she looked directly at her son and said, "I'm sorry, Jack. I know I told you your father was dead, and I never told you about the fire, either. Joe and I thought it best not to upset your young life any more than necessary. You were very happy with us and we with you, so we left it that way. But when Jenna told me all these things about the man she called Jake, I knew I had to do something. There were too many similarities, I knew it had to be your father. It would have come out sooner or later anyway. Please forgive me!!" Then as she glanced toward Tim, she tearfully said, "And Tim, I am so happy that Jenna found you!"

Mary looked so vulnerable, so misty-eyed at this point, that, without a word, Jack walked over to her and hugged her. "Of course, I forgive you, you did what was best for everyone, and Mom, you've been a wonderful mother, I couldn't have asked for a better one!"

She broke into sobs, partly from remorse for thirty-five years of withholding the truth, but mostly from relief and happiness. She was truly happy that Tim had returned, that he had found his family at last!

"Guess that makes you my grampa!," Jenna fairly shrieked, as she put her arms across the shoulder of the man in the chair. "I can't believe it - I found my own grandfather! Wait till I tell Tom!"

"Dad!" Jack said, as misty-eyed as his mother. "This is incredible! I can't believe all this is happening, I knew Joe was my adopted father, but I never in my wildest dreams believed I'd ever find my real father, and to think Jenna stumbled on you by accident. I can't believe it! Miracles actually do happen!" The usually calm and collected Dr. Lauren was overcome with emotion. He hugged his father and wiped the tears that were falling down his face.

"So this is my family!" Tim beamed. "I should have known - there was something about Jenna - a bond I couldn't explain. We seemed to take to each other immediately! I - I can't believe it! Thank God for all of you!" He attempted to embrace them all with his long arms, as tears of joy streamed down his cheeks.

"If I had only known; I've been living here for fifteen years now. I suffered from amnesia for twenty years, all the while I lived in Seattle. I didn't know for sure my right name or anything else about me, so I gave myself the name of Jake Miller. I married a wonderful lady in Seattle, but she died in 1971. You all would have loved her! Shortly after she died I finally realized my true identity and I came back. I tried to find you, son, I guess I didn't know quite how to proceed. I checked newspapers until I was led to believe that I was implicated in the fire. Then I'm afraid I shied away from searching, thinking it may be best if I left you to live your life without interference from me, or possibly that you didn't even live here anymore, and to think you were right here in town, working in the same hospital that I used to work in - it's incredible!"

"Tim, you were in no way implicated, it was an explosion,

no one was to blame!" Mary interrupted. "It was an accident!" she emphatically added.

"But I've had to live with the fact that I ran from the scene, and left everyone wondering why - why I didn't come back to claim my son. But it was because of that - amnesia -." He almost hated to say the word.

Dr Lauren was overwhelmed, "It's all right, Dad, don't give it another thought. It can happen, but you're here now! And we've got so many years to catch up on, Dad, so many things to talk about. All those years you were in Seattle, you can tell me what your life was like there, and I can fill you in on my childhood with the two wonderful people who raised me. We sure have got a lot of catching up to do!"

"And now I can go back to being Tim Rogers, if I choose to, although I have to admit I've grown quite fond of Jake Miller these past thirty-five years, we've gone through a lot together," Jake laughed.

There was a tremendous amount of happiness and relief shared by the five occupants of that hospital room at that moment, the joy of a family being reunited, of a father finding his son, and a son finding a father he never knew he had! And as for Tim, alias Jake, he learned the true meaning that day of that simple truth - *the Lord works in strange and mysterious ways!* Dr. Timothy Rogers had finally assembled the pieces of his past and was home at last!

Made in the USA
Charleston, SC
07 August 2012